Praise for Penny

AN UNTIMELY FROST

Lilly Long Mystery #1

"Penny Richards has created a fascinating heroine, a great mystery, and an exceptional play on history. For any lover of history and / or mystery, this is a must-read author!"
— *New York Times* bestselling author Heather Graham on *An Untimely Frost*

"A strong heroine and the intriguing Pinkertons make this historical mystery a cozy way to spend a weekend. Lilly Long's independence and stubborn spirit will immediately endear her to many readers. The case is well constructed, and the tone of the prose casts an almost gothic mood over the story. This is a solid start to a new series, and the introduction of a potential work and romantic partner for Lilly adds an extra element of appeal for a variety of readers."
— *RT Book Reviews,* 4 Stars

"[A] riveting series launch . . . Strange undercurrents of sorrow and menace swirl around our intrepid heroine, drawing her into a vortex of cruelty and long-buried evil. Richards provides just the right amount of melodrama in this lively tale."
— *Publishers Weekly*

"Penny Richards has written a fun, feisty protagonist in Lilly Long. The prose is crisp and the tempo paces nicely to a finish that sees Lilly needing every bit of her cunning."
— Historical Novel Society

LILLY LONG MYSTERIES

AN UNTIMELY FROST

THOUGH THIS BE MADNESS

MURDER WILL SPEAK

Published by Kensington Publishing Corporation

MURDER WILL SPEAK

PENNY RICHARDS

KENSINGTON BOOKS
www.kensingtonbooks.com

KENSINGTON BOOKS are published by

Kensington Publishing Corp.
119 West 40th Street
New York, NY 10018

eISBN-13: 978-1-4967-0607-2
eISBN-10: 1-4967-0607-2
Kensington Electronic Edition: May 2018

ISBN-13: 978-1-4967-0606-5
ISBN-10: 1-4967-0606-4
First Kensington Trade Paperback Printing: May 2018

10 9 8 7 6 5 4 3 2 1

Printed in the United States of America

This book is dedicated to all the women past, present, and future who have been victims . . . whether physical, mental, or sexual. May those from the past rest pain-free and in peace at last; may those in the present find a way to survive and heal mentally, physically, and spiritually; and may those in the future be protected from this evil by ever-increasing knowledge of how to protect ourselves and those we love, vigilance of law enforcement, and constant awareness of our surroundings . . . always.

For murder, though it have no tongue, will speak . . .

—Hamlet, *Hamlet,* act 2, scene 2

CHAPTER 1

1881
Chicago
Pinkerton Offices

"Hello, McShane."

Lilly Long approached the man leaning against the brick façade of the Pinkerton offices, engrossed in the newspaper he was reading.

Andrew Cadence McShane, the often dour, sometimes charming man who'd been assigned as her partner, glanced up. Seeing her approach, he pushed away from the building and folded the paper. His bold, blue gaze raked her from the flowers atop her white chipped-straw hat to the toes of her stylish, white leather shoes. He arched a dark eyebrow before doffing his bowler and sketching a bow.

"Good morning, Miss Long. You're looking remarkably cool and fresh this hot summer day."

Though his words were not personal in any way, Lilly could not deny they pleased her or that she'd spent an inordinate length of time fussing over her attire before settling on the simple white eyelet dress adorned with teal ribbons. The fact that she'd taken such care filled her with a sense of dismay.

To hide the feeling, she raised her auburn eyebrows and regarded him with innocent brown eyes.

"Feeling flirtatious today, Mr. McShane?" she queried, looking him over from head to toe.

"Just being truthful, Miss Long."

"Well, thank you, McShane. You're looking very dapper yourself."

Instead of reacting to her compliment, he frowned. "McShane? What happened to calling me Cade?"

She hadn't expected him to notice. Flustered, she said, "I've decided it's a bit too personal. McShane sounds more like a business partner."

"In other words, you've been thinking about how Timothy Warner slipped through your defenses, and you're determined not to get too close to a man again. Not even a working colleague."

Tim Warner was the man Lilly thought she'd married several months earlier. His physical attack on her and the theft of her savings had compelled her to leave her acting career and seek employment with the Pinkertons, so that she could aid other women.

"Nonsense! It occurred to me that it would be better all around if we keep things businesslike."

He regarded her with a thoughtful expression. "I'm sure you're right," he concurred with a brusque nod. "So, let's get down to business. Do you know why William has called us in?"

"I haven't an inkling."

Cade made a sweeping gesture toward the door and then held it open while she slipped inside the dim lobby. She took his proffered arm with the barest hesitation, and he guided her toward the stairway.

When they entered the outer office, Harris, William's secretary, rose and greeted them.

"Good afternoon, Miss Long. Agent McShane."

"Good afternoon, Harris," they said in unison.

"Any idea what's up?" Cade asked.

"Mr. Pinkerton is not in the habit of sharing his agenda with me," Harris said, sounding every bit like a prim spinster. His toothy smile softened the statement. "Let me see if he can see you now."

Without another word, the thin, balding man rapped on the door with William Pinkerton's name stenciled onto the milky looking glass. Heeding their boss's summons, Harris stepped inside, only to return in a moment. "Please go in."

"Thank you, Harris." Cade placed his hand at the small of Lilly's back and ushered her into the office.

As usual, William came around the desk to greet them. "Good morning, Miss Long," he said, taking her hand in a hearty grip. Then he turned to Cade. "McShane." Niceties over, he gestured toward the leather armchairs in front of his desk. "Please, have a seat."

Ensconced across from Allan Pinkerton's elder son, Lilly folded her hands in her lap and waited. As usual, William got right to the point.

"I'm sure you're wondering why I've called you in."

"We assumed you have another assignment for us," Cade said.

"Actually, I have some correspondence for Miss Long."

"Correspondence?" Lilly echoed. "Something more from Mr. Linedecker?"

When she and McShane had finished the Fontenot case in New Orleans, she'd found a letter awaiting her from the attorney she'd hired to procure her divorce from Timothy. That letter had informed her that there was no reason to start divorce proceedings, since her marriage had been an elaborate hoax.

Nothing about her nuptials had been real. Not the minister. Not the witnesses. Not the license she'd signed, and certainly not the love Tim had professed. Now she wondered if her attorney had learned something new about the man who'd done such an excellent job of deceiving her.

"No. Not from Mr. Linedecker." William pulled open the middle drawer of his desk and removed two packets.

"I don't understand, sir. Why didn't you just send the letter to my boardinghouse by courier?" she asked.

A pained expression flashed in William's eyes as he handed one envelope across the gleaming expanse of wood. "It's a bit . . . complicated."

There was no return address on the cheap white envelope. Impatiently, she tried sliding her finger beneath the flap, but her lacy gloves impeded her. Cade held out his hand. Without a word, she handed him the missive, and he opened it with a smooth flick of his pocketknife.

"It's from an actor friend of yours," William said. "Miss Nash."

"Nora?" Why would Nora send her mail here?

"It appears she needs help."

"Help?" Good grief! Lilly was beginning to sound like a parrot she'd once seen that mimicked everything those around him spoke. Her mind was awhirl with thoughts and memories, searching for . . . what?

"What kind of help?" Cade asked, cutting through the chaff and getting to the heart of the matter.

"Why don't you tell McShane about Miss Nash before we get to her problem," William suggested.

Problem? Lilly didn't like the sound of that at all. What could have happened? Confused, and starting to worry, she said, "Nora was with the troupe back in the days before Pierce became the manager. I ran into her last spring in Vandalia, and she told me she was tired of traveling around and wanted to settle down and have a family. She'd signed up to become a mail-order bride."

"Gutsy lady," Cade said. "Or incredibly naïve." A dry smile

made a brief appearance. "However, in my limited experience, that seems to be the norm when it comes to dealing with females with a background in the theater."

William smiled, and Lilly's eyes narrowed the slightest bit.

"Don't go all prickly on me, Miss Long," McShane said. "I'm sure you're aware that the unlikely combination of guts and innocence can be quite disconcerting to us mere males. In your case, it has served you well, though I feel my life span has shortened since we've been working together."

The always serious William dared to chuckle. "As we here at the agency well know."

Lilly knew William was referring to the way she'd gone about applying for her job. To make up for her inexperience, she'd devised a plan to apply for the position as three completely different women. The tactic had infuriated the Pinkerton sons, but impressed Allan no end, since his motto was "the ends justify the means."

"The two of you can discuss Miss Long's headstrong tendencies at a later date, Agent McShane. As for Miss Nash . . . suffice it to say that she left the theater to follow her dream some time ago," William said. "I believe that's enough information for now. Read the letter to us, Miss Long, and then we'll discuss it."

Apprehension gripped her as she stared down at the envelope in her hands. His vague comments had stirred up an uneasy feeling that churned in her gut. Knowing she could not put it off forever, she pulled the lined pages from the envelope and began to read.

> *Dear Lilly,*
> *I am writing to you because I can think of no one else who might be able to help me. Since I know your work requires that you travel a lot, I felt the best way to make sure you got this letter was to send it to the Pinker-*

*ton office. I only hope and pray that it is not intercepted
and that you can find some way to help. You were right
about Elijah Wilkins.*

Lilly's heart took a plunge. When Nora had first mentioned her decision to go to Texas and marry a stranger, Lilly
had been skeptical of the whole notion, especially since she'd
learned of the decision soon after her own marriage to a vir-
tual stranger had left her penniless and wallowing in self-
doubt.

Nora had brushed aside Lilly's worries, reminding her that
even people who met and courted in conventional ways often
found they didn't know much about their mates once they
began to share a life, something Lilly could not deny. But now
it seemed her fears for her friend had come true. She turned
her attention back to the letter.

*As you know, I was looking forward to starting a new life with my
husband, but it took me less than a day to realize I'd been lied to. Eli
met me at the train station in Ft. Worth. He was nothing like the
man who had exchanged letters with me.*

Lilly's fingers tightened on the missive. She knew firsthand
what it was like to learn that the one you loved had feet of clay.
She read on, words that were difficult to decipher since they
were blurred in spots where Nora's tears had splashed onto the
coarse paper.

> *Oh, Lil, there is so much to say and no easy way to
> say it. Suffice it to say that the man whose words I fell
> in love with works as a procurer of women for several
> bawdy houses here in Ft. Worth. He lures women to this
> place with the promise of marriage and then sells them
> to whichever madam gives him the most money.*

Lilly's gasp of shock sounded loud, even to her own ears. Lowering the hand holding the letter to her lap, she looked up at Cade and then to William.

"Nora has been sold as a . . . a . . ." Lilly couldn't bear to even connect the ugly word to her friend.

"He's selling women into prostitution," Cade said, summing up the whole miserable mess in one blunt commentary.

"Yes."

"Proceed, Miss Long," William told her.

> *I tried to escape one night, and when my madam found out, she had me beaten and put me back to work two days later. There are children, too. . . .*

Lilly's voice faded to a whisper. She'd heard about children who were abused in heinous ways, but it was one of those tragedies that always happened somewhere far away. She'd never expected to have any connection to it. What kind of sick person would hand over an innocent child to be used as a sexual plaything?

She thought of Robbie, the ten-year-old orphan who had followed her and Cade all the way from Chicago to New Orleans. Realizing that the same fate might have befallen him sent a shiver of fear down her spine. The idea of something so dreadful happening to him was unbearable.

"I know this is difficult, Lilly," Cade said, reaching out and curling one scarred hand around hers. "But please finish the letter."

"Of course." She picked up where she had left off.

> *There are children, too, Lilly. With the help of a friend, I managed to get some of them on a train back East. That time, I was handed over to a bunch of cow-*

boys straight off the trail who were looking for a good time.

I almost didn't make it. I'd heard that a lot of girls kill themselves rather than stay in the life, but until that night I never really understood how anyone could sanction such a miserable death. Now I see that perhaps it's better than the miserable lives we live.

Oh, Nora! Lilly's own teardrop splashed onto the page.

Not me, though. When my body started healing, I decided that taking my own life is the coward's way out, and I've never been a coward. Instead, I decided to get well and find a way to take down this evil operation. And then I'll come home.

I know it's asking a lot, but will you come, Lil? I've been laying low and letting myself heal, and I can hang on for a while, I think. There is no way you can let me know if you're coming or not, but I hope to look up one evening and see you walking through the door. If you can come, hurry. There are too many lives at stake. If not, I understand and will do what I can for the others. Take care, my dearest Lilly.

> *Your friend,*
> *Lenora*

Lilly refolded the letter with slow, deliberate movements and stuck it back into the envelope. Her tearful gaze moved from Cade to her boss.

"It's . . . unthinkable." Her voice broke. "All she wanted was a home, a good man, and a family. This is . . . obscene." She met William's gaze directly. "You knew." It sounded like an accusation, even to her own ears.

He nodded. "She sent me a letter, too."

"I must go and help her, Mr. Pinkerton."

"Holy mother of pearl, Lilly!" Cade cried before William could respond. "You can't just run off on a lark. You have responsibilities to the agency."

"Lark!" Lilly sprang from her seat and turned on him, her color and her voice high. "I hardly think going to help a friend who has been abducted and sold into carnal slavery can be considered a *lark* by anyone with an iota of common sense. Or decency!"

In her state of agitation, she failed to see the look of admiration cross William's face.

"Please be seated, Miss Long."

The authoritative tone halted Lilly mid-sentence. Horror filled her. Not only had she raised her voice, which was very unladylike, very unmannerly, but she had raised it in front of her boss! She felt whatever progress she might have made with the agency would slip away.

"Sit, Miss Long," he said again.

This time, she did as she was commanded. She dared not look at him. She could only imagine what she might see on his broad face. As for McShane, she really didn't give a fig what he thought of her outburst. Really! The man had so few sensibilities!

"You're both right," William said, after letting her stew in a heavy silence for a moment. "McShane is right in saying that you have responsibilities. You're right in saying that your friend needs help and that helping will not be an adventure."

"*Will* not?" Cade asked. "What exactly are you getting at?"

"As I said, Miss Nash sent me a letter, too, along with two hundred dollars she'd saved for her new home when she got there. She somehow managed to keep it hidden from Wilkins, just as she managed to get these letters to the post office.

"She's offered the cash to me as payment to the agency to send you to find out who, if anyone, in the district they call Hell's Half Acre, is behind Wilkins's enterprise."

"She wants to *hire* the agency?"

"Yes. But I'm telling you, Miss Long, there is absolutely no way I can take the case for that amount of money. We try our best to help people, but we are a business. There are salaries, expenses. . . ." His shrug seemed to encompass everything left unsaid.

Money. Why did it seem everything came down to money? she thought in disgust. "I understand that, sir, but—"

William held up a large hand to silence her. "Your devotion to your friend is admirable, Miss Long. Indeed, she is fortunate to have someone like you on her side. I was about to say that even though the agency is unable to take the case, I've talked with my father, and we are willing to give you time away to deal with the matter. Unpaid, of course."

"Count me out."

Lilly looked at her partner in astonishment. He shrugged. "I can appreciate your concern, and I agree that what's happened to your friend is terrible, but with Robbie living with Meagan and Seamus, I'm responsible for part of his upkeep."

"I understand," she told Cade, and she did.

From their time in New Orleans, Lilly knew the boy ate as if there would be no tomorrow. Seamus had two children and one on the way, while trying to support a family on a policeman's salary.

She drew in a deep breath and exhaled slowly. "Thank you for your understanding, Mr. Pinkerton. I promise I'll do what I can and try to find Elijah Wilkins, or whoever it may be, as quickly as possible, and I promise not to take advantage of your generosity."

"Surely you aren't considering going to Texas alone, to a

place called Hell's Half Acre," Cade said. "From what I've heard, the name doesn't begin to describe it."

She lifted her chin to its familiar, stubborn slant. "I admit that I would feel more comfortable with you along, of course, McShane," she told him, doing her best to sound blasé about the whole thing. "And I'll have to give my plan some careful thought. But Nora is an old friend, and I would never be able to sleep at night if I didn't try to help her."

William and Lilly looked at Cade. His eyes narrowed, and his lips, beneath his neatly trimmed mustache, thinned in anger. He turned to William.

"I cannot work for nothing, sir! And neither can Miss Long, truth be told!"

"My finances are none of your concern!" Lilly told Cade in a huffy tone.

"Please," William said, once again coming between the sparring partners.

"Sorry, sir," they said in unison.

"Surely, we can work out something," Cade said.

Lilly chewed on her bottom lip, thinking hard. McShane was right. She did need to be paid while she worked, but if it came down to it, she would do what she could to help Nora and borrow money from Pierce and Rose to get by. If ever a woman needed justice, it was naïve Nora Nash. All those poor women deserved justice. And the children . . . ah, sweet heaven! The children deserved much more than that, those poor, innocent souls.

"What about charging Miss Nash the lowest agency rate and using the money she sent to cover the bill until it runs out?" Cade suggested. "That way we know exactly how much time we have to solve the case." He looked at Lilly and offered her a grim smile. "There's nothing like a deadline to make an operative work hard and fast."

"What if you can't solve the case by then?" William asked.

"Then we'll shanghai Miss Nash, extricate those we can, and come home."

Lilly gave Cade a tentative smile of thanks. Once again, her partner had considered all the angles and chosen a way that might work. It was a good plan, if only William would accept it.

He looked from one to the other. "Agreed. By my calculations, at three dollars a day, you'll have just over two months to find out who's behind the prostitution ring Wilkins supplies. If you don't have an answer by then, you either come home and we're done, or you work for no pay. Your choice."

Cade seemed mollified, and Lilly was ecstatic. She had no doubt that she and her partner could bring about justice for those women who were being used so cruelly.

She threw off the feeling. "Tell me about this Hell's Half Acre," she said. "I've never heard of it."

"Count yourself lucky," William said. "Basically, it's an area at the southern part of Ft. Worth roughly between Rusk and Calhoun streets to the east and west, and Seventh and Front at the north and south. The train depot is nearby, so it's handy for railroad workers, as well as the passengers coming into town to find entertainment. An optimal location, actually."

"And then there are the cowboys," Cade added. "Sitting in a saddle and eating trail dust for weeks on end is thirsty work. Ft. Worth is their last chance to indulge in a little gambling and carousing before heading north. I've heard a cattle drive can take anywhere from two to four months, depending on the market and the weather."

Lilly lifted her eyebrows in surprise. "There are no towns along the way?"

William shook his head. "There's nothing but Indian territory between there and Abilene or Dodge. To sum it up, Miss Long, the Acre is a crime-filled hellhole, chock-full of every vice known to man. Something to provide whatever pleasure and desire a man has the money to pay for."

Depression settled over Lilly. This is where Nora was.

"It sounds as if Wilkins is nothing but a flunky, since he procures for everyone, so I expect we're looking for someone with a little more clout."

"How will we find Nora?"

"I'm not sure. It would have been a great help if she'd said which madam she worked for, but since she's new and fresh it's pretty safe to say she's at one of the sporting houses and not in a crib."

Lilly glanced from one man to the other. "Crib? What's that?"

"A crib is nothing more than a pen on the streets," William said. "It's where the women go when they're no longer attractive or have contracted some sort of disease.

"Boarding, or sporting houses, dance hall, or whatever you want to call them, are better-class establishments with more sophisticated settings and a higher class of girls, so they can charge more per transaction."

There was an emptiness in Cade's eyes, as if he were seeing a vision in his mind he'd rather not. Then he seemed to shake off the feeling, and his mouth twisted into something almost resembling a smile. "They even have fancy parlors where the girls and the clients can mix and mingle before a choice is made for the evening."

"Unbelievable," Lilly whispered. Sex for money. A *transaction*.

"We haven't any time to muck around," William told them, smoothing his mustache with a thick finger. "The first thing we need is some plausible reason for the two of you to be there. If you just show up as Pinkerton agents and start asking questions, you'll never get any answers. Posing as a married couple isn't the right cover in this instance."

"Agreed," Cade said.

Lilly was not surprised to hear William say, "I have an idea brewing." Their boss was known for his quick thinking. "I'll need to do some checking around and confirm a couple of legalities with Simon. We'll meet back here first thing in the morning and see if we have a viable plan."

"Simon?" Lilly echoed.

"Yes," William said, smiling. "Your friend Linedecker appeared to have such an honest and practical approach to the law, I persuaded him to come work for us. It never hurts to have someone on the team who can help with legal issues."

The announcement stunned and pleased her. Simon was struggling as an attorney. Working for the Pinkertons was just the step up he needed to attain success.

Before she could comment further, Cade said, "What's your idea?"

"I was thinking that you could play a gambler from back East who got the dance hall from Dusty Knowles."

"Who is Dusty Knowles?" Lilly asked.

"Just a no good gambler who let his 'appetites' get in the way of how he took care of his business. He wound up owing a lot of money, so he packed up and moved to California and let his dance hall go back to the bank. You can say you won it from him in a poker game or bought it from him because it was a good deal."

"It could work," Cade said with a nod.

"As I said, you can't just waltz into town and start asking questions, but if Agent McShane goes in pretending to be a gambler with an eye to opening a new business, he's free to ask all sorts of questions. Any potential owner would want to know what to expect before deciding whether or not to move ahead with his investment."

William had a point, Lilly thought.

"After all," he said, looking to Cade, "I'm sure you plan on putting in a pricey operation that will appeal to the bigwigs. And hopefully, when word of your arrival gets around town, it will bring your friend out of hiding."

Lilly had listened to it all in silence. "And what would my role be?"

"I thought you could be McShane's paramour."

"Why can't I be the new owner?"

McShane had the audacity to laugh. "You're shaping up to be a good operative," he said, "but you don't have nearly enough experience to deal with the likes of what we'll be mixed up in out there. To say it's a nasty business is putting it mildly."

"And I'll need to check on the legalities with Simon before we move with this. It may be moot."

Lilly decided to give in without a fight. She knew they were right, but she'd had to try. Would she ever get to be the top agent in one of their cases?

"I think it's a good plan, but we need someone else to be the potential buyer," she said. "Cade is more suited to being a bodyguard or a bouncer."

"She has a point," her partner said.

"I can't deny that has merit," William said with a nod. "He's certainly got the experience at cracking heads. What about your friend, Wainwright?"

"Pierce?"

"Yes. Where is the troupe these days? He did such a bang-up job in New Orleans; he'd be ideal for this."

"They were in Terre Haute, the last I heard, but he can't get away from the troupe every time we need help. Too many people rely on him for their bread and butter."

"Of course," William said. "You're right. Any other ideas, McShane?"

"Erin," he said without a moment's hesitation. "She'd be perfect."

"Who's Erin?"

"My sister."

Once again, William agreed with a slow nod. "Can you speak with her and see how she feels about it?"

"If I can find her," Cade said with a lift of his shoulders.

"Excuse me," Lilly said, "but what am I missing here? How can your sister possibly help us with this assignment?"

The expression in his eyes grew as bleak as a winter day. "Erin is a prostitute," he told her. "She knows a lot about how the business works."

CHAPTER 2

After the three had agreed on a meeting time for the next morning, Cade suggested that he and Lilly go somewhere to formulate a workable strategy, a common practice when they were given a new assignment. Everything they said and did during the operation needed to be designed so that the people they connected with believed their cover. Everything from their relationships to each other, their backgrounds, and the personalities of the characters they would be portraying—the smallest details needed to be addressed if they didn't want to ruin the chances of finding Nora and bringing justice to those who deserved it.

Lilly's curiosity warred with her upbringing. She was eager to know more about Cade's sister, especially how she'd come to be a lady of the evening, but good manners forbade her asking. McShane would tell her what she wanted to know—or at least part of it—when he wanted to tell her.

"What about a restaurant?" she asked instead, glancing at the pendant watch hanging around her neck and seeing that it was approaching the supper hour.

"Normally I would agree, but today I think we should go to my brother's place. He should be home soon, and he and Meagan have been asking to meet you for months. We won't have to worry about someone overhearing us, and they probably know how to get in touch with Erin."

The thought of meeting Cade's brother and his brother's wife and his sister who was a real, honest-to-goodness soiled dove caught Lilly off guard. "I . . . I don't know," she said.

"They won't mind," he assured her, almost as if he'd read her mind. "And Robbie will be there."

She couldn't deny that the thought of seeing the ornery, mischievous boy brought a surge of pleasure. "Are you certain it will be all right?"

"Positive. And I know for certain that Meagan is making shepherd's pie and brown bread for supper."

"All right," she said, bowing to his wishes. "It sounds delicious."

"It will be."

Neither of them spoke much on the way to the McShane home. Lilly imagined Cade was concocting some sort of plan to get them all assimilated into Hell's Half Acre and back out again, unscathed. She was busy wondering how and why his sister had become a tart.

Remembering the men who had paraded through her own mother's life and bed didn't help. As far as Lilly knew, Kate Long had not sold her body, but neither had she been averse to sharing it with one man or another, whenever it suited her fancy.

When Lilly was old enough to understand what was going on, she'd hated her mother, but that had faded with the passage of time. No one could help loving Kate, and her daughter was no exception. To this day, Lilly could not fathom why her mother had done what she'd done, been what she'd been, and love aside, she had never condoned Kate's behavior.

To squash any similar, errant tendencies she might have inherited, Lilly had done her best to negate her own beauty with every unappealing style of hair and dress she could imagine. More important, she had remained a virgin until she'd wed Timothy Warner. Except that she hadn't really married him.

Memories of her sham marriage took her thoughts back to William's announcement about Simon Linedecker's association with the agency. She smiled at the memory of the tall, rather untidy man with the tortoiseshell glasses. Without the advantage and influence of the wealth that most young attorneys possessed, Simon had been struggling to keep his offices open when Lilly approached him about her divorce. His association with the Pinkertons would be a good move for him in many ways. She hoped she'd have the opportunity to see him again one day.

"I don't suppose you'd tell me about Erin before I meet her?" she asked, breaking the growing silence.

Cade slanted a sharp glance her way. "You're right."

She wasn't surprised by the answer. How many times had he told her that she asked too many questions?

"Don't pout, colleen," he said, calling her by the name she despised. "I'm not trying to be difficult, but it's not my story to tell."

Lilly frowned. "You're angry with her. Will you tell me why?"

"Beyond the obvious, you mean?" he snapped.

Lilly nodded.

"No."

"I thought not," she said with a sigh.

"Then why ask?"

How could she tell him that everything about him was of interest to her when it was all she could do to admit that fact to herself?

"'Hope springs eternal. . . .'" she quoted with a wan smile.

"Indeed, it does." And that was the end of the conversation.

Thirty minutes later, they arrived at the McShane residence, a small apartment in an Irish area located in the northern part of the city. The moment Cade opened the door, Lilly's senses were awash with the wonderful aromas of freshly baked bread and some other wonderful combination of ingredients.

Hearing the door open, the woman working at the small metal basin turned with a smile on her pretty, freckled face. The smile faded a bit when she noticed Lilly standing next to Cade. Rallying, Meagan McShane dried her hands on the apron tied around her protruding belly. He had failed to mention that his brother's wife was expecting a child. And soon. She crossed the room and gave Cade a hug. "What brings you here, *dearthàir beag?*"

Lilly loved hearing their native language, though she had no idea what they were saying. Cade flashed his rare grin. "She called me younger brother, though I'm older than she is."

"Ah . . ."

"Well, you're younger than Seamus."

"That I am. And speaking of Seamus, I saw him earlier, and he said there was shepherd's pie for supper." He plastered a pitiful look on his face. "Since I'm so hungry I could eat the back door buttered, I thought I'd avail myself of a good home-cooked meal. Besides, you know I never pass up shepherd's pie."

"Shepherd's pie, stew, potatoes, doesn't matter. You never pass up the chance for food, is what you never pass up," Meagan said. "Now away with ya."

She gave him a push toward the living area and turned to Lilly with a bright smile and an extended hand. "Something tells me you're Miss Long."

Lilly was somewhat surprised by the woman's friendliness.

"Yes. I hope my coming along isn't too much of an imposition."

"Not at all. We've plenty. I never know who Seamus might bring in from the streets. It's nothing for him to come dragging in some homeless person or another." She gestured toward the parlor area. "Please have a seat. Would you care for something to drink?"

"Nothing for me, thank you," Lilly said, settling into a corner of the worn sofa.

Cade asked for a glass of water and took a seat in a rocker with a woven rush seat, while Lilly looked around the combination living and kitchen area with interest.

The camelback sofa was a faded green stripe; lace curtains hung at the windows. Coveted Irish lace, Lilly was certain. A painting of a lush green countryside, cottages with thatched roofs, stone fences, and grazing sheep hung above the fireplace, whose ashes had been swept out for the summer. An intricate Celtic cross of bronze hung next to the rock fireplace. On the other side hung a framed, embroidered piece with an Irish blessing and a border of shamrocks. The home was small, but scrupulously clean.

They had just gotten settled when a child's voice squealed, "Uncle Cade!"

The McShane daughters had just come through a door that no doubt led to one of the handkerchief-size yards that some of the ground-floor apartments possessed. The two ginger-haired girls, clad in flower-sack dresses, raced across the room to their uncle in a flash of bare legs and wide smiles. Their small bodies hit him so hard that the rocker threatened to topple over under their combined weight and speed.

"Easy there, lassies!" Cade cautioned, somehow wrapping an arm around each one and drawing them onto his lap. He planted loud, smacking kisses on their heat-flushed cheeks.

"Goodness, Isibeal," he said to the youngest. "You've grown a foot since I saw you last." He turned to the older child, somewhere around five or six. "And you, Keely, get prettier every day."

"I'm pretty, too," Isibeal said, her little mouth puckering in a pout.

Cade flashed Lilly a look that seemed to hold a plea.

"Of course you are." The comment drew their attention from their uncle to the strange woman sitting on their sofa.

Isibeal pulled the two middle fingers she was sucking on from her mouth and asked, "Who are you?"

"Yes," Keely asked. "Who are you? You're very pretty."

"I'm a friend of your uncle's, and thank you."

"You're very pretty." Isibeal repeated.

"Your hair is redder than ours," Keely noted.

"It is, isn't it?"

"All right, girls, give your uncle a hug and go back outside to play until your da gets home," their mother said.

"We want to see Uncle Cade."

"He'll be stayin' fer supper. Robbie will be here soon enough. He said something about bringing you a peppermint if you're good."

"We're always good," Keely said. Meagan, who was checking the oven, cast her gaze toward the ceiling, as if she expected a lightning bolt to head their way. "Outside. See if you can find a fairy house."

Heaving matching sighs, the girls hugged their uncle, who told them he loved them, and the tiny sprites headed back down the hallway, that no doubt led to the bedrooms and a back door.

"They're adorable," Lilly told her hostess as she tried to subdue the sudden ache in her heart.

"Aye, they're that all right. They're also a handful. I'm not sure what I'll do with another, but I keep tellin' myself that the

Lord never gives us more than we can handle. And Robbie's a huge help."

"I'm glad for that," Lilly said.

Satisfied that the meal was coming along as it should, Meagan joined them, taking a seat next to Lilly. "Sooo," she said, drawing out the word and looking directly at Cade. "I know you well enough to realize something's going on."

He smiled. "You're right. We needed a place to talk over a case." He wasted no time in telling his sister-in-law the situation in Texas with Nora. Meagan offered sympathetic murmurs throughout the tale. "I wanted to get some input from Seamus and Erin. I figure she can give us a lot of important information."

"That's true." A cloud seemed to dim the brightness in Meagan's eyes. "We've not seen her in weeks, so I assume she's doing well. We never know."

"I've not set eyes on her in more than a year," Cade confessed. "Do you have some way of getting in touch with her?"

"We can send Robbie to her flat when he gets back. Assuming she's still living there."

"Where is Robbie?" Lilly interjected, glad to have an opportunity to change the subject since this topic was obviously painful for both McShanes.

"He's supposed to be helping Mrs. Malone with some chores. He says he needs to earn some money."

Cade chuckled. "So, he's really turned over a new leaf, has he? I guess between me and Seamus, he's afraid to step too far out of line."

"Partly," Meagan said, nodding. "Robbie's coming along nicely. I think he's starting to understand that we *care* where he is and what he's doing. And he's beginning to understand that the rules are as much for his own good as our peace of mind."

There was a commotion at the door, and a burly man who stood a good half head taller than Cade stepped inside. Like his brother, Seamus McShane also had a mustache and a shock of untidy hair. His hair was a deep auburn, and his eyes were so dark they looked black. His face was broader and more lined, and he was a few stone heavier, but the shape of the brothers' mouths, chins, and noses was the same. That they were blood relations was obvious.

Smiling, Meagan rose and hurried to the door. Seamus pulled her into a loose embrace and pressed a loving kiss to her lips. Only twice had Lilly witnessed such a tender moment between two people who so obviously cherished each other: Pierce and Rose and Rollo and Neecie in New Orleans. An almost painful longing to experience that for herself filled her heart. She blinked back the tears of self-pity.

"Supper will be ready in a tick," Meagan told her husband, and, with a graceful whirl, went into the kitchen area.

Seamus, wearing a somber expression, neared Lilly's chair and held out his hand. "Miss Long, I presume."

"Yes," Lilly said, placing her hand in his.

"I'm very pleased to meet you and would like to offer my condolences."

"Condolences?"

"I understand you're stuck working with my younger brother." The comment was spoken only partly in jest.

"Yes, well, we have butted heads a time or two, but I'm learning a lot," she said, shooting a teasing look at her partner.

"I believe that," Seamus said, releasing her hand. With a sigh, he took the spot on the sofa his wife had vacated. "He's very good at his job."

"He's also in the room and can hear every word the two of you are saying about him," Cade reminded them.

"I just thought your memory could use some jogging," Seamus told him. "What brings you here? I didn't expect to see you after we spoke this morning."

"Besides the shepherd's pie, you mean?" Cade countered.

"Well, yes."

"Lilly and I have a new case, and we needed somewhere to discuss some ideas. We wanted input from you, and I really need to pick Erin's brain."

"If there's anything to pick," Seamus said in total disgust. Like the other two, he seemed unable to accept his sister's behavior.

"Meaning?"

"Meaning, I've offered to get her a job at the meatpacking plant, and she refuses. She'd rather . . ." His voice trailed away, and he shot a look of apology in Lilly's direction. "I'm sorry, Miss Long. I'm certain ye've no desire to hear about our sister's shenanigans."

"Lilly knows what Erin does for a living. Actually, we're sort of depending on her to help us out."

Cade explained the situation and their idea for infiltrating the dark world of corruption that made up Hell's Half Acre.

"We thought of using Lilly's friend Pierce again, but he has responsibilities. Then I thought of Erin. Who better to play a madam than someone who knows the business?"

"True," Seamus said, rubbing a finger over his heavy eyebrow. "She can certainly bring authenticity to the role."

"Do you think she'll be interested in going to Texas?" Lilly asked, speaking up for the first time since Cade had explained their assignment to his brother.

"If she's smart, she'll do anything to get away from her life for a while. But I've no notion what she'll say. One of the things I assigned Robbie to do is keep an eye on her. She might be a proper mess, but she's still my sister, and I, at least, need to know she's all right from time to time." The last was offered along with a sharp look at Cade.

He ignored the jab. "Is she working for anyone?" he asked in a neutral tone.

"Not the last time we spoke. She says the money's better on her own, and she's tough enough to handle it."

"No doubt."

"She's your sister, Cadence," Meagan reminded from across the room. "We're not to judge, just love."

"I'm not judging," he countered. "I just think she's daft, living the way she does. It makes me furious with her."

"I know, brother, but until she's ready to change, there's nothing we can do."

There was a sound at the door, and young Robert Jenkins burst into the room with all the might of a small whirlwind. "Meagan, you should see . . ." His voice trailed away, and he stopped just inside the open portal. "Holy mother of pearl, McShane! What are you doing here?"

Lilly tried not to let the disappointment she felt show on her face. She and the child who had taken up with Cade during a bad patch in his life were not on the best of terms, but for him not to acknowledge her was a bit of a blow. After all, Robbie was the one responsible for helping to save her life not so long ago in New Orleans. She'd walked away from that assignment feeling they were on better terms. Her mistake.

"Is that any way to make a man feel welcome, Robbie?" Cade said, rising, as if he thought the child might run to him.

Lilly knew that the tough little boy might want to be hugged by the man he'd grown so fond of, but she also knew him well enough to know that letting a weakness of any kind show was forbidden. Robert Jenkins would sooner die than let anyone know he had a soft spot for his Irish hero.

"You might say hello to Lilly," Cade suggested.

"I might." Then, wearing a deliberately pompous expression that looked absurd with his faded denims and the smear of dirt across his face, he made a formal bow. "Miss Long. I trust the world is treating you well."

Despite her irritation and hurt feelings, it was all Lilly could do to keep a straight face. She never knew what to expect from him. She had to press her lips together to keep from laughing. When she gained control of her amusement, she said, "The world is treating me quite well, Robbie. And you?"

"Can't complain," he quipped. Then, dropping the veneer of manners, he turned toward the kitchen. "What smells so good, Aunt Meg?"

"Shepherd's pie and brown bread."

"Sounds good enough to eat."

"That's lovely, then, isn't it?" she said. "You can eat, and then Cade has something he needs you to do for him."

A gleam of excitement leapt into Robbie's eyes. "Need help with an assignment, McShane?"

"In a way," Cade hedged. "I need you to find Erin and bring her back here."

The boy's head drooped, and his shoulders slumped, and then he shot a pointed glance at Seamus. "You're not gonna arrest your own sister for bein' a workin' girl, are you, Uncle Seamus?"

"No, Robbie," the policeman said with a heavy sigh. "Cade just needs to talk to her about an assignment he and Miss Long will be leaving for soon."

"Do you know where she is?" Cade asked.

"She's still at that little flat," Robbie said. "Saw her taking a swell inside no more'n two days past."

"A swell?" Cade asked.

"And why not? Yer sister don't deal with no riffraff. This gent came across as right respectable." Robbie gave Cade a look that seemed to ask if he was blind. Or stupid. "She's very pretty, is Erin, and she don't look for her men in the dives. Her place is right nice, too, so I figure she's doin' okay for herself."

The fact that Robbie understood the workings of such

worldly, adult topics, much less could speak about them in such an offhanded manner made Lilly more than a little uncomfortable.

Cade's eyes narrowed. "And how would you know what her place is like inside?"

Robbie's reply was to cock an eyebrow at his mentor.

Lilly had heard how the boy had climbed through an open window and pilfered through a bedroom when he and Cade had driven Dr. Ducharme to a tryst in the country. The child was quite adept at getting into and out of places he shouldn't think of going. Usually without anyone being the wiser.

"She came out the next morning, so I guess she's okay," Robbie said, ignoring Cade's question. "She's been seein' this one a lot lately."

"No more talk," Meagan said. "Robbie, wash your hands and face. Supper's ready."

Lilly was anxious to get the meal under way. Not only was she starving, but the sooner they ate, the sooner she would meet Erin McShane, Cade's hooker sister.

CHAPTER 3

After the meal, Lilly helped Meagan clean up the kitchen while they waited for Robbie to return with Erin. Lilly didn't know what she expected. Some poor, downtrodden, used-up shell of a woman whose face bore the ravages of the life she'd lived, perhaps. Or someone like Colleen, the woman from MacGregor's tavern that Timothy had taken to bed. Painted up, cheap, and coarse.

The woman who followed Robbie into the flat was neither.

Erin McShane blew through the door like a breath of fresh air. Framed in the aperture, she looked over the room's occupants with both hands on her slim hips and her head held high. She was dressed simply in a navy-blue skirt and gingham shirtwaist. Raven-black hair was pulled away from a perfectly oval face and caught at the nape of her neck with a length of yellow ribbon.

Her complexion was what one expected to see in the Irish, smooth and creamy white. No attempt had been made to hide the abundance of freckles scattered across her face. In fact, Lilly would have bet a month's pay that Cade's sister wore no cosmetics, even though her eyebrows were a perfect arch above her violet-hued eyes, eyes so large they looked as if they belonged on china doll. Even from where Lilly sat, it was obvious that the newcomer's eyelashes were enviably long and thick.

A rather strong nose, full lips, and a too-wide mouth—a mouth that seemed designed to entice—delivered her from mere prettiness. As one might expect, her chin was set at an angle that dared anyone to criticize her. She did not look jaded and exploited or tired and used up. She looked fresh and unspoiled and, though no one would consider her beautiful in the traditional sense of the word, she was arguably the most striking woman Lilly had ever seen.

"Well, well, if this isn't like old home week . . . minus a few," she said.

"Hullo, Erin," Seamus said, smiling. "It's good to see you."

"Is it now?" she countered, answering with a question as the Irish were wont to do. "I'm wonderin' if Cadence feels the same way."

"Erin, come meet Cade's partner, Lilly Long," Meagan urged, forestalling any comment Cade might have made.

Lilly stood to meet the McShane sister and found that she was a full head taller than the other woman, who extended a hand in cordial greeting. "Miss Long."

She was aware of Erin McShane's scrutiny. She saw curiosity in her amethyst eyes. Curiosity coupled with a sharp intelligence and a considering expression. Was Erin wondering why her brother was working with a woman, or if there was more between them than work?

"I'm very pleased to meet you," Lilly said. "Please call me Lilly."

"I'm Erin."

"I just made some fresh coffee, Erin," Meagan said. "Would you care for a cup?"

"I would, thank you."

"Who else wants coffee?" Meagan asked, her pleasant gaze moving from one guest to the other. The conversation, or confrontation, whichever it turned out to be, was set aside while their hostess sent Robbie and the two little ones back outside so the adults could talk, Robbie complaining all the way.

After everyone was seated and coffee was served, Erin crossed one knee over the other in a most unladylike action and turned to Cade, foot swinging. "Well, *daor dearthái,* what on earth have you gotten yourself into that you'd ask your dreadful sister for help?"

"No trouble, Erin," Cade assured her, his tone one degree above arctic. "Lilly received a letter from a friend who's in a bit of trouble. I wanted to get your input on how best to go about solving things."

Rather than trying to explain Nora's situation to Erin, Lilly passed her the envelope, and the group sat in silence while Erin read the letter. The expression on the other woman's face changed from borderline indifference to outright anger. Her dark eyebrows drew together in a frown, and her lips thinned.

When she finished, she looked up, folded the message, and said a word Lilly had never heard before. From the expressions on Seamus's and Cade's faces, she surmised that not only was it derogatory, it was vulgar. Seamus's face was a dull red, and Cade looked both disgusted and furious.

"Mind your mouth, sister," he said. "We've a lady present."

Erin shrugged and shot Lilly an indifferent look. "I supposed as an actress she'd be well acquainted with that sort of language." She offered Lilly an unrepentant smile. "My apologies."

"Certainly."

"I'm assuming you want to go and get your friend out of that nightmare," Erin said.

"Yes. We want to bring her home as well as find out who's

snatching women and children and selling them into . . ." Lilly's voice trailed away. She was reluctant to say the word describing Erin's occupation.

" 'Prostitution' is the word you're looking for, I believe," the dark-haired woman supplied. A bleak look crept into her eyes. "No child should have to endure what those children will experience," she said. She looked toward her brother. "What did you have in mind?"

Cade explained their plan to go in as prospective dance hall owners, so that they would have more freedom to ask questions about the workings of the businesses in the Acre.

"If it's my opinion you're wanting, the idea has merit," Erin said.

"That's fine, then," he said. "As you know, Lilly and I play various roles to bring criminals to justice, and it occurred to me that you might be willing to take a little break and give us a hand."

Lilly thought she detected a glimmer of interest in the other woman's eyes.

"How?"

"I thought that we could say that one of your favorite 'clients' won the place in a poker game and gave it to you as a thank-you for giving him so much pleasure through the years. As a prospective business owner, you'll be checking things out, getting the lay of the land, feeling out the law, all those things, before deciding if you want to move west and open a place of your own."

"Go on."

"I can go as your protection, and Lilly can play your best friend and my paramour. Perhaps among the three of us we can get some solid information in a short time. We've only got a bit over two months to wrap things up."

"Why?" she asked. "I'm not certain that's enough time to do all that."

"I tend to agree, but that's what we're up against." He explained their financial limitations. "If you go, the only thing you'll get is a trip to a different place and your food. There's no proper pay involved."

"I see."

Erin glanced at Lilly. "Are you ready to play a fellow prostitute, Miss Long, since even speaking the word seemed so difficult?"

Lilly felt as if she were being tossed a challenge. "I'm a fairly accomplished actress, Miss McShane. I believe I can pick up the behavior of the ladies in no time. And if you're referring to the imaginary intimacy between me and your brother, we shared a room for several weeks in New Orleans, and I've grown accustomed to his snoring."

If she hadn't known better, Lilly might have thought she saw a hint of laughter in Erin's eyes. But this was no laughing matter.

"So, I go as . . . ?"

"Erin O'Toole," Cade suggested.

"Mother's maiden name." She gave a slow nod. "Why not? It will be easy to remember."

"Good," Cade said. "We go playing the people I've suggested and try to find out as much as we can about how things work in Hell's Half Acre, bust the organization wide open, get the offenders arrested, and bring back Nora Nash."

"I'm tellin' ya it won't be that easy," Erin said, her attitude toward her brother softening for the first time. "Even with the best intentions, things can go bad fast, if you'll recall."

Cade's face drained of color. "I've forgotten nothing."

Ignoring the coldness in his voice, she asked, "Do you think your Miss Long is ready for what might happen?"

"Miss Long knows the dangers that go along with this job. She signed up for it."

"But she's never been to a place like Hell's Half Acre, has she?"

"I'm no shrinking violet," Lilly said, weary of them talking about her as if she weren't hearing every word. "I can take care of myself."

Erin did smile then. "We'll see, won't we?"

"You're going to help?" Seamus asked, clearly surprised by the decision.

"Against my better judgment. There's a . . . situation I need to think long and hard about," she said. "And being away from it for a time might give me a better perspective. Besides," she added, "it seems the very least I can do under the circumstances."

"You're right," Cade snapped. "It is. We'll be leaving in a day or two. Be ready."

"Ever the bossy one," Erin said, and this time she did smile, albeit sadly.

When Erin left, Cade and Lilly took Robbie out for a walk and to buy him a scoop of ice cream. They chose a small table near the ice-cream parlor's window where they could watch the pedestrians pass. The usually crowded streets were almost deserted. Most had gone home to their families.

"So how are things going with Seamus and Meagan?" Cade asked.

Robbie, who had just popped a huge bite of the vanilla ice cream into his mouth, swallowed quickly and then grabbed his head and gave a loud groan. "I'm dying!"

Cade and Lilly exchanged a smile. "You're not dying, though I'll agree it feels as if you might," Cade told him.

"And for a moment, you wish you would," Lilly added.

Somehow managing to keep a straight face, Cade said, "It's just a cold headache. The good Lord's way of telling you not to eat your ice cream so fast. Or take such big bites. It lasts longer."

Robbie just glared at him. After a moment, he recovered. "Things are going okay. Like I said before, Meagan's a bit of a nagger, and likes to keep tabs on me, but she's a right proper cook, and she keeps my clothes mended and washed." He shrugged. "What more could a boy want?"

"What about Seamus?"

"Seamus is a very important man. Did ya know he made sergeant and got a pay raise?"

"He told me."

"That's nice with the wee babe coming soon. I worry that me staying there will put too much of a strain on their pocketbook."

Cade and Lilly exchanged another smile. If Robbie had reached the point that he was concerned about other people, he was coming along very well.

"Don't worry about that, lad," Cade said. "I give them some money along to help out."

"That's good, then." Robbie took another bite of ice cream.

"I'm glad you're happier there than you were before," Cade told him. "At least I know you're fed and warm and have clean clothes. And I don't have to fret so much about something happening to you. I worried before, especially after you followed us to New Orleans."

Robbie looked chagrinned. "I'll admit that weren't the smartest thing I ever did, but I met Mrs. Fontenot and Bernard and the others, and I'm glad for that."

"So am I."

"The girls seem very attached to you," Lilly said.

"They are a royal pain in my behind. Always wanting me to do something when I'm there. Read to them. Play hopscotch. Build a fairy house. Have a tea party." He cast his eyes toward the ceiling. "Girls!"

This time, Lilly and Cade didn't even try to hold back their laughter.

"The whole family cares for you, and those little girls look up to you, Robbie," Lilly told him. "See that you're a good example."

"I'm doin' my best."

Lilly reached across the table and gave his hand a pat. "I know you are."

"Ya know, it's really not so bad. I admit it's nice knowin' someone would worry if you didn't come home at night."

That was as close to his admitting he was happy as Lilly and Cade were likely to get. They finished their ice cream and walked him back to the apartment. On the way, he regaled them with a tale of Isibeal's picking up the dead mouse that Callie, the calico cat, had left in front of the door as a gift. Meagan had managed to snatch it from her hand just as she was about to put it in her pinafore pocket.

It was just the sort of tale a boy like Robbie would find funny. Neither Lilly nor Cade missed the twinkle in the child's eyes as he told the story. They left him, satisfied that, at least for the moment, everything was all right in his world.

CHAPTER 4

With their tentative plans in place, they caught a cab, and Cade instructed the driver to take Lilly home first. He sat next to her, his arms folded across his chest, his outstretched legs crossed at the ankle. Now and then, whenever the buggy hit a depression in the road, his shoulder brushed hers.

She took a great deal of satisfaction in the fact that she no longer panicked at his merest touch, nor did she go all atwitter and breathless. They'd spent so much time together that his occasional, casual touch seemed almost natural. Thank goodness! She did not think she could maintain a working relationship in a constant state of awareness.

"Robbie seems well, don't you think?"

"What?" He turned toward her. The blank expression in his eyes told her that his thoughts had been far away.

"I said that Robbie seems to be doing very well with your brother and Meagan."

"He does, and I'm thankful for that."

"He seems serious about his schooling." She gave a lift of

her shoulders. "He seems serious about everything, really. Even though he complains, I think he's happy."

"Yes," Cade said with a slow nod. "More than anything, he needed some stability, and to feel wanted and cared for. And purpose. A boy who's grown up the way he has needs purpose, or he'll fall back into old habits. Helping the neighbors, keeping an eye on Erin, and doing what he can for Seamus keeps him out of trouble."

"An idle mind is the devil's workshop?" Lilly queried.

"Something like that."

"Tell me about Erin," she asked for the second time.

He scowled. "Have I told you lately that you ask too many questions?"

"You have."

"Then what about the answer that it's none of your business?"

"Perhaps it isn't," she countered, "but Meagan and Seamus had no problem talking about this new client of hers in front of me."

"Nosey, are ya?"

"Curious." Without waiting for him to comment, she launched into a description of what she'd been told while Cade went outside to play with the girls before he left. "While we were doing the dishes, Meagan told me that Erin stopped working the streets several months ago, choosing to wait in the lobbies of the better hotels until some gentleman of means showed up. Most of them tended to be more than a one-night stop. Seamus confirmed it. Then Robbie says this new fellow has been around for a few months now and seems to be her only client. What do you make of that?"

"That she's getting more money for her services," Cade said. "And that he's probably helped with her flat, as well. It also tells me that our story that one of her gents gave her the saloon isn't too far off base." He faced Lilly. "Why this morbid interest in my sister's life?"

Lilly's natural curiosity had been piqued by the older woman, who was at least four years her senior. She wanted to know everything about Erin McShane, who was in some ways very much like Lilly's mother. Why would a woman sell her body? Even more thought provoking was why a woman would give away her favors for nothing, as Kate had done? Lilly could hardly tell Cade she hoped to get a better perspective on her mother's behavior by learning more about his sister's.

"I'll be working alongside both of you," she improvised. "And I can't be worried that every little word I say may set one of you off whenever we are together."

"All right. If ya must know, I don't approve of her lifestyle."

"I gathered that. You haven't mentioned any of your other siblings having gone to the wrong side, as you call it, so why did she choose that path?"

"I really don't know. But I suppose four out of five staying on the straight and narrow is splendid, considering."

"Tell me about them."

"What?" he asked, frowning.

"Tell me about your family. After all these months, you know a lot about me, but I hardly know anything about you. Tell me about your parents. What brought them here from Ireland?"

"Are you serious?"

"Never more so."

After regarding her with a searching gaze, he nodded. "All right. Not that I understand why you want to know, and it's really none of your business."

"So, you've said. Humor me. Please."

"Fine. My parents were Padraig and Margaret McShane. Da always called my ma Maggie. They came to America in 1844, a year before the potato blight."

"Why?"

He cut his blue gaze to her. "Why does any man do what he does? Things happen. Change. I dinna have any idea. Looking for the promise of a better life, I suppose."

"They're both gone now?"

"For a while now," he said with a nod. "Ma married a nasty piece of work named Josep Boguslaw a year or so after Da passed. Everyone was out on his or her own except me and Erin."

"How old were you?"

"I was sixteen and she was fourteen."

"There are five of you?"

"Aye. Madden's the eldest. He's a family man who owns a little grocery shop a few blocks from Seamus's. Fiona—Fee—is two years younger than Maddy. She works in a textile factory. Seamus came along just a year after Fee, and there are two years between him and me. Erin's the baby."

"Tell me about your father?"

The expression in Cade's eyes turned to nostalgia. "He was big and fun lovin', and he loved Ma and his whiskey and crackin' heads if necessary." He shot Lilly a pointed look. "He was never mean when he drank, though, and never missed a day's work.

"He served in the War. I was just eight when it broke out, and when he left, Ma was devastated. She was afraid she'd never see him again. He wasn't in but a bit over a year when he got shot in the leg and couldn't march, so they let him come home. It destroyed him. He wanted to fight for his new country."

"I've heard the Irish fought hard."

"How would you know that?"

"Pierce and I had long talks about a lot of things while I was growing up."

"War hardly seems a fit topic for a girl to be discussin'."

She flashed a grin. "I know. He and Rose could never have

children, and I think, since I was all he had, he treated me like the son he always wanted."

"He seems like a good man."

"He is." She turned to Cade. "Do you ever see the others?"

"Oh, yes. On holidays and such. Whenever I'm in town."

"So, you're on good terms with everyone except Erin," she stated.

"We're not on bad terms," he argued.

"Well, it certainly seems that you are. The tension between you is as thick as the fog on the lake in the early morning."

Once again, Cade regarded her with a composed expression. She refused to move or look away.

"She tried to kill herself more'n a year ago. Erin."

The news hit Lilly like a blow to her middle. It was hard to imagine the vivacious Erin cold and lifeless. Even harder to imagine her losing hope enough to take her own life.

She realized that most Catholics considered suicide a mortal sin, which would explain Cade's anger and disgust with his baby sister. Lilly thought he should try to be more forgiving, but as he often said, it was none of her business, and she had no intention of offering him advice.

He looked away, watching the buildings go by. She suspected he saw nothing but the past. "It's no way to live, the life she's chosen."

"She has other options, I'm sure."

"O' course she does. My da used to say we're all one choice away from a completely different life. Fee could get her on at the factory, or Erin could go to work for Madden at the grocery. We don't understand it, but there's nothing we can do."

"Has she ever talked about why she chose that lifestyle?"

"No. It almost killed the lot of us when we found out, and then, when she cut her wrists . . ." He swallowed and couldn't seem to find the strength to finish the sentence.

"What about your stepfather?" she asked, hoping to change the topic. "Why was he a nasty piece of work?"

"No more questions." Almost simultaneously, the buggy pulled up in front of her boardinghouse. Cade leaped to the sidewalk, and she placed her gloved hand in his so he could help her alight. Instead of letting go, she clung to it for a moment longer than good manners dictated, taking comfort in its strength and warmth.

"Thank you for telling me. I believe that if I understand Erin better we'll be able to form a better working relationship once we get to Ft. Worth. And perhaps I won't irritate you with some little misstep."

Without commenting, he turned and walked her to the door.

"I'll see you in the morning," she said.

"Nine sharp. Don't forget to secure your door."

She recalled Timothy's forcing his way into Rose's room, attacking them both, and stealing the money she had kept hidden there. It was a painful memory, yet something she never wanted to forget.

"I always remember to lock it."

CHAPTER 5

When Lilly stepped into the Pinkerton office the next morning, Cade was already ensconced in one of the leather side chairs. His legs were crossed ankle to knee, one foot bouncing in a nervous rhythm, just as Erin's had the day before.

When he saw Lilly, he stood at once, proving he'd garnered some manners somewhere along the way. Harris, the Pinkerton secretary, followed suit.

"Good morning, McShane. Harris," she said, smiling.

Cade scowled. Harris responded with a pleasant, "Good morning, ma'am." He went to the closed door leading to William's office, gave a sharp rap, and stuck his head inside. "Miss Long and Agent McShane, sir."

"Send them in."

Lilly preceded Cade into the office and, after shaking hands with her boss, took her customary seat across from him.

"Did you send word about the meeting to Mr. Linedecker?" William asked his secretary. There was a hint of irritation in his eyes.

"Yes, sir. He must be running late."

Simon? Had he been called in to give his opinion about their plan? A quiver of pleasure shot through her at the thought of again seeing the young attorney. At that moment, there was a commotion in the outer office, including murmuring, footsteps, and a slamming door. Lilly and Cade turned. A man who stood head and shoulders taller than Harris was positioned directly behind him.

"I'm sorry I'm late, sir," Simon said from the doorway. "The horse pulling my cab threw a shoe, and I had to walk several blocks."

"That happens. Come in, Mr. Linedecker," William said.

He did as he was bidden, and Harris closed the door behind him. Smiling, Lilly turned toward the man who had helped her in a time when others had turned her away. Cade had risen and was looking over the newcomer.

"Simon, I believe you know Miss Long," William stated.

"Indeed, I do," the attorney said, taking both her hands in his and giving them a squeeze. "How are you, Miss Long?"

"Never better, Mr. Linedecker." She cast a surreptitious glance at her partner, who looked as if he'd just taken a bite of a green persimmon. What on earth was the matter with the wretched man, anyway? He was always in a foul mood over something or other.

"That's good to hear." Simon frowned. "I do hope you've recovered from the bad news about your marriage."

"Oh, yes," Lilly said in a breezy tone, doing her best to pretend that learning that she had given her purity to a man she was not really married to had not destroyed another bit of her belief in love. She laughed lightly. "I'm fine. Though it was a blow to my self-esteem and shredded what reputation I had, it was a blessing in disguise."

Cade cleared his throat—more as a way of ending the little tête à tête than anything—and William introduced the two men. Simon pumped Cade's hand, his nervousness obvious. Cade wore his most stern, professional countenance.

"Did you speak to your sister?" William asked Cade as Simon settled onto the small settee.

"I did, and she's willing to help us."

Simon made a noise, and when everyone looked his way, he smiled and covered a cough.

"Excellent. I spoke to my banker friend who has direct knowledge about the Dusty Knowles property."

"Who is Dusty Knowles?" Simon asked.

"I forgot you weren't here yesterday," William said. "I need to catch you up on what's going on." He quickly outlined Nora's situation and their tentative plan. Simon appeared to be both fascinated by the situation and sickened.

"Mr. Knowles packed up and moved his operation to California. Fortunately for us, his place in Ft. Worth is right in the heart of the Acre. We can use it as the place that was given to Erin." William looked from Cade to Lilly. "The three of you can decide who her generous benefactor is."

"Why would anyone just leave a business for the banks to repossess and not try to sell it instead?" Lilly asked the question that had been bothering her since she'd heard the story the day before.

"My guess would be that Dusty ticked off the local law or owed someone money," Cade offered. "He probably needed to get out of town fast."

"What do you mean? Who would he owe besides the bank?" Simon asked, pushing his glasses up with a forefinger.

Cade's impatience with the unsophisticated attorney was evident to everyone in the room except, perhaps, Simon. "It's common for people who break the law to give money to shady law enforcement officers, so that they will look the other way, and it's important to stay on their good side. Maybe Dusty wasn't keeping up his end of the bargain."

"Are you saying that law enforcement is paid to turn a blind eye to crime?" Simon asked.

Lilly was as shocked as Simon. She had always assumed that law officers were law-abiding citizens.

"That's exactly what I'm saying."

"B—But isn't that wrong? Illegal?" she asked.

"Of course it is. I thought you'd figured out that the world isn't always a nice place, Lilly."

Clearly, she hadn't, but it was something she was learning fast.

"My friend has contacted the banker who took the dance hall when Dusty defaulted," William said. "And since it's been sitting vacant for so long, he's agreed to let us use it for our undertaking." He turned to Simon. "Do you think you can have the papers drawn up showing the transfer of the building and furnishings to Cade's sister, Erin McShane, by this afternoon?"

"She'll be going as Erin O'Toole," Cade corrected.

Simon looked from one man to the other, and his face paled. Still, he met his boss's gaze squarely. "I'm sorry, sir, I can't do that."

William's mouth tightened in disapproval. "Any particular reason?"

"Simply put, in my mind, this arrangement isn't a legal transaction. If I draw up papers deeding that building to Agent McShane's sister and someone other than the actual owner signs them, not to mention that Miss . . . McShane will be signing as Miss O'Toole, I fear I could be disbarred or lose my license. I can't let that happen."

Since Lilly knew nothing of the law, she didn't know what to make of Simon's refusal. It was clear, though, that he was unaware that the agency operated on the premise that the ends justified the means, which meant the truth could be stretched and the rule of law taken to the very edge of its legal limits . . . and sometimes beyond. A lesson she had learned in New Orleans.

"Good grief, man!" William barked. "It isn't as if we're defrauding anyone. We're trying to save some lives here."

"I'm sorry, sir." Simon looked like an obstinate little boy daring to defy his father. "If you feel you must replace me with someone who doesn't mind"—his voice trailed away, and he gave a vague wave of his hand—"this sort of thing, I understand."

Lilly recalled how the struggling lawyer had been only too happy to take on her divorce case when no one else would. Leaving his struggling practice for steady employment with the premiere detective agency had been taking a giant step of faith, and refusing to comply with the agency's wishes was a huge risk. To be willing to toss a budding career away for your morals and ethics was definitely brave and decidedly unwise.

William regarded the younger man for several seconds. "Fine. That will be all, Linedecker."

Simon looked stricken at having been dismissed without further dialogue. He unfolded his lanky frame from the settee and strode toward the door, his head high.

"I'll have Harris type it up for us," William was saying.

"Sir?"

"Yes, Linedecker?"

"Am I to still consider myself an employee of the agency?"

"For the love of all that's holy," William said, running short of patience. "Of course, you still work here. I may not be happy with your thinking, but I admire it, nonetheless. Now go! We have things to do."

Simon left without another word.

"Lilly, you can sign for Erin, and I'll sign as Dusty. It will be ready by this afternoon. I'll get tickets for you all on the next train headed that way. Can your sister be ready?"

"She will be."

CHAPTER 6

The long rail journey was over. The three of them had taken a train from Chicago to St. Louis, where they switched to the St. Louis, Iron Mountain and Southern Line. Those rails headed south through Poplar Bluff, Missouri, and into Arkansas, rattling through Bald Knob, a small place that had been established just that year.

From there the train rumbled on to Malvern, which, according to the line's information, was only twenty-two miles from the healing baths at Hot Springs. After sleeping in a Pullman, the thought of a hot, healing bath sounded wonderful, and Lilly vowed she would visit the popular spa one day.

They rolled through the southwest portion of the state, to Texarkana, where they once again changed lines. The Texas and Pacific would take them straight into Ft. Worth, depositing them in the heart of the infamous "Paris of the Plains."

If Lilly had imagined that she would form some sort of bond with Erin during the trip, she was mistaken. Cade's baby sister was not inclined to much talk, though she did answer any and all questions Lilly had about how to conduct herself once they reached their destination. Erin's advice was to act unafraid of anything, and to stick as close to Cade as possible.

"The last thing I need is for something to happen to you."

The intensity in Erin's voice was unexpected. Why would Cade's sister think she would be blamed if anything happened to Lilly?

"I can take care of myself," she'd said, not at all sure she could.

"Then see that you do, and everything will be peachy, won't it?" had been Erin's reply. And that had been the end of the conversation.

Lilly had expected to remake her wardrobe to be more in keeping with her new station in life, but to her surprise, Erin pointed out that they were infiltrating the infamous red-light district under the premise of setting up a tasteful, high-class establishment that would appeal to the successful men of the city. They would dress with style and class instead of dressing like what they were pretending to be.

Erin told them that her arrival would not endear her to the owners of the many established sporting houses, but then, the object was to get information, not make friends.

Darkness was fast approaching when they pulled into the station. Several men almost knocked down Lilly in their eagerness to quench their desire for a drink and a woman. When Cade grabbed one of them by the arm and told him to apologize, she expected to see a fight, but after meeting Cade's cold, blue stare, the man showed more sense than he looked to have, murmured the requisite expression of regret, and went on his way.

She expected Cade to whistle for a buggy, but, instead, Erin beckoned to a young man standing next to a plain wagon, looking for a fare. When he saw her waving, he lost no time getting to her side.

Lilly looked askance at her partner.

"I'm just the bodyguard, lass. She's the boss, remember?"

Lilly's eyes widened. She hadn't remembered. She needed to be on her toes, or she'd be making some horrible mistake that could put their whole operation in jeopardy.

"Need to go to a hotel, ma'am?"

Erin bestowed a brilliant smile on the driver. "Actually, we'd like to be taken to Dusty Knowles's old place."

"That'd be The Thirsty Traveler," the youth said. "It's only a few blocks from here. You know it's closed."

"I do," Erin said in a teasing voice, "but it may not be for long." The driver looked intrigued, and Lilly knew that he would waste no time in passing on the gossip as soon as he dropped them off.

The baggage was loaded, Cade helped the ladies into the dray, and they were rolling down the street. Some men from the train had rented a buggy and were yelling and waving, as if they'd spotted someone they knew. Looking up, Lilly saw several doves hanging over the balconies of their respective houses, almost as if they were checking out the new arrivals.

Some were seated on the railing, clad in frilly chemises and bloomers, newly curled hair hanging over their shoulders, while wavy tendrils of smoke from their cigarillos drifted up toward the darkening sky. Others leaned forward, showing their wares off to their best advantage. As Colleen McKenna had been, they were all underdressed and overly made-up.

If Lilly was fascinated by the ladies of the evening waiting to go to work, the men gathered outside the various establishments were equally interested in the two respectable-looking women riding in the wagon. No doubt they were wondering what the women were doing in this part of town with only one lone male to accompany them.

"You thinkin' about opening up Dusty's place?" the driver asked, unable to contain his curiosity. "No offense, but you

ladies don't seem the type to fit in here. You look more . . . re-
fined."

"Why thank you, sir," Erin said, with a little laugh. "I certainly take no offense to that. But I am considering reopening
The Thirsty Traveler."

Lilly listened. She was certain that anything said would be
common knowledge by this time tomorrow.

"I'm here trying to gather all the information I can before
making my decision," Erin told him. "Tell me, is this place as
bad as rumors have it?"

"Worse," the man told her without a second's hesitation.
"There's not a night goes by without someone getting knifed,
shot, or robbed. If there's only a fracas or two, it's a slow evening.
I don't remember the last time we had a slow night."

"It sounds pretty rough," Cade said.

"I guess it is, but what else can you expect from a bunch of
buffalo hunters, cowboys, and gunmen? Add the morphine,
cockfighting, and the horse racing, and this place is just a calamity
waitin' to happen."

Morphine? Lilly had heard all about the addicting drug, but
had never imagined that she would come into contact with
anyone using it.

"What about the law?" she asked.

"They pretty much leave the gamblers and drinkers alone,
but the dance halls and the girls, now that's another thing.
They get rounded up pretty regular."

"Are these cowboys and gunmen you're talking about
cruel with the girls?" Erin asked, playing her role to the hilt.
"If they are, I need to put out the word that I won't have it. I
plan to run a quality establishment."

"Aw," he drawled. "I guess a fella gets out of hand from
time to time. That's just the business, ain't it? A lot of the doves
kill themselves to get out of the life."

So, Nora hadn't been exaggerating. Thank goodness, she was made of sterner stuff. Lilly could still sense the strength of the words in her friend's letter when Nora had vowed to hold on and fight until help arrived.

"They found one of the gals nailed to an outhouse a while back."

Lilly's stomach lurched. Even Erin looked a little queasy. "Who would do such a thing?" Lilly asked.

The man took off his hat, scratched his greasy head, and resettled the dirty headpiece. "Hard to say, ma'am."

After a block or so, Lilly saw a peeling red sign that read THE THIRSTY TRAVELER in stark white. The rest of the place didn't look much better. Unlike some of the businesses that had been left unpainted to brave the harsh Texas weather, The Thirsty Traveler had been whitewashed at some time. But the same sun and wind that bleached cattle bones white and blew grit into noses and eyes had taken its toll on the once-pristine exterior.

"Are you sure this is the place you want?" the driver asked, angling the rig to a stop in front of the building.

"Well, no one led me to believe it was the Oriental," Erin said, tossing a wry smile over her shoulder toward her companions. "This is it."

During one of their talks, Erin had told Lilly that Tombstone's Oriental was considered one of the finest places of its kind east of California. Visitors told tales of brightly lit, Brussels-carpeted gambling rooms that were stocked with reading material. Lilly had also learned that, contrary to popular belief, saloons and gaming halls were strictly for men. If a man wanted a woman, he needed to find a boardinghouse or dance hall. One thing was for certain: This wasn't the Oriental.

Cade placed his hands on Lilly's waist and swung her down before doing the same for his sister. "D'you have the key?"

Without a word, Erin rummaged through her reticule and

pulled out a skeleton key with a string of twine attached. Cade took it from her, and, while she paid the driver, he set about unlocking the door. In a few seconds, it swung wide, and they got their first look at the place that would be their home for the foreseeable future.

Erin planted her hands on her slender hips, and the trio surveyed their temporary lodging in contemplative silence. The downstairs room was large, and there were four doors that led to unknown places. A staircase with a landing led to the upper floor where the girls plied their trade. A waist-high, turned-spindle railing bordered all four sides of the upper floor, with doors that led onto a balcony that overlooked the street.

A large fireplace with the ashes of a long-cold fire was centered on one wall of the lower floor. The bar was on the opposite side of the room with the requisite painting of a scantily draped woman hanging behind it. Shelving for the liquor bottles flanked either side of the portraiture, with one row below, in easy reach of a busy bartender.

Fortunately, it didn't look as if anything had been destroyed. All the awful, gaudy gold tables and red upholstered chairs, where the "ladies" and "gentlemen" could sit, share a drink, and converse before heading upstairs, looked to be in fair condition, with only the usual signs of wear.

"Thank heaven I'm not really considering buying it," Erin said at last. "It's a bit of a mess, isn't it?"

"It is that," Cade agreed.

"Shall we have a look around?"

They soon learned that the doors on the lower floor led to an office with a battered desk, a functional, but far from fancy kitchen, plus two smaller rooms that served as bathrooms for the girls and their male visitors. The ladies' necessary featured a large wall mirror, two vanities, and two slipper-shaped tubs with small hand pumps at one end.

"Very smart," Erin said with a nod of approval. "Carrying

bathwater upstairs for so many people would keep a couple of strong men very busy. My hat is off to Mr. Knowles for being so forward thinking."

Personally, Lilly did not feel that a man who used women for his own means was forward thinking, but rather was a reprobate.

"Ready to go upstairs?" Cade asked.

"By all means."

He made a sweeping gesture toward the staircase, and he and Lilly followed Erin. As Lilly had noticed earlier, the narrower gallery at the front of the building led to an outdoor balcony, much like the ones they'd seen as they'd driven from the station. There were two closed doors on each of the three remaining sides.

"So, it looks as if there were six girls working here," Lilly said, still trying to get her mind around the routines of this alien world.

Erin looked over her shoulder as she continued up the stairs. "Hm. Most places only have three or four girls. The other two rooms are probably for the madam—or Dusty, in this case—and the bouncer."

Lilly sighed. The bouncer and his paramour. During the time they'd spent together in New Orleans, she had grown far too friendly with her partner. Learning that her "marriage" to Timothy had been a sham had brought her to her senses. She would never allow herself to be taken in again, not even by her handsome, bewildering, exasperating partner.

The next time she fell for a man, *if* she ever allowed that to happen, she would make certain it was someone far different from Cadence McShane. Someone malleable, who thought she was the most wonderful thing since Borden's condensed milk. A good and uncomplicated man. Someone like Simon Linedecker, perhaps. Certainly not the likes of Cadence McShane.

They'd reached the first room, and Cade swung the door wide to reveal a small, but garishly appointed bedroom done all in scarlet and gold with lots of filigree, fringe, and tassels. The second was a replica of the first, but the décor was purple. The two remaining rooms were copies of the first two, decorated in royal blue and emerald green. Making a face, Erin stepped back out into the hall and started toward the last two rooms.

Cade stood in the doorway and gestured for Lilly to follow. As she passed him, her elbow brushed his arm.

"Which one do you want?" he asked, mischief dancing in his eyes.

"I thought I was supposed to share with you."

"Missed me, have ya?" His face, still handsome despite the scar that ran through his eyebrow and down his cheek, wore his maddening boxer's grin.

"Did anyone ever tell you that you are insufferable, Mc-Shane?"

"Once or twice," he told her after pretending to think on it for a bit. "Rest your fears, Miss Long; we don't have to share a room since there's no one here but us."

She felt her cheeks grow hot. How could she have forgotten *that* small detail? If not for that fact, she and Cade *would* be sharing a room.

Hoping to make the best of her blunder, she quipped, "I'm a novice, remember? How can I possibly think of everything? That's why I'm paired with you."

"All right."

"And while we're on the subject of our fictitious relationship, I would like to lay down some rules."

He leaned against the doorjamb and crossed his arms across his chest. "You would, would ya?"

"Yes." She lifted her chin to look him directly in the eye.

"I want to make it clear that there is to be no flirting, no pseudo seduction . . ."

His eyebrows rose in question. "Pseudo?"

"Yes. Pretend. We both know it's only a childish game you and others like you enjoy playing with women whenever the mood hits."

He regarded her soberly for a moment, then nodded. "So, you think I'm playing games. I see."

"And do you understand?"

"Explicitly. Is there anything else?"

"Yes." Heat flamed in her face once again. "No more kisses."

A half smile curved his mouth. "You had no objections at the time."

He had her there. "Well," she blustered. "How could I? We were playing a married couple. But even so, we shared far too much . . . intimacy."

Even as she spoke the words, she knew they were only somewhat true. She hadn't objected, partly because he had taken her by surprise, but also because she'd enjoyed it, blast it all!

"Children!" Erin chided, poking her head out the doorway of a room down the way. "Stop quarreling! Cade, come and see if this room is acceptable."

He pushed away from the doorframe and went to join his sister. The room had a definite masculine feel with a simple oak bed, dresser, and small wardrobe. There were no frills, no gold or filigree. The curtains were simple white panels, and no knickknacks adorned any surface. A shaving stand with a plain white bowl and pitcher sat near the window, taking advantage of the light.

"It's perfect," Cade said. "Have you seen your room?"

"Oh, yes," Erin said. "It's a cross between those of the girls and this one. I'm not certain if Dusty liked things a little fancier than his bouncer, or if he added the gewgaws and pretties to try to please some woman or other."

To Lilly's surprise, Cade smiled at his sister. "That's something that's hard to do."

Erin gave a matter-of-fact lift of one shoulder. "It depends on the woman, *daor deartháir.*"

"What about you, Erin?" he asked. "What would it take to make you happy? A millionaire? A big house? A place like the Crystal Palace?" Though the moment was light, Lilly sensed the question was serious, that he really wanted to know.

Her smile was sweet, even whimsical, tinged with the slightest hint of mystery. "None of those things."

"No?" He regarded Erin with a quizzical expression.

"The answer would surprise you, Cadence. It really would." Without waiting for him to comment, she whirled and left the room, heading down the stairs. "You bring the bags up. Lilly and I will check the armoires and see if there are some clean linens so we can all have some fresh bedding. Then, perhaps we can find a place to get a bite of supper."

"That sounds like an excellent plan," Cade said, already clomping down the stairs. "I'm starving."

Because they were doing the case on so little money, it was necessary to spend it frugally. They planned to eat a proper supper and eat simply for breakfast and dinner. The small snack they'd bought from the news butch on the train was long gone. Like Cade, Lilly was ready for something hot and filling.

"Which room, Lilly?" he called from the bottom of the stairs.

"The green one," she said, for no other reason than that green was her favorite color. It certainly had nothing else to recommend it. As garish and tasteless as it might be, she would only be sleeping there, so what did it matter?

CHAPTER 7

They walked down the street and around a corner, settling on a small restaurant that was situated in a narrow building squeezed between two larger ones. It wasn't fancy, but was reasonably clean, and the coffee smelled good enough to kill for. No one expected the food to be the best, and they all agreed that it ranked one notch above filling, but it gave them an opportunity to be seen by the locals.

Newcomers, whether they were cowboys looking for one final fling before heading out on a long trail drive, or just strangers coming to town to sample the pleasures, were bound to stir up a lot of curiosity, and curiosity led to questions. Which worked to the trio's advantage. They needed everyone talking about them so that they could strike up some conversations and spread the word about why they were here. The hope was that if Nora heard about new people arriving, she would brave exposure to check them out and realize that her plea for help had been answered.

The establishment was busy, and diners came and went at a

rapid pace, though Lilly and her companions took their time, eating their stringy beef slowly, and watching and commenting on those who came and went. They were halfway through a half-decent brown sugar bread pudding when a tall, rangy fellow in denim jeans, a chambray shirt, and a leather vest with a badge pinned to the front stepped through the doorway. He stood there for a moment, surveying the occupants. Looking for someone.

"I think we've attracted the attention of the law," Cade said, spooning up another bite of the sugary dessert.

It was all Lilly could do to keep from turning around to see, but instead, she kept her eyes dutifully on her bowl. Erin, though, deliberately lifted her head and stared across the crowded room at the newcomer. There was a challenge and a dare in her amethyst eyes. And just maybe a hint of interest.

Without a word, the stranger started toward them. Either they were who he was looking for, or he was accepting Erin's challenge. Hooking his thumbs in his pockets, he stopped at their table. "Someone told me one of the drivers dropped off two women and a man at Dusty's old place. That wouldn't happen to be you all, would it?"

"As a matter of fact, it would," Cade told him, standing and extending his hand. "Cadence McShane."

The lawman took his hand. "Sam Davies. I've been the marshal since I beat out Jim Courtright a couple of years ago."

Before he could say anything else, Erin held out her hand. "Erin O'Toole."

Looking directly into her smiling gaze, Davies took her hand. She gestured toward Lilly. "This is my friend Lilly. Mr. McShane is here to"—she smiled—"make certain that Lilly and I come to no harm. We hear the Acre can be very unhealthy for some ladies."

At first Lilly was shocked at Erin's high-handedness, but,

just as quickly, she realized that Cade's sister had deftly taken the lead in the conversation, establishing that she was the one in charge. Just as they'd planned.

"Would you care to join us?" she asked, indicating the fourth seat at the table.

"I'd be pleased," he said, pulling out the chair and settling into it.

"Would you like some dessert? Coffee?"

"No, thank you, Miss O'Toole. This time of day my taste starts turning to something a bit stronger, and they don't serve liquor here."

"Then please excuse us while we finish."

"Certainly."

While he watched Erin, both Lilly and Cade watched him.

"What brings you to our little Paris of the Plains?" he asked at last. "And more specifically, to Dusty's? I'm assuming you're a friend of his."

"Alas, no," she said with a melodramatic sigh. "I'm afraid I don't know Mr. Knowles. It's my understanding that when he left, he defaulted on the loan on his property, which then passed from one banker to another until one of my longtime *friends*"—she gave the slightest weight to the word—"wound up with it and made it a gift to thank me for all the wonderful times we'd had together."

Davies had no problem getting the drift of her meaning.

"Mighty generous of him," he said.

"We've had some *very* good times," Erin confided with an artful smile and an audacious wink.

"So, do you plan on opening up the place?"

"That remains to be seen, Marshal. That's why we've come. To check out things, see if there's room for one more . . . boardinghouse."

"There's always room for another first-rate place," he said.

"Why, Marshal, I thought sporting houses were against the law."

"They are." For the first time, he looked a little uncomfortable.

Erin laughed. "Well, there seems to be a lot of law breakers here." She rested her chin on her hand and looked at him with mischief in her eyes. "I thought it was your job to shut them down."

Lilly had to press her lips together to keep from smiling. Erin was certainly good at confrontation. The words were damning, but her flirtatious manner made it hard for the marshal to take offense.

For just a moment, he looked taken aback by her bluntness, but then he seemed to gather his thoughts and his composure. When he replied, he seemed a trifle wary, as if he was wondering just what Erin O'Toole was up to.

"Oh, I make arrests, Miss O'Toole, and I've shut down several places, but most everyone in town, including a good number of the bigwigs, agrees that the girls not only provide a valuable service, but they bring a lot of revenue to the legitimate businesses. I try to be fair-handed with the arrests."

"How's that?" Cade asked.

"When the men come in off the trail, they're dead-dog tired and have a lot of dust to wash down. They spend their pay at the bathhouses, get a shave and a haircut, buy new duds at the mercantile, drink a little, play some cards."

"That makes sense," Cade said.

"Sure it does. And as a man, I'm sure you understand that they crave the pleasure of some feminine companionship before they start out on that long, gritty trek from here to Kansas City or Dodge."

Davies gave a slight shrug and turned his attention back to Erin. "As long as things don't get too out of hand, we just look the other way. I'm sure you understand, since you're in the same line of work."

Hm. He could give as good as Erin, it seemed.

"Indeed, I do, and you've helped me with my decision."

"I have?"

"Yes." She offered him a sultry smile. "I'm sure you understand that I need to have a handle on how things work here and see if there would be any opposition to my opening up another place."

Davies laughed. "Oh, there'll be opposition, all right, but not from me. Believe me, some of the madams will be spoiling for a fight."

Erin smiled a knowing smile. "They're afraid I might upset the pecking order?"

"Some of them will be concerned."

"Who's at the top of the ladder?"

"That would be Velvet Hook and Rosalie Padgett."

"Velvet Hook?" Lilly repeated, forgetting for a moment that this was Erin's show. "That can't be her real name."

"Naw. Everyone says that, once she gets her hooks into a fella, he ain't got a chance. Others say it's 'cause she was a hooker durin' the war."

"I can't wait to meet them," Erin said. Lilly thought it sounded perfectly horrible.

"I'm sure you'll have the opportunity." Davies stood and plopped his hat back on his head. "How long do you expect to be here?"

"It's hard to say, Marshal. We want to check out the situation thoroughly and then, if it seems feasible, come up with a plan to renovate the place. Then I'll get some cost figures together and see if my lawyer thinks it's a viable undertaking."

"Lawyer?"

From the expression on Davies's face, he was astonished by the notion that a woman who made her living selling her body would have enough business sense to have an attorney help her with a potential new venture. Lilly saw his wariness turn to respect.

"Yes." Erin didn't elaborate. "I seldom make any decisions these days without consulting him." Her smile was derisive. "I'm not getting any younger, Marshal Davies, and I need to make the best use of my . . . *assets* as possible. All my assets."

Lilly realized that Erin had chosen the word on purpose. It was an impressive play on words that was titillating and show-cased her intelligence. She was as good an actor as her brother. But then, perhaps it wasn't an act. Cade was intelligent. Why should Erin be less clever? To think such a thing was the height of condescension, especially from another female.

Davies's smile could only be described as slimy. Lilly imagined that he was envisioning disrobing Erin to better appreciate those "assets."

"You're a very interesting woman, Miss O'Toole. I look forward to hearing what you decide. And perhaps being one of your first clients." His gaze traveled around the group. "I'm sure I'll see you here and there, since you plan to stay a few days. Have a good night, now, ya hear?"

"You too." Lilly and Erin watched as he turned and left the room.

Cade was looking at his sister as if he'd never seen her before. Lilly suspected that he'd never before seen this side of her.

Erin leaned against the back of her chair and blotted her lips daintily with the napkin. "Well, how did I do?"

"As well as I expected," Cade told her. "Better. Lilly? What was your impression?"

"I think Erin handled herself very well. It's obvious she knows her business and that she can hold her own with the likes of Sam Davies."

"Do you think he bought our story?" Lilly asked.

"Yes." Cade took a sip of his coffee, even though it had to

be stone-cold by now. Lilly knew he liked to drink something to kill any lingering flavor of the sweet dessert, a little quirk of his that she'd noticed from the weeks they spent together. Something they had in common.

"He was feeling us out, trying to see what we're up to and if we'll be any problem. I think he was impressed with Erin. He has to know she's no fool." Cade smiled. "The part about consulting your lawyer was genius."

"Would it surprise you to learn I do have a lawyer?" Erin asked with a lift of her dark eyebrows.

"Not really. You've always managed to surprise us in one way or another."

That seemed to give her pause. "Well, for your information, I do." She reached into her reticule and handed Cade some money. "Go pay the bill, brother, and let's go back to our little home away from home. I'm exhausted."

CHAPTER 8

Lilly's sleep was light, restless, interrupted by the sounds of cursing, yelling, and the pounding of horse hooves. Once a single gunshot piercing the night sent her bolt upright in a second of pure terror. The darkness of the unfamiliar room did little to comfort her; the thought of Cade sleeping just down the hallway did. Whatever else she thought of the man, she trusted him to take care of her and his sister. . . .

The scent of something cooking wafted up from downstairs and woke Lilly. Not bothering to hide a yawn, she raised onto her elbows and glanced out the lacy curtain that hung between the fringed edges of the green velvet draperies. Morning. Finally. What time was anyone's guess.

Swinging her legs over the edge of the bed, she scurried behind the dressing screen to make use of the chamber pot, then poured some tepid water into the china washbowl and washed up. Without bothering to dress, she grabbed the robe draped over the walnut footboard of the bed and shrugged into it on her way down the stairs.

The tantalizing aroma of baking bread and frying bacon came from the small kitchen area where they'd guessed Dusty's cook had prepared meals for him and his "girls." Lilly was surprised to see Cade buttering a slice of the brown bread the Irish were so fond of, while Erin used an egg turner to bathe some eggs with bacon grease. All seemed well, so the siblings must have called a truce, at least for the moment.

Sensing her in the doorway, Cade turned. "Ever the sleepyhead."

Lilly smothered a yawn and said, "I hardly slept a wink last night. Didn't all the commotion keep the two of you awake?"

"Not really."

"I heard it, but it didn't bother me," Erin added.

"Where did the food come from?"

"I sent Cade out a bit ago to see what the grocer had to offer. Do you cook?"

The very notion of trying to make a meal took Lilly aback. Traveling from place to place, the troupe had stayed mostly in rooming houses and eaten their meals there or at some restaurant or another. She didn't recall ever having a kitchen.

"No." Both of her companions looked at her as if she had two heads. "I've never had a proper home, so I've never learned to cook."

"Then it looks like you'll do the washing up," Erin told her.

"That sounds like a reasonable exchange," Cade agreed. "Don't you agree, Lilly?"

"It is." Her voice held a confidence she was far from feeling. She had no idea how one went about doing that either, but how hard could it be?

An hour later she was finding out. After the three of them had shared the breakfast and planned their day, Erin got dressed and set out with Cade to explore the area that would be their temporary home. Lilly was left to wash the breakfast dishes, which was proving more difficult than she'd imagined.

The greasy remains of the meal refused to come off the plates no matter how much of the harsh lye soap she used.

Irritated, she stood with her wet hands on her hips, looking at the dishes sitting in the revolting dishwater with its skin of congealed bacon fat floating on top. Helping in the kitchen had been her job in New Orleans, and Lamartine had never seemed to have this problem. How did Lilly always get stuck with mundane chores when everyone else was out looking for clues? And how was she going to explain the unwashed dishes to her two partners? She was debating her next course of action when she heard a knock at the kitchen door.

She stood transfixed, staring at the dark wood and wondering if she should answer it. She wasn't expecting anyone, and she could think of no one except perhaps the marshal who would have reason to stop by. She'd about decided to ignore the summons when the rapping started up again.

It didn't sound like a man's knock, and, because her curiosity had gotten the best of her, she snatched up a towel and dried her hands on the way to the door. Flipping the lock, she pulled open the door.

The woman standing in the aperture looked near her own age, but there was something, almost a haunted expression in the depths of her dark eyes, that hinted of seeing and experiencing things Lilly could only imagine. She was clean and dressed in a plain white shirtwaist and brown skirt.

"May I help you?" Lilly asked, wondering why the woman had come. She didn't miss the nervous twisting of the hands clutched together at the stranger's waist.

"Are you Miss O'Toole?"

"No. I'm Miss Long. Lilly. Miss O'Toole's friend."

"I'm Bonnie Brady, and I'd like to speak with her for a moment. Is she here?" The question was accompanied by a quick glance over her shoulder, as if she were afraid someone had followed her into the alley and might see her.

"I'm afraid she's out, Miss Brady. She and her . . ."—just in time, Lilly remembered that Cade was playing Erin's body- guard, not her brother—"associate have gone to look around town."

She was about to suggest that Miss Brady come back later when she blurted, "Do you mind if I come in?" Once again, Lilly's visitor checked behind her. Was she hiding from someone?

Recalling the uncomfortable feeling she'd experienced when someone had been watching her, Lilly stepped aside. "Certainly. Come in." She waved a hand toward the doorway leading to the parlor. "We'll sit in there."

Bonnie Brady settled into the corner of one of the faded settees, and Lilly sat in a chair across from her.

"I hope I didn't interrupt anything important."

Lilly attempted a smile. "I was doing dishes. Or trying to."

Bonnie frowned. "What do you mean?"

"No matter how much soap I use, I can't get the grease off."

"Then your water must have gotten cold."

Gotten cold? Lilly had no idea the dishwater was supposed to be hot. She looked at Bonnie, who broke into laughter.

"Don't tell me you didn't know that the wash and rinse water is supposed to be hot."

"I didn't," Lilly confessed. "My . . . family traveled around a lot, and I've never had a proper home."

Bonnie jumped to her feet. "Come on, I'll show you." Without waiting for Lilly, she headed toward the kitchen.

"You seem familiar with the place," Lilly said, following her new self-designated helper.

"I used to work for Dusty."

Moving around as if she knew exactly what to do, Bonnie set about adding more kindling to the stove. Once the small blaze was burning, she picked up the dishpan and, balancing it against her hip, opened the alley door and poured out the murky water. She used the kitchen pump to refill the kettle and added water to both the dishpans before setting them on the stove.

"Were you the çook?" Lilly asked.

The comment elicited another laugh. "No. There's no money cooking for a living. I was one of Dusty's doves. That's what he called us. Dusty's Doves."

Lilly wasn't surprised by the announcement that the stranger sold herself for a living, but like Erin, Bonnie Brady wasn't what Lilly had expected from a lady of the evening.

A possibility leaped into Lilly's mind. Maybe being left to clean up while Cade and Erin looked around had been a blessing. If anyone knew who the main players were and the intricacies of how the politics worked in the infamous Third Ward, it would be Bonnie Brady or someone like her. Becoming Bonnie's new best friend might be just what was needed. She was bound to know *something* about Nora's situation.

Even though Lilly couldn't ask direct questions about Nora, perhaps something connected to her disappearance would come up during the conversation and give Lilly the chance to ask questions. She refused to act as Cade's lover and cling to his arm while pretending the lack of a brain or any common sense while he and Erin worked the case.

Their assignment in New Orleans had involved more people, and she'd been glad for his help, but in their positions as house servants they could do little but observe the family until their day off. She'd felt as if she were a servant and not an agent of the most prestigious detective bureau in the country. Thank goodness, the roles they were playing now were far different. This time, they were not confined by so many rules and had more freedom to explore various avenues.

She and Cade might be partners, but Nora was *her* friend. This was personal, and Lilly vowed to leave no stone unturned to find out where Nora was and take her home, to safety.

Her decision made, Lilly said, "Why did Dusty leave town?"

"He got behind on his payments to Longhair Jim, and he didn't have much choice but to skedaddle in the middle of the night."

One of the things Lilly had learned since becoming a Pinkerton operative was that, when you were involved in anything shady, "skedaddling" in the middle of the night was common practice. Bonnie's comment confirmed what Marshal Davies had told them the evening before.

"Who's Longhair Jim?"

"Jim Courtright. He was the marshal here until a couple of years ago. They wanted him to clean up the Acre, and he did make a lot of arrests, but just like Marshal Davies, he usually let the girls out the next day. The madams wanted him out because he never bothered the gambling parlors or saloons.

"When the outlaws started coming in, the law started cracking down again, but then the businessmen griped, saying that cleaning up the place was bad for business."

"So, the local companies are willing to accept illegal activities as long as they profit from it." Again, just as the marshal had told them the night before.

"That about sums it up. Before Courtright came up for re-election, the *Democrat* pulled its support, and Davies beat him," Bonnie said, testing the temperature of the heating water with her fingertips. "Personally, I think Velvet and Rosie had something to do with it. They're both mighty fond of Sam." She tossed Lilly a towel. "Here. I'll wash. You dry."

Lilly was mortified. "Oh, no! That isn't necessary. I don't even know you."

"Hopefully you will, and in case you haven't noticed, I'm trying very hard to make a good impression." She swished the rag over the plate in the now steaming water, and then placed the plate in the clean rinse water.

"Why?"

"I came to talk to Miss O'Toole, hoping she'll consider hiring me once she gets things set up and ready to open."

Word had certainly traveled fast! Lilly should have known that's why the woman had come. How could she tell Bonnie that they weren't really going to reopen the dance hall? She couldn't. Their job was to find Nora and get her to safety and do their best to expose the mail-order bride organization. In the meanwhile, it wouldn't hurt to find out what she could from her unexpected visitor.

"Where are you working now?" Lilly asked.

"I work for Velvet."

"And you aren't happy there?" Lilly set the plate she'd just finished drying aside.

"I can't imagine anyone who's happy working for Velvet." Bonnie gave a little shudder. "She has a real mean streak. If she knew I was here, no telling what she'd do."

That explained why Bonnie had been so uncomfortable standing outside. She didn't want anyone seeing her at another establishment and reporting back to her boss.

"What brought you to Texas?" Lilly asked, wondering why someone would come to a place so rough and violent.

"It's a long story, but basically, I couldn't find work in New Orleans. They told me my speech and manners weren't good enough for those fancy bordellos down there. Then, someone told me a girl could always find work here if she was disease free and halfway decent looking, so here I am." She turned to look at Lilly. "What about you?"

"Me?"

"Is Miss O'Toole a hard taskmaster?"

Lilly brought out the story they'd made up for just such an occasion. "Oh, she's not my boss. We met a couple of years ago, working at a place in Chicago. We're just friends."

"So you ain't a workin' girl anymore?"

"Not for a while now," she heard herself saying without a second's hesitation. "Cade—he's the man who keeps the peace for Erin's place back in Chicago—and I are together now. I haven't worked for a living since."

The ease with which the lie tripped from her lips amazed her. Untruths became easier every day. Lilly supposed she could console her smarting conscience by telling herself she lied to help others.

"That's nice," Bonnie said, scrubbing on the last plate. "Finding someone to take us away from here is what we all want, but so far no Prince Charming has come along for me."

Sadness washed over Lilly. A man to take them away. The thing all young women wanted. A home. Husband. Family. It was what she'd wanted when she married Timothy, and what Nora had wanted when she'd signed up to marry a stranger and traveled to this godforsaken place.

"I have a friend who signed up to be a mail-order bride in hopes of finding that dream," Lilly said, thinking that it was a logical way to bring up the subject of Nora.

"More and more women seem to be doing that, and I hear it works well for some," Bonnie told her. "Others . . ." Her voice trailed away, and she gave a shrug that said nothing, but Lilly saw an emptiness in her eyes. Bonnie shook off the moment's darkness and smiled. "How did it work out for your friend?"

"I think it's too early to say."

Bonnie wrung out the dishwashing rag and hung it on the edge of the table. "That's done."

"I can't thank you enough," Lilly said, as Bonnie slung the water out the back door. "I'll know what to do next time."

"I'm glad to help," Bonnie assured her. Then she sighed. "I guess I'd better get back. I don't want Velvet waking up and missing me."

"I'm sure we'll be spending time at various places around town, so maybe I'll see you again."

Bonnie smiled. "I hope so. I like you."

Somewhat taken aback, Lilly replied, "I like you, too." She realized as she spoke the words that she meant them. Bonnie, like so many of the women who worked as prostitutes, did so out of necessity. What they did to make a living did not make them bad people any more than being an actress did.

"Don't forget to tell Miss O'Toole I stopped by," Bonnie said as Lilly followed her to the door.

To her surprise, Bonnie pulled Lilly into a loose hug. Then, releasing Lilly, Bonnie said, "There's something about you that's different, Lilly Long. I don't know what it is, but it's very nice."

Without a word, Bonnie opened the door and slipped outside.

CHAPTER 9

When Cade and Erin returned to Dusty's, they all dressed for their first night of observing the nocturnal mating rituals in the Acre.

Erin looked stunning in a simple gown of soft blue-green satin with a matching metallic gauze insert smocked at the throat and waist. The simple, flowing lines of the gown were in direct contrast to the popular corset and bustle style made so fashionable by Parisian designers.

In contrast to the usual madams' attire, her gown was tasteful, elegant, and promised the locals a hint of what she would bring to the Acre if she chose to reopen Dusty's. She exuded class and refinement, just what they wanted everyone to see in her. Only truly confident women could defy convention with such elegance.

As her friend, Lilly wore a simple dress she'd used in her first leading role as Priscilla Dunlap, a spoiled young woman from a wealthy family. The soft gown was of finely woven cotton muslin with narrow green and white stripes. The fitted bodice boasted an unadorned, proper scoop neckline and three-quarter-length sleeves. The solid green ruffles at the elbow and hem were the only adornment.

Cade wore one of his simple black sack suits that showed off his intimidating physique to its best advantage. Carrying a sweet-smelling cheroot, and wearing a scowl along with his bowler, he looked the part of a no-nonsense bouncer . . . especially when you added the jagged scar that ran down the left side of his face.

Rosalie Padgett's Silver Slipper was the first place they visited. The moment they stepped through the door, Lilly realized the sporting house was aptly named. The large common area, where men could mix and mingle with the doves, was decorated with sofas and chairs upholstered in royal blue velvet and satin. Dainty tables, too small in scale for the overstuffed seating, were done in silver leaf. A large replica of a ladies' dancing shoe—also done in silver—and at least five feet in length and three feet high at the heel, was situated on a pedestal against one wall. A large portrait of a blond woman with her hair done in a style suited to a young girl hung above the oversized footwear. The famous Rosalie Padgett herself.

Cade led them to a table, and they all three ordered sarsaparilla, much to the barman's surprise. Though she didn't know a lot about her partner, Lilly did know that for a time after the death of his wife, Cade had partaken of a wee too much alcohol and been fired from the Pinkerton Agency. Since he'd come back to work, he'd been as sober as the proverbial judge. Though she sometimes indulged in a glass of wine, Lilly was not a drinker, and she assumed Erin had made the choice to abstain so that she could keep her head about her while they watched and learned.

The women who worked for Rosalie made no attempt to approach them, but the tingling at the nape of her neck, that same feeling she'd experienced when she'd gone looking for Timothy in MacGregor's Tavern, alerted Lilly that every move the trio made was being observed, which wasn't surprising. Unless they were employed there, women were seldom spotted in sporting houses. Those females who craved the male counterpart of the establishment's entertainment were more discreet and found it on the sly. In secret rooms and backdoor assignations.

It looked as if there were four women working the room. All of them were reasonably attractive, though once again, they had been too heavy-handed with their powder, rouge, and kohl. They were not so scantily clad as Tim's harlot had been, and if their bodices were too tight and low cut, they were not so cheap looking. Lilly supposed this was what was meant by having a higher class of woman.

Nora wasn't among them. Common sense told Lilly that it was silly to feel disappointment. Had she really expected to find her at the first place they entered? Still, it was discouraging to think of how many of these dens of iniquity she might have to patronize before finding her friend.

She scanned the room's occupants again. The customers were no doubt wondering what two women were doing there, even if they were accompanied by a man who looked as if he could take care of them, as well as himself.

"Do you see your friend?" Cade asked.

"No." Even she heard the heaviness in her voice.

"Never mind." He lifted his glass in a toast to the two women, and murmured, "To our success." The mugs clanked together, and they all took a sip.

"We're causing quite a stir," Erin said, sotto voce, as she allowed her gaze to travel around the room and its occupants.

"That we are, little sister."

"Do you think there's any chance of learning anything just sitting here?" Lilly asked.

"Who knows? I'll make a trip to the necessary in a few moments and see if I can strike up a conversation. It's my experience that a man in his cups will spill his guts if properly approached."

"And you would know," Erin quipped, wearing an innocent expression.

Cade's blue eyes darkened to a stormy steel, but he only offered a tight smile and made a *tsking* sound. "No sense being unpleasant, Erin."

"You're right. Sorry. Oh! Don't be obvious, but I think I see the illustrious lady in the portrait standing near the bar talking to some man."

"No surprise there," Cade said, sipping at his drink once more. "She'll be keeping an eye on things."

"She's looking right at us."

"Talking about us, too, I'll wager."

Lilly sneaked a peek. A tall man with his back to them stood nearby. Rosalie Padgett looked very much like her portrait. Tall and shapely, she projected an air of cool confidence that bordered on coldness. Her honey-hued hair was waved back at the sides and tortured into a mound of coils atop her head. The shorter front was curled and fell across her forehead in artful abandon.

As Lilly tried to assess the woman without bringing attention to herself, the madam placed her hand on her companion's arm, and he turned to get a glimpse of the newcomers. Lilly drew in a sharp breath, and the man turned away at once, as if he were afraid of being seen. Why?

"My, my, my," Erin cooed, smiling at her brother as if they were talking about something pleasant. "If it isn't Marshal Davies with Miss Rosalie."

"Davies?" Cade echoed, sneaking a peek for himself.

"Yes. And from the way she's cozying up to him, it doesn't look as if he's here to arrest her."

Cade took another swallow of his drink. "I'm guessing he's telling her everything he learned about us."

"I imagine you're right. Knowing how things work here, I didn't expect him to keep the news to himself," Lilly said. "Did you?"

"Not really."

"He'll probably make the rounds of all the madams to let them know there's a possibility of new competition coming to town. If they're paying him off to stay in business, he owes them that much," Cade said.

"Good point."

As they sat, pretending to enjoy their carbonated drinks, Lilly saw another man approach the couple. Tall, well built, and dressed in jeans and a plaid shirt, he swaggered, rather than walked. Like Rosalie, he oozed confidence. For those who liked a rugged man with a rough beard and a high opinion of himself, he might be considered attractive. Judging by his clothing, Lilly pegged him as a cowboy or a rancher. She immediately wondered what he could have to discuss with the madam. Rosalie listened to what he had to say without comment.

"I wonder who that is?"

Erin looked up and frowned. "I couldn't say. Brother, I think it's time you took yourself to the toilet."

"I believe it is." He scooted back his chair and stood. "You ladies keep an eye on things, and I'll see what I can find out."

Lilly and Erin conversed in a desultory manner for a few minutes. Finally, Erin said, "When Cade gets back, I'm ready to move on to Velvet's. Isn't that where your new friend works?"

"Yes. I'm thinking she'll be a good source of information if we can figure out how to get her talking."

"I'll leave that to you," Erin told her with a careless wave of her hand. "I'm here as your cover, not as a detective. All I'm concerned with is trying to decide if I want to make the most of my lover's gift. There's no reason I'd be interested in anything except the potential to make money." She smiled a saucy smile. "Of course, one never knows when—or how—I'll pick up a little nugget of information."

Lilly hadn't thought of it that way, but Erin was right. Her role as a potential new madam was their cover. Knowing the business as she did was what gave credibility to their presence. On the other hand, since Lilly was playing a former working girl, it was only natural that she'd be curious about her contemporaries . . . who or what had brought them here and why they'd turned to this way of life.

As a peacekeeper, Cade could question the bouncers, bartenders, and clientele about the girls, the troublemakers, and get a little deeper into how the "wanna play, gotta pay" scheme worked.

"Uh-oh!" Erin said under her breath, "the newcomer is coming over."

Before Lilly could reply, her companion's lips curved into an enticing smile. "Hello there, handsome."

Lilly looked up and saw the good-looking man who'd been talking to Davies and Rosalie standing next to her. His thumbs were hooked into the pockets of his jeans, and he was smiling down at her with a devilish grin. He was even better looking up close, and she decided his scruffy beard wasn't so bad after all.

If it hadn't been for the expression in his eyes, he might have won her over. His mouth smiled. His night-black eyes didn't. His tone was jovial. His eyes held secrets. Coldness. The same coldness she'd sensed in Rosalie Padgett.

He looked from her to Erin. "Mind if I join you, ladies?"

"Not at all," Erin assured him, patting the place next to her with a well-manicured hand.

The stranger pulled out a chair and sat down. "I hear you're looking to open up Dusty's old place."

Listen and learn, Lilly, she told herself, picking up her mug and taking another swallow of her drink.

"I'm considering it," Erin said. "I need to think on it long and hard." She extended her hand. "Erin O'Toole. This is my friend, Lilly Long."

He took Erin's hand. "Elijah Wilkins."

Lilly choked on her drink and went into a fit of coughing. As she searched in her reticule for a handkerchief, her mind whirled with disbelief. *Elijah Wilkins*. The man who'd lured Nora into a trap by promising her the things she'd always wanted. Then, when she was away from safety and security, with no one to call on for help, he'd sold her like a slab of meat from the market.

Either Erin hadn't made the connection, or she was as good of an actress as her brother was an actor. Lilly had never imagined locating Wilkins would be so easy. She prayed her horror wasn't written on her face.

"Are you all right?" Erin asked as Lilly gained control of her coughing.

"Yes," she wheezed, dabbing at her mouth with the frilly square. "I just swallowed wrong."

Before she could regain her dignity, Elijah Wilkins extended his work-roughened hand, leaving her no choice but to take it. Somehow, she managed a smile. "Mr. Wilkins."

"I'm glad you're all right, Lilly."

She bristled. He dared to call her by her given name? Never mind that they had just met. To him, she was nothing but a tart, and, as a man, he was her superior. "I know you're not working, but I came over to see if you'd like to take a walk around town with me. I've always had a thing for redheads."

Lilly's startled gaze flew to Erin, who raised her eyebrows and smiled as if to say, "You said you could take care of yourself, so how are you going to get out of this one?"

How *would* a lady of the evening respond to such a request? "I'm sorry, Mr. Wilkins, but I'm afraid—"

Before she could finish, she felt a heavy hand on her shoulder. "She's afraid I wouldn't like that very much."

Lilly looked up toward the familiar voice and felt all the tension ease from her body. McShane. Thank goodness he'd come back when he had!

Wilkins studied Cade from head to toe, taking in the scar, the breadth of his shoulders, and his beat-up hands. "I'm sorry. I thought you were just the ladies' protection. I didn't know your relationship was a more personal one."

"Well, now you do." Playing his role to the hilt, Cade offered his hand. "Cadence McShane."

"Elijah Wilkins." Trying to make light of the tense moment, Wilkins looked at Erin and said, "Maybe you'd like to take a walk with me, Erin. I can introduce you to some people and explain how things work around here."

Erin's expression was colder than a grave on a winter night. "I'm not the kind of woman who likes being second choice, Mr. Wilkins," she informed him in a haughty tone.

Then, while he tried to find a way to get out of the hole he'd dug for himself, she offered him a bright smile. "But then, I have a thing for men with beards, and I need all the information I can get."

She stood, and Wilkins followed suit. "I'll see the two of you back at Dusty's in an hour or so," she told Cade and Lilly. Without another word, she tucked her hand in the crook of the pretender's elbow and let him lead her out the door and into the night.

CHAPTER 10

"Will she be all right?" Lilly asked as Erin and Elijah Wilkins left the building. "I don't trust him."

Cade leaned over and reached for his mug, cutting her a sideways glance. "I don't like it, either, but leaving with strange men is what she does, remember?" He lifted the mug. "Ma used to say 'if I let myself I'd worry myself to death over that.' Well, that's how I feel about Erin. I've done all the worrying I intend to do for her."

Lilly heard the disgust in his voice and understood what he meant. She'd gotten to know him better over the past few months, and she knew he didn't mean it. Like her, he was cautious about letting himself care too much for anyone. Caring about someone increased your chances of getting hurt, tenfold.

He downed the remains of his beverage, placed some money on the table, and said, "Let's get out of here. I'd like to go to another place or two before we go home."

She nodded. "Velvet's?"

"That's exactly what I was thinking."

Outside the bawdy house, Lilly tucked her hand into the crook of his arm, and they strolled down the dimly lit street toward Velvet's. The sounds of coarse laughter, blistering curses, and the music of "Oh, Dem Golden Slippers" being pounded out on a tinny-sounding pianoforte mingled with the shuffle of horses' hooves, the yelling of spectators at a cockfight on the next block, and the low keening of a woman somewhere in the shadows.

The sounds reminded Lilly of the night she'd searched the streets of Chicago for her thieving husband. Only he wasn't her husband, thank the good Lord. It was almost worth losing every penny to know she'd never been bound to the cheating liar.

"I gather that was the no-account who persuaded your friend to come out here as a bride," Cade said, breaking the silence stretching between them.

"It was," she acknowledged with a nod. "When he told Erin his name, I almost choked on my sarsaparilla."

Though she could barely make it out in the dimness, she saw the hint of a smile. "I noticed from across the room."

"Did you learn anything while you were gone?"

"The bouncer said that Davies and Rosalie are thick as thieves, which is why we saw them talking together."

Lilly turned to look at him. "Thick, as in he thinks there's something more between them than her paying for protection?"

"He seems to think so."

"Hm. That can't be proper, can it?"

"Have you seen much of anything proper since we've been here?"

"Now that you mention it, no. It's just that I can't imagine people choosing to live this way."

"I'm sure that some, like your Nora, didn't choose it, and others, like your new friend, Bonnie, had little choice."

He was right. Since becoming a Pinkerton, she was learning some hard truths. Circumstance often handed out limited options.

"When we get there, you try to talk to Bonnie, if you can. I'll check with the bouncer, just like I did at the Silver Slipper."

"Fine." They walked a few more steps, but Lilly was not ready to give up on the conversation just yet. One question begged to be answered. "Is that why you're so angry with Erin? She had other choices?"

"Did anyone ever tell you that you ask too many questions?" he asked, reiterating his standard reply when he thought she was delving too deeply into his past, or his feelings.

"You do, on a regular basis. I keep hoping to wear you down."

"Doubtful."

He stopped and held out a hand to help her step from the wooden sidewalk onto the dirt street. Velvet's was directly across from them. Like Dusty's place, it was a two-story building. The lights on the second floor were muted by the drawn blinds that spent more time down than up. A large black sign edged with a fancy scroll border hung over the roof of the porch. VELVET'S was emblazoned across it in white, flowing script. Lights blazed from behind the double swinging doors, and the sounds of "Camptown Races" drifted into the night.

Lilly found the rollicking song contrary to her taste. She longed for violins and horns warming up in the orchestra pit before a performance. Hell's Half Acre with its dancing girls singing naughty songs on stage was a far cry from Shakespeare.

She missed it. The theater. The performances. Pierce and Rose. She missed it all, just as Pierce had predicted she would. Still, she would not go back. Even though she hadn't been a detective long, it was long enough for her to know that the work she did made a difference.

A short time later, Cade was holding one of the swinging

saloon doors for her, and she stepped into another of those once-alien establishments that were fast becoming commonplace.

Velvet's was a cross between Dusty's place and MacGregor's. As in the others, there was a bar. The mirror behind it was newer than the one in MacGregor's had been, and it was framed in gold leaf. The parlor-type setting had circular, tufted seating, upholstered in black velvet. Round tables, made just to fit the center, held statues of cavorting cherubs with bows and arrows.

Cupid? Really? Did Velvet Hook actually believe love was connected to her tawdry business in any way? As in MacGregor's, there were women working the floor . . . pausing at tables to smile and flirt and laugh at whatever the men said. And as in MacGregor's they wore far too much powder and paint. But instead of bloomers, chemises, and corsets, these women had on mesh hose and black satin costumes with ruffled petticoats beneath full, knee-length skirts.

Though their low-cut bodices exposed generous portions of their chests and shoulders, they were far from indecent. In fact, many fashionable storefronts displayed respectable ball gowns with a similar cut, yet those gowns were considered quite stylish and not at all improper. Colorful ostrich feathers were attached to the women's upswept hair and bounced with every move they made.

The stage curtain was drawn, and an ornate easel sitting in front held a sign that stated that the Dancing Quartet would be performing the French-inspired cancan at nine. Lilly scrutinized each woman carefully. She didn't see Nora or Bonnie anywhere. *Now what?* she wondered as her sense of futility deepened.

She followed Cade to a table near the bar, and, once again, he ordered two carbonated beverages. Once again, he received a strange look from everyone around him. Lilly watched him shrug and smile and pick up the foam-topped mugs. He was still smiling when he reached the table.

"What's so funny?"

"Everyone is shocked that I don't order a shot of whiskey, or at least a beer."

"What do you say to them?"

"That I have to keep my wits about me to protect the lady."

"That makes sense, but I doubt you'll be needing to protect me from anyone."

"You never know, lass, you never know," he said, setting one of the mugs in front of her. "Some men don't mind a sharp tongue as long as the lady's face is pretty enough. And," he told her, "Elijah Wilkins was quite taken with you."

Lilly glared at him and reached for her mug. "Don't remind me." She looked around. "I don't see Bonnie anywhere."

"Is she one of the dancers?" Cade asked.

Lilly frowned. "No." She shook her head. "I don't know. I guess I just thought that Velvet would use the girls however she could."

"I suppose it's possible, but I imagine in a place like this that Velvet has dancers *and* working girls."

Lilly was thinking about that when she caught a movement from the corner of her eye. Her gaze moved upward. A man was exiting one of the rooms. As he started toward the staircase, he grasped the edges of his striped gray vest and gave it a little tug to settle it over his paunch.

Her troubled gaze met Cade's. "Do you think she's . . . upstairs then?"

He shrugged. The expression in his eyes looked almost apologetic. "Possible. Even probable."

The image that rose in Lilly's mind was not pleasant.

"Are you all right?"

She brought her gaze to his. "I'm fine," she lied. "Why?"

"You just turned a rather sickly white."

"It's just that I can't comprehend . . . this life."

He allowed his gaze to move around the room, taking in the people, no doubt gauging which of them, if any, was a threat. "Neither can I."

One of the dancers headed in their direction, her gaze fixed on McShane, but she caught Lilly's eye and stopped, turned, and walked the other way.

"What was that all about?"

"What?" she asked, all innocence.

"The glare you gave that pretty little thing."

Lilly placed her elbow on the table and propped her chin in her palm. "It meant, 'stay away from my man.' We're supposed to be lovers, remember?"

"How can I forget, when you're such delightful company?" He straightened suddenly. "Hullo! There's a lass coming down the stairs. Is that your friend?"

Thinking it might be Nora, Lilly turned to see Bonnie coming down the flight of stairs, running her hand along the polished bannister as she made her slow descent. Her face was devoid of expression, and Lilly knew that if she were close enough to see, her new friend's eyes would be bleak. Empty. As empty as her own heart had been when she'd discovered Tim's betrayal.

"D'ya want me to approach her? See if we can buy her a drink?"

Lilly thought about it a minute and then shook her head. "No. I think it's time you went to talk to the bouncer. I even give you permission to flirt with that dancer. Just don't be too obvious, and don't let me see you."

Cade sketched a sharp salute and left her sitting alone at the table. The act caught Bonnie's attention. Spying Lilly, she changed direction, passing McShane on the way.

Lilly gestured toward the chair he'd just vacated. "How are you?"

"Just peachy." Bonnie sat down and, rubbing at the red places on her upper arms, signaled for the barkeep.

"What'll it be, Bonnie?" The stocky man smiled at her, transforming his average-looking face into something very attractive.

"Whisky."

"I'll be back with it in a minute."

"I think he likes you," Lilly noted.

"He does. I like him, too." She didn't seem happy about the notion.

"Then why not try to see where those feelings go?"

Bonnie's mouth curved upward at the corners in a sad smile. "Charlie can barely support himself, much less another person, and I don't know much besides what I do."

"You know how to clean and wash dishes. Maybe you could find work as a housekeeper for some rich family."

"You're sweet, Lilly," Bonnie told her, attempting a smile. "But for someone in the business, you seem a little naïve. Do you think Velvet would just let me quit?"

"Why wouldn't she?"

Charlie brought her drink and set it in front of her. Bonnie gave his hand a pat. "Thanks, Charlie. You're a dear."

She downed the shot glass of liquor in one huge gulp, cringed and shuddered and coughed a little. Taking a frilly handkerchief from a pocket, she dabbed at her watering eyes.

"Velvet is very protective of her girls," she said when she could speak again. "She expects us to toe the line and considers me one of her best moneymakers."

Lilly's heart broke a little more. She looked around the room and saw McShane in a far corner with the dove who had been so interested in him. He had placed his hands against the wall on either side of her head, effectively pinning her there. She didn't seem to mind. Lilly was a bit surprised to realize she did.

Reminding herself that he was only doing his job, she brought her attention back to Bonnie. "What about the dancers? Is that all they do? Dance?"

Bonnie gave a sharp little laugh. "Of course not." She held her glass aloft, catching Charlie's eye. "I'm not sure how they do it where you're from, but Velvet treats her dancers especially well. It's hard to find a girl who can kick up her heels the way they're expected to, so when she finds someone who can, she gives them a little more leeway than she does the rest of us."

"What do you mean?"

"They don't have to give a 'performance' until after they go on stage. Until then, they just pass on any interested men to one of us."

"Why aren't you a dancer?"

She smiled wryly. "Probably because I have two left feet." Charlie came and switched out the empty glass for a full one. This time Bonnie sipped at the fiery liquid. "When an actress happens to come this way, there's a bidding war between Velvet and Rosie to see who gets her."

Lilly couldn't stop the gasp of shock that escaped her. "Bidding war? The madams haggle for the girls?"

Bonnie shrugged. "They do."

"Where do the girls come from?"

"Here and there. Everywhere. Some, like me, come because they know there's work in town that provides food three times a day and a roof over their heads."

"Is that a fair exchange, considering what you go through?" Lilly looked pointedly at the marks on Bonnie's arms.

"Everything's a transaction of some kind, isn't it?" She took another sip of her drink and frowned at Lilly. "Things must be really different where you come from."

"I guess they are. You must understand that Chicago is much more cosmopolitan than Ft. Worth."

"I hadn't thought of that."

As dismayed as she was, Lilly was determined to know

more and perhaps get a hint about where Nora was. "Do many actresses come here looking for work?"

"A few."

Lilly was about to delve more deeply into that, but Charlie approached the table and leaned over to whisper something in Bonnie's ear. Apprehension filled her eyes. He gave her a pat on the shoulder and flashed Lilly an apologetic look before heading to the bar.

"I have to go," Bonnie said, scooting her chair away from the table. "Velvet isn't happy that I'm socializing instead of working. And she'll be wondering what we were talking about."

From the expression on Bonnie's face, Lilly surmised that an angry Velvet was not a good thing. "Which one is Velvet?"

"The one in the gold gown sitting in the corner."

Lilly saw a short, plump woman playing a game of solitaire, smoking a cheroot, and sipping a drink of some sort while managing to keep an eye on everything happening in the room. She caught Lilly staring. If Rosalie's eyes were cold, Velvet's expression radiated fire. She didn't look like anyone Lilly would want to cross. Bonnie's apprehension was understandable.

"I'm sorry. I didn't mean to cause any trouble. Just tell her that my friend owns Dusty's, and I was asking questions about the business."

"Sure," Bonnie said. "I'll try to come by as soon as possible." With that, she turned and walked away.

Lilly sat waiting for Cade, nursing her sarsaparilla, and thinking of what she'd learned. It was no wonder the suicide rate among the women was so high. The idea that Velvet expected Bonnie to go back to work when she'd just come downstairs was detestable, but was there anything that could be done about it?

Having lived a secure, relatively trouble-free life, Lilly confessed to looking down on women who'd chosen this path.

But the incident with Nora was teaching Lilly that sometimes there was no choice. A single woman alone in the world had few viable options for making a living, and for the unlearned or perhaps those who were not strong-willed, prostitution seemed their only way to survive.

Her perception was changing. Though she didn't condone the occupation, she no longer condemned the unfortunate women who had no other choice. It was not her place to pass judgment, but to reach out to those she could and try to show them a better path. She knew she could not help every woman used or abused by a man, nor could she end the terrible practice that had been in existence since the beginning of time, but she could help one woman at a time.

While she sat waiting for McShane to finish his flirting, a murmur swept through the room. A gaunt man of indiscernible age shuffled toward the bar. Thirty, perhaps, even though his hair was going gray at the temples and his emaciated state and jerky movements made him look much older. Yet despite the ravages of life, she realized that he'd once been attractive, without being overtly handsome. He had a "kind" face as Rose was fond of saying.

As he came closer, his haunted gaze collided with Lilly's, and if it had not been too absurd to be considered, she might have imagined she saw a glimmer of recognition there. Ridiculous! She'd never seen the man before. He looked away, and the moment passed.

She watched him take a seat at the bar and order a drink. Charlie set a mug of beer in front of the newcomer, who propped his forearms on the bar top, slumped over the brew, and stared into the foamy head, as if all the answers to his problems could be found there. A promise and a lie believed by far too many.

Sorrow enveloped him. It was there in the defensive way he'd entered the room, as if he wasn't certain how he would be received. It was in the unhappiness etched on his gaunt face. It was in the drooping of his shoulders, the way he seemed to block out everything around him. And it was in his eyes, which, for a brief second when they had met hers, had reflected the pain he carried deep inside.

She wondered who he was and what had happened to rob him of his youth and his joy. The man downed his beer faster than most, and, wiping his mouth on his sleeve, he left. Only then did it seem as if the room took a collective sigh of relief.

Why?

Who was the man, and why did everyone look at him as if he were a pariah? Maybe Charlie knew. Bonnie would tell her, if Bonnie ever managed to speak to her without fear of Velvet's retribution.

Lilly looked around the room, taking in the drunkenness, the overt, seductive moves between the men and the women hired to provide them pleasure. How many of those men were married? Had homes and wives? Children? How many would partake of the sordidness available and then go home and profess their love and devotion to their families?

She'd studied the Bible enough to know that no sin was larger than the next, but, by its very nature, this seemed worse. Overwhelmed by the enormity of the problem and her inability to fix it, she felt the sudden urge to cry. Then, remembering Robert Pinkerton's face on the day she'd been hired by his father, she stiffened her spine and her resolve. She would not give the younger Pinkerton son the satisfaction of quitting in the middle of an operation. She would do what she could and go back to Chicago.

And then, she would see.

CHAPTER 11

Cade returned to the table just minutes after the stranger left. He looked rather pleased with himself. Despite her determination to keep things between them on a purely professional level, Lilly could not quite forget the kiss they'd exchanged when they'd gone to New Orleans as a married couple. Her annoying awareness of him, and the fact that he had been flirting with the dancer, made her cranky.

"Stop grinning like a jackanapes," she said.

Mischief danced in his eyes. "My, aren't you the cross one? Don't tell me it's past your bedtime already?"

She glared at him. He flicked a finger toward her beverage and asked, "Are you going to drink that?"

"No."

"Then I am." He reached for the mug and took a healthy swallow.

Lilly watched in surprise at the intimacy of his drinking from her glass, from the very place her lips had been.

"Did you find out anything from your friend?" he asked, after draining at least half the contents.

"Not much. The dancers are expected to offer private per-formances once they finish their cancan. Evidently dancers are much sought after and relatively rare. Former actresses often fit the bill."

"That makes sense," he said, nodding. "Anything about Nora?"

"No. The conversation had just turned in that direction when the bartender—Charlie—came to tell Bonnie that Vel-vet was not happy about her shirking her duties." Lilly sighed. "And I learned that it's a miserable, horrible life."

"She said that?" Cade asked, frowning.

"She didn't have to. The implication was in every word she spoke, every expression on her face. Just hearing her talk about it is heartbreaking."

Cade didn't say anything.

"Enough of that. What about you? Did your little dove tell you anything of use?"

"In fact, she did. I found out the competition between Vel-vet and Rosalie for top madam is fierce, and they've competed with each other for years. Goldie said that—"

"*Goldie?*" Lilly interrupted. "Her name is *Goldie?*"

"Probably not," Cade said without missing a beat, "but that's neither here nor there, now, is it?"

"I suppose not," Lilly said, properly chastened.

"Goldie said they're the top two madams in town and that they'll do whatever they can to try to best each other. They've even been known to go after each other's girls every chance they get."

Lilly frowned. "Go after? What do you mean?"

"Steal them away. Offer them more money."

"Why on earth would they do that?"

"To have a better stable for the men to choose from."

Lilly gave a fierce shake of her head. "Don't."

"Don't what?"

"Don't refer to them as a stable. It sounds so . . . I don't know, as if they're . . . animals. They're just poor, miserable women, and most of them would rather be anywhere else doing anything else."

"You prefer that I call them prostitutes?"

Lilly shook her head and rested her forehead in her palm. The whole sordid situation troubled her in ways she couldn't begin to understand. Or explain. "I'm sorry. It's just . . ."

His tone softened. "Look, lass, I know a lot of what's been thrown at you these past months must have shaken you to the core. I know that some of what we've had to do has been contrary to your beliefs."

Lilly looked up. His eyes held concern and understanding. She knew he was referring to what had happened in New Orleans. He'd been in the business longer than she had. He was older. He'd been playing roles to aid the Pinkertons for so long that he'd become an expert at hiding his feelings. For him to show concern for what she was going through was a little surprising. What he said was true.

She started talking, everything that had been building inside her spilling out in a rush of words. "Preachers are supposed to be godly men, not thieves and worse," she said, referencing her first case.

"They are," Cade agreed. "It's unfortunate that there are some who abuse their position for their own gain."

Recalling the ugly state of affairs they'd discovered in New Orleans, she said, "Marriage is a sacred union, and those vows should not be taken lightly."

"I agree."

"And now this." She spread her hands palms up. "I'm ashamed to say that all my life, I looked down on women who sold themselves for money. I thought of them as terrible, weak creatures." Her earnest gaze bored into his. "But since we've been here, I've learned that for some of them, this life was their only option. And women like Nora, who are lured into it under false pretenses, have no choice at all in the matter."

"You're learning," Cade said. "Life is hard."

"Yes," she said with a nod. "And things aren't always black-and-white."

His lips twisted into a sardonic smile. "There are definitely many shades of gray in between."

Indeed, there were. "I wanted to become a Pinkerton to help women who'd been misused by men, and there are many, many of them. This place confirms that. But almost every day I'm learning that wickedness isn't just a male trait. Women can be just as evil. That's very troubling to someone who was taught that women are to be nurturing and gentle as well as strong."

Even though her mother's life paralleled those of the women here in many ways, Kate Long had possessed those basic feminine qualities, and Rose certainly did.

"Wickedness doesn't concern itself with gender, Lilly. It just looks for weakness of character. Selfishness. Avarice. Any chink in our armor that offers a place for it to enter. Make no mistake, lass, the devil will take whomever he can, man or woman."

"I don't know if I can do this, Cade," she said, forgetting in the despair of the moment to keep their relationship on a professional footing.

"Don't know if you can do what?"

"Do the work we need to do without letting all the ugliness consume me."

"You get used to it."

Irritation surged through her. Irritation and alarm. His answer wasn't what she wanted to hear. "That's just it. I don't *want* to get used to it. I want to do the work, but I don't want it to change me. I don't want to get hard and uncaring."

She saw that her comments alarmed him, and McShane

was never nonplussed. He stared into her eyes, as if he were searching for the right thing to say.

"Only you can decide if you're right for the work, Lilly," he told her in a gentle tone. "And I'd never try to sway you one way or the other. It isn't easy. It does change you. I won't deny that. We do have to get tougher mentally, even if it goes against the grain."

"Even you?"

"D'ya think I was happy when I shot my first man?" he countered. Bleakness darkened his eyes. "I vomited afterward, and I didn't sleep fer weeks. But he'd killed someone else . . . and he had a gun pointed at me. Only one of us was walking away, and I decided it should be me."

Unexpectedly, he reached out and placed a scarred hand over hers. "You knew when you went into law enforcement that it would be difficult, yet you chose it anyway. The very nature of our business means we're often forced to do things that are foreign to our nature . . . even our values. All we can do is ask the good Lord each night to help us hold on to our compassion, not lose our humanity. If that happens, we're in trouble."

She nodded, trying to take in everything he'd told her. His fingers tightened around hers.

"You're becoming a good operative, Lilly Long, and the fact that you do care so deeply about what you do is one of the qualities that makes you so effective."

He released her hand and finished off the sarsaparilla, then set down the mug with a thud. "I think it's time to go back to Dusty's and call it a night. Things will look different in the morning."

He was right. Things would look different, but would they look better? Lilly let him scoot back her chair, and they left Velvet's together. She wasn't even aware of the warmth of his hand against her waist.

★ ★ ★

There was little talk between them as they walked back to their temporary home. Cade couldn't rid himself of Lilly's very genuine concerns about their work and if she had what it took to continue as an agent. Tonight was the first crack he'd seen in her determination to continue as a Pinkerton. It troubled him. And surprised him.

During the time they'd been together, he'd seen many different sides of her personality—from her stubbornness to her tender heart, her intelligence to her insightful instincts. She was quick and bright and spirited. She met things head-on. The life she'd lived as part of a traveling theater troupe had instilled a confidence and a certain level of fearlessness in her, yet the very fact that the theater was a somewhat cloistered environment had left her unsullied in many ways. And, though she might not realize it, she was still nursing wounds inflicted by her mother's lifestyle and tragic death.

He suspected that worry about Nora and seeing firsthand the life she'd been forced into was disturbing Lilly. She might have even noticed the similarities of her mother's life with that of Bonnie or the other girls working in the bordellos. The only difference was that Kate Long had not taken pay from her men.

Lilly turned to look at him, and he realized that without being aware of his actions, he had covered the hand resting on his arm with his free one. Thankfully, they were at the edge of the sidewalk. "Watch your step," he cautioned.

"Thank you."

When he forced his thoughts from her, an image of his sister came to mind. An unexpected pain stabbed him. *Ah, Erin, how did it come to this?* They'd been close growing up, and, as any big brother should, he'd shielded her with an intense protectiveness from those who tried to make her life difficult. Erin had been feisty and lippy and happy and forever wearing an impish grin.

She'd begun to change when she was fourteen or so. Her smile lost its contagious brightness. Laughter became rare, replaced with a mocking smile and a caustic tongue. Their mother said it was just something girls went through at that age, that she would soon outgrow it and their bonnie Erin would be back. It hadn't happened.

She'd been seventeen and he'd been nineteen when their stepfather had been killed in a buggy accident while driving home from a night of drinking. A wheel had come off, and the carriage had flipped over on top of him. His absence had put a strain on their already tight finances, and, with the older Mc-Shane siblings gone from home, it had been up to him and Erin to step up and help bring in money to support themselves and their mother.

A short two months later, he'd learned what Erin did for a living. When he had confronted her, she'd refused to talk about it. He'd been so furious that he'd pushed her away.

From then on, their relationship had been rocky at best, but the day his wife, Glenna had been killed and Erin had attempted suicide, the chasm between him and Erin had widened so much that he didn't think there was a bridge long or strong enough to span it. But, just because he blamed Erin for Glenna's death and disapproved of how she made a living, didn't mean he'd ever stop loving her. That love was what made accepting her choices so hard.

He did appreciate her help with the current assignment. Maybe this was as good as it would ever be between them. Maybe he should be thankful for that much.

CHAPTER 12

To Lilly's surprise, the aroma of fresh-brewed coffee greeted them as soon as they opened the doors of The Thirsty Traveler. Erin, wearing a rather tatty wrapper, sat at one of the tables, cradling a cup in her hands.

"I'm surprised to see you back so soon," Cade said.

"Believe it or not brother, I don't lift my skirts for everyone in trousers."

Lilly wondered if Cade noticed the pain in his sister's eyes. As a woman, Lilly realized that Erin had used the crude comment to deliberately shock and hurt him. Something inside Lilly told her that whatever it was that stood between the two was more than Erin's occupation. If there was ever a chance for them to be together alone, and Erin seemed in an expansive mood, Lilly would try to find out more about the strained relationship.

"There's coffee in the kitchen." Erin acted as if the brief exchange had never occurred.

Cade headed that direction. "D'ya want a cup, Lilly?" he called over his shoulder.

"Why not?" She needn't worry about the coffee's keeping her awake. Her current role allowed her to sleep late if she wanted.

He returned with two mugs and set one in front of her. Then he sat down between her and his sister and took a sip of his. "Did you learn anything from Mr. Wilkins?" he asked Erin.

"Nothing much beyond the fact that he is an arrogant blowhard who thinks every woman should fall at his feet. Or into his bed. He did impress upon me that he had valuable connections if I decide to stay and reopen the place. And he assured me he could produce whatever I needed to gratify the carnal preferences of both men and women, no matter what it might be."

"To which you replied . . . ?"

"I'd keep it in mind."

"That's it?"

"Yes, Cadence, that's it. I spent the rest of the time trying to keep his hands off me." Done with sparring with her brother, she turned to Lilly. "Did you see that girl who stopped by yesterday?"

"Yes, but only for a moment. She came down from one of her . . . appointments and sat with me long enough to have a drink, but then the bartender came over and told her that Velvet was getting upset because she wasn't working the floor." Despite herself, Lilly heard the break in her voice.

"Are you sure you're up to this?" Cade asked, his cup halfway to his lips.

"I'll be fine," she assured him. But would she?

"What am I missing here?" Erin's dark eyebrows were drawn together in a frown of genuine concern. "Did something happen?"

"Lilly is having a bit o' trouble dealing with the realities of the lives these women live."

"I see." Erin drew in a deep breath and released it. "I'm not certain if I should apologize, be offended, or be happy that someone recognizes what it's really like."

"Please don't be offended," Lilly was quick to say. The last thing she needed was conflict between her and Cade's sister.

"Trust me, it would take more than that to really upset me."

"It's just that when I look at Rosalie and Velvet, all I can think of is that beneath their veneer of civility and beauty, there's nothing but coldness, heartlessness . . . a hardness of heart that is beyond my understanding. They haven't a single qualm about using those women to feather their own nests. It's horrible! I don't understand why the girls don't just walk away. Buy a train ticket and move on to a new life somewhere."

"That isn't always as easy as it seems," Erin told her. "Especially if there's nothing to move on to."

Hadn't Bonnie said something similar? "But some must have some family or friends. Bonnie has something. Charlie—that's the bartender—seems to care for her, but she says he can't support them both."

"That may just be her excuse."

"What do you mean? Why wouldn't she want to escape the life?"

Erin looked pensive. "It may sound silly, but it's hard to separate yourself from your past. A lot of women get worn down physically and mentally. They think they're not good enough for a decent man." She looked up at them, a challenging look in her eyes. "Take a girl like me. What if I give a decent man a chance, and someone finds out about my past? If I love this man, I certainly don't want to see him suffer shame and embarrassment because of me. And then, what if he wanted to be rid of me? I'm right back where I started. And can I ever truly believe a respectable man will trust me around other men?" She shook her head. "It isn't as cut-and-dried as it may seem."

Strangely, Lilly understood. Wasn't her own vow to live a life different from her mother's her way of distancing herself from her past?

"I understand," she said. "I didn't mean to turn this meeting into a discussion about me and my feelings. I'll be fine. Let's get back to the investigation."

Erin seemed to return to the present slowly. "You're right. Cade, were you able to get any new information?"

He told her about the competition between the two top madams and how they'd steal girls from each other.

"Well, that's certainly different," Erin said. "It makes a certain amount of sense in a twisted sort of way. Wilkins told me about a woman they found nailed to an outhouse. I wasn't sure if it was a scare tactic to keep me from settling here or a warning to the other girls to tread lightly."

"Bonnie told me about that too, and I can only imagine it was a warning."

"Of course, it was," Cade said. "Whoever killed her was saying, 'Watch your step. Don't cross us, or you could be next.' "

Lilly looked from one sibling to the other. "The question is, who is 'us'?"

"That's yet to be found out," Cade said. "It could have been any one of the madams. Or even some cowboy passing through who got carried away. We'll probably never know." He looked from his partner to his sister. "Don't you find it interesting that Davies is saying it will be fine to open up another place, but Wilkins is being less than enthusiastic?"

"That is interesting," Erin said. "Do you think it's some sort of game they play? Are Wilkins and Davies enemies, or do they have something going on together that they'd prefer no one know about?"

"I couldn't tell much when they were standing there with Rosalie," Lilly said.

"Davies is going to make things harder for us," Cade said.

"How so?" Lilly asked.

"He seems like the type of man who holds his cards close to his vest. He may tell us he'll help and that there's plenty of room for new places, but I doubt he gives us any truly useful information since we'll be in direct competition with his two favorite ladies."

Erin gave a little shiver. "Even though he makes my skin crawl, I'm going to keep working on Wilkins. The more comfortable he gets with me, the more he's likely to open up or let something slip."

"Good thinking, sister. I'm going to try to find a good poker game tomorrow and see if I can get anything from some of the locals. I may even take in a horse race."

"Don't you think you should be working instead of playing?" Lilly asked.

"I will be working. You should have figured that out by now."

She knew his words were true, but it irritated her that he would be somewhere else and not at her side. And *that* irritated her as well. She was getting entirely too accustomed to his being around, and that wasn't good, not if she ever hoped to make it on her own as an agent.

"I might try to find out the identity of the man who came in just before we left."

"That skinny fellow everyone was watching?" Cade asked. "Why on earth are you interested in him?"

"Don't you find it strange that everyone stared at him when he came in and they seemed glad to see him go? I want to know why." She didn't add that if she talked to the man, she would ask him why he'd looked at her as if he knew her from somewhere.

"It sounds as if we all have busy days ahead of us," Erin said, around a yawn. "I'm for bed."

"I'll go to the market in the morning to get what we need

for the day," Lilly offered, hoping that one of them would take pity on her and do the dishes. And there was always the chance that she could strike up a conversation with someone who could shed a little light on Nora's whereabouts.

"Thanks, Lilly," Erin said, heading for the stairs. "Good night."

"Good night."

When Erin reached the landing, Cade turned to Lilly. "Don't forget to take your gun when you go."

The prompt grated on her, even though she knew he was only looking out for her. She did have a bad habit of forgetting her derringer, or it not being handy when she needed it.

"Thanks for reminding me," she said, and, without another word, went upstairs. She thought she heard him chuckling.

Lying in the darkness of her room, Lilly couldn't sleep. She kept recalling the events of the evening and her conversation with Cade. She couldn't believe she'd opened herself up the way she had, especially not to him. He had listened and told her what he felt, but he had not mocked her for being too soft, or tried to influence her in any way. He'd sounded as if he understood.

This wasn't the first time she'd questioned her choice to leave her family and the stage and become a detective, but it was the only time she'd considered her choice with such a heavy heart. Corruption, lawbreaking, and debauchery were not pretty in any form, but what the procurers and madams— even the marshal, who made a pretense of keeping the law— condoned was beyond contemptible.

If she got through this assignment, and she had to for Nora's sake, what sort of loathsome offense against women would she encounter the next time . . . and the next? Lilly knew she was headstrong and stubborn, but were those traits enough to sustain her?

Do you believe in what you do, Lilly?

The little voice inside her whispered the question, demanded an answer. She did. Wholeheartedly. Was knowing she was helping some women enough? She didn't know. But if she decided to stay with it, it would have to be.

CHAPTER 13

The next morning, Lilly took the small grocery basket they'd found on a shelf in the kitchen and walked the short distance to the mercantile. The Texas sun beat down on her shoulders, even though it was barely eight o'clock in the morning. At least there was a breath of breeze. A few strands of hair tickled her neck.

Hardly anyone was stirring, which suited her just fine. The doves and madams were sleeping, as were those men who had not passed out early from too much drink. She was surprised to see the doors to the drinking establishments were open. Did they open at such an early hour to cater to those who might wander in looking for some hair of the dog?

As she strolled down the street, she studied the buildings on either side of the thoroughfare. Besides the requisite saloons, gambling parlors, and bawdy houses, she spied a butcher, a drug emporium, a combined barber and bathhouse, and a haberdashery where the men coming off the trail could buy themselves a new getup before heading out to sow their wild oats.

The difference in the people here from those she was accustomed to dealing with was vast. Thanks to the cattle market, Ft. Worth was a growing city, and its people, just like the place itself, were rough and raw. In comparison, Chicago, Springfield, and even the small town of Vandalia, with their theaters and nice restaurants, seemed more evolved. Sophisticated.

Still, as disturbing as the Ft. Worth lifestyle was, she could not deny that it was riveting, much like the time she'd almost been run down by a carriage. Though she'd been frightened, she had been unable to run from the danger.

Danger. At precisely that moment, she felt the unmistakable sensation of being watched. Her heart began to pick up speed. Knowing she couldn't turn around and look, she slipped her free hand into the pocket of her olive-green skirt and felt a sense of relief when her fingertips brushed the cold metal of her derringer. Thank goodness, the grocery was only a few doors down.

The relief she felt when she stepped into the store was overwhelming. Feeling safe in the confines of the market, she stood in the doorway, letting her eyes adjust to the dimness and her heart rate slow while she looked around. After a minute or so, she felt more herself and began to shop for the day's groceries.

Neither Cade nor Erin had specified what she was to bring back, so she would buy what she wanted. It should be something easy, since none of them wanted to be stuck in the kitchen when they could be out on the street gathering information.

She put some butter into her basket, along with a dozen eggs, three fresh peaches, a jar of apple butter, and asked the grocer to slice her a wedge of red-rind cheese. She was looking at the potatoes when she felt the presence of someone behind her. She stiffened and was about to turn when her basket was snatched and the thief went running through the store, straight for the open doorway.

Too startled to be afraid, all she could think of was that they had only a certain amount of money to spend on any given day. While she was gathering her skirt to chase him, the man reached into the basket, as if to take something from it.

"Stop!" she cried, taking a few running steps.

The sound of her voice drew the attention of the clerk behind the counter, who was wrapping her cheese in brown paper, unfazed by what was going on. He looked up just as the thief paused and turned to look at her.

Recognition set her reeling. The man from the dance hall! Any tender feelings she might have had for him and his plight vanished as she realized he was nothing but a robber.

Neither moved for long seconds, and, for a moment, she thought he was about to say something. Instead, he set the basket down, turned, and dashed outside. Running to the entrance, she watched the culprit race down the street and disappear around the corner.

"That man!" She turned toward the shopkeeper, who had stood watching the entire exchange without making a move to help. "Who is he?"

The clerk was tying a knot in the twine. He glanced up, unconcerned. "I'm just goin' to add this here cheese to your tally."

"Fine!" Lilly snapped. "Who was that man?"

"That guy who just left? That's Monty." The clerk pulled a stubby pencil from behind his ear, gave the lead a lick, and began to write on a scrap of paper.

"Monty who? I think he's been following me. Who is he? Is he dangerous?" She blurted off the questions in rapid fire. "And why didn't you try to stop him?"

"He didn't have any of the store's merchandise, and he set down your basket. Besides, he works for me sometimes, and he ain't never took nothin' that I know of. Just one of his pranks, most likely."

Irritated by the grocer's indifference, she leaned over and grabbed the handle of her basket. "What's his last name?" she asked between gritted teeth.

"Newton. Monty Newton." The clerk tapped his temple with a broad finger. "He ain't all there in the head, if you know what I mean. I don't think he's dangerous."

Lilly felt like screaming. Why wasn't he taking this more seriously? "What do you mean, you don't think he's dangerous?"

"A while back, I'd have said he wouldn't hurt a hair on your head, but now, it's hard to say."

"Why?"

"About half the folks around the Acre say he killed that woman. But I figure there can't be any evidence against him or else Marshal Davies would have done thrown him in jail."

"What woman?"

"One of those gals who worked for Velvet or Rosalie. I can't remember."

"The one they found nailed to the outhouse?" Her breath seemed to hang in her throat while she waited for his answer.

"You heard about that?" He shook his balding head.

"Yes. Please. Tell me what you know."

"Don't know much, but I recollect her name now. That gal was called Dottie. This was a different one. I heard say she was Monty's favorite, so it don't make any sense that he'd hurt her, but sometimes it's hard to understand why folks do the things they do, ain't it?"

Lilly felt as if she were running in circles. She was getting nowhere fast with this man. "That is strange. Why do they suspect him?"

"Well, he's a regular down at the houses."

"Regular?" Lilly was so eager to learn more about the man that she wasn't concentrating on what the clerk was saying.

"You know," the grocer said, his face turning bright red. "He went to one place or another from time to time to find his pleasure."

Lilly regarded him expectantly, waiting for more. "So, Monty goes to the houses to find his pleasure," she prompted, stifling the urge to reach across the counter and give the man a good shaking.

"Right. But word is he didn't. Couldn't."

Didn't? Couldn't? "I don't understand."

The merchant shook his head. "Please, don't make me spell it out for you, ma'am."

It hit Lilly then just what he meant. Oh, dear! From her experience hearing her mother with her lovers and her own experience with Tim . . . Well, she had never imagined that a man . . .

"I don't think this is a proper conversation to be having with a young woman like you."

Good grief! He was worried about her sensibilities! Once, Lilly would have agreed with him, but this was different. She was different. This was a serious case to be solved, and for all intents and purposes, she was not an innocent young woman.

Relying on her acting skills, she gave a throaty laugh. "I appreciate your concern, but I'm not the unsophisticated woman you think I am. I'm one of 'those women.' In fact, my friend is here to see if opening The Thirsty Traveler again would be a good business decision."

"All right, all right. But you don't go tellin' anyone what I say, ya hear? I don't want no trouble."

"My lips are sealed." At least until she got back to Dusty's.

He threw back his shoulders and drew in a fortifying breath. "Like I was sayin', scuttlebutt has it that Monty can't . . . perform."

Despite what she'd heard about the stranger, she felt a rush of sympathy for him. What a terrible thing to be bandied about by everyone in town.

"It didn't matter what girl he chose, he just couldn't uh . . . carry out his task. Problem was, he had to pay for the time he spent with them, anyway. Everyone said he got real mad and blamed the women. They started worryin' about what he might do, and the madams stopped making the girls take him upstairs." The clerk shrugged. "It wasn't enough to hurt business, so they just cut him off. Then this new curly-haired blond gal come along, and he seemed to take a real shine to her."

Lilly's heart sank. Nora! "Do you know her name?"

"Nah. She came in a few times. Seemed nice. Real pretty and seemed almost smart. For a whore."

The insensitive label sent Lilly's fury soaring.

"Pardon me, ma'am," he said, realizing his blunder. "No slight intended."

"None taken," Lilly lied, her head reeling.

"Her and Monty musta hit it off real good," the shopkeeper said. "It sorta makes sense now when I look back at it."

"What makes sense?" Lilly was having a terrible time following his thought process.

"Well, I heard she wasn't too happy about bein' here, and she even tried to run once, but Wilkins caught her and brought her back."

"Elijah Wilkins?"

"Yeah. You know him?"

"We've met."

"Then you probably know that he not only finds and sells for a lot of the houses in the Acre, but he's the enforcer, too."

The word conjured up images she would rather not have envisioned. Images like Wilkins nailing a woman to an outhouse . . . and turning Nora over to a gang of cowboys. She wanted to ask the grocer if he knew anything about what had happened to her friend after Nora had helped to get the children out of town, but she couldn't without destroying her cover story.

"What did you mean when you said it made a lot of sense for them to spend so much time together?"

"Well, her wanting to get away and Monty with his problem . . . Maybe there was something else between them." When Lilly looked at him questioningly, he lifted his narrow shoulders in a shrug. "Maybe she didn't mind his problem, since it meant she got a break from her work. All I know for sure is that they spent a lot of time together."

"Have you seen her lately?"

"No. She's the one everyone thinks Monty killed."

It took every bit of acting skill Lilly possessed to pay for her purchases without breaking into tears. Out on the street, she lifted her face to the sky and drew in deep breaths while she fought the urge to fall onto the board walkway and give her grief free rein. Or maybe kick the posts supporting the overhang. It wasn't fair or right that someone who wanted nothing but a home and family had come to such a wretched end.

She walked back to Dusty's in a grief-induced haze, while the times she'd spent with Nora before she'd left the Pierced Rose Troupe flashed through her mind one after the other.

Those times were gone for good.

Thankful that no one was stirring when she got back to the boardinghouse, Lilly headed straight for the kitchen to replenish the fire, make the coffee, and put some eggs on to boil. She was fighting to hold back the tears and memories while she sliced and buttered the leftover bread when Cade came into the room and peeked over her shoulder. "No meat?"

"No." Her voice was sharper than it should have been, and that made her teary, too. She sniffed and blinked hard. "It's too expensive to have every day. Pierce says you get the same nutrition from eggs that you do from meat."

"Then I hope you're boiling plenty."

She refused to look up from her task, fearful that any small bit of kindness would send her into a fit of caterwauling. He poured himself some coffee and leaned against the table, sipping the dark brew and watching her. She knew it wouldn't take him long to figure out that something was wrong.

"Why've you been crying, lass?"

Lass, not colleen. McShane's way of showing sensitivity toward her. And why was it that his Irish brogue seemed more pronounced when he spoke tenderly? His gentleness was her undoing. The misery she'd tried so hard to hold in check spilled over, and tears ran down her cheeks.

Moving slowly, she laid the knife aside, and turned to face him. More than anything in the world, she wanted him to put his arms around her and let her cry out her sorrow against his chest. But, of course, he didn't. She'd laid down the rules, after all.

"Nora's dead."

He didn't move for several seconds. "Are ya sure?"

She nodded and swiped her fingertips across her cheeks.

"Who told you?"

"The grocer."

With a little push of his hips, he straightened and set his cup onto the worktable. He set the eggs off the stove and refilled her cup. "Let's sit," he said, handing her the mug. "And you can tell me everything."

Minutes later, they were seated at one of the tables near the bar. She related the incident with Monty Newton and told Cade what the clerk had said about Monty and the murdered woman.

"Are you sure he didn't take anything?" Cade asked.

She wiped at her tears with her handkerchief. "It looked as if he was going to grab something out of it, but there was only butter and peaches in it, and it was all there."

Cade frowned. "It doesn't make sense for him to grab the basket and not take it, or at least steal something from it."

"Maybe I scared him when I yelled." It was as much question as statement.

"Maybe." But he didn't look convinced.

She took a sip of her coffee while watching her partner's changing facial expressions. "What now?"

He pulled himself away from wherever his thoughts had taken him and met her gaze. "Did the grocer say how she died? I mean, wasn't she recovering from an assault?"

"Yes, she was." Lilly gave her head an angry shake. "He didn't say, and I was so upset I didn't ask. All I could think of was getting out of there with my dignity intact."

"Never you mind. Someone will tell us." He reached out and touched her hand with a single fingertip. The action brought her head up until their gazes met. "I want you to know that I'm very sad about Nora. Losing someone you care about is hard. I also know you're going to be angry as well as sad, and that rage can make you do stupid things. Don't."

She knew he was referring to his actions after his wife's death. She nodded in compliance. "Thank you. I'll try to keep my wits about me. So where do we go from here?"

He wrapped his hands around his cup and stared at a spot across the way, as if he were collecting his thoughts. "Well, we came to find Nora and take her back home, and we wanted to help bring down Wilkins for the ploy he's using to get his hands on new women.

"The fact that Nora is dead makes this a murder investigation," Cade continued. "We need to remember that there's a chance her killer is someone different from the mail-order bride mastermind. Like this Monty character."

"You don't think it was Wilkins?"

"I'm saying that at this point we can't be sure of anything. We need more information."

"I agree, but how will we ever find out anything?" Lilly asked. "These people cover for one another, and the doves are afraid to say too much for fear of paying the price. I'm not even sure I trust the marshal."

He smiled. "I didn't say it would be easy, lass, but people make mistakes. They say and do things to incriminate themselves without realizing it. We need to be vigilant and watch for every little thing. Shakespeare got it right in *Hamlet*."

When Lilly frowned at him in confusion, he said, " '*For murder, though it have no tongue, will speak . . .*' It's been my experience that murder victims speak to you from the grave, if you only listen."

"I'm not sure I understand."

"You need to think back over everything Nora said to you the night you had dinner together," he told Lilly.

"That was months ago."

"I know, but you may recall something. Anything. And we need to read her letter again, and see if there's anything we missed that might point us in a new direction."

"We do the same thing we've been doing, only harder."

"That's a good way of putting it. One point we need to remember: We're working on two different cases. Who's behind the bridal fraud, and who killed your friend."

"I hadn't thought about it in that way."

"My gut tells me that the two will overlap in some way, since the people in the Acre are united in their desire to protect what they have." He shook his head in disgust. "They all have a sort of mutually beneficial arrangement with one another. Almost incestuous."

Incestuous. Leave it to the experienced agent to put things into perspective. It was a good word for the relationships that bound the residents of the Acre to one another, all so that they could continue to exploit women and children to make the almighty dollar. You scratch my back; I'll scratch yours. Pay me, and I'll leave you alone. Need something; I'll get it. Look the other way so my legitimate business will thrive.

The list went on. To find out who murdered Nora they needed to find out who, if anyone, besides Velvet, had anything against her. Should Monty be at the top of the list?

"I guess we start with Monty. According to the grocer, the town is split between those who think he's the killer—even though there's no evidence against him—and those who say he could never hurt anyone."

"Then we need to see what we can find out," Cade said. "As for the brides, I'm betting Wilkins is in it neck deep."

"I agree. I wanted to ask the shopkeeper if he knew anything about Nora's helping the children, but I figured that was something I shouldn't know about."

"You figured right. Be very careful, Lilly. It will only take one small misstep to bring this whole case down around our ears." He emptied his cup. "So, we follow our plan and try to get evidence," Cade continued, "The last I heard, you can't put anyone in jail on hearsay and supposition, no matter how nasty he may be."

"Why do you think Monty Newton is following me?"

"I'm not sure, but I can make an educated guess. Nora's letter to you said she had help from a friend. She also said that she hoped to look up one day and see you coming through the door."

"Did I tell you that he seemed to recognize me when he came into Velvet's?"

"No, but if he did, it's probably because she told him you'd be coming, and asked him to keep a watch out for you. That's what he's doing. Maybe he's following you to try to find a way to contact you."

"I hadn't thought of that, either," Lilly admitted. "But I

have considered the possibility that he's the friend who helped
her get the kids out of town, and that he knew about the letter. He may have even sent it."

"It makes sense."

"So, you don't think he's dangerous."

"Good morning."

The sound of Erin's voice stalled whatever answer he was
about to make. Fully dressed, she was coming down the stairs,
a quizzical expression on her face. "What are you two looking
so serious about?"

"Lilly found out some valuable information at the grocer's
this morning."

"Oh?"

"First, it seems pretty certain that her friend is dead."

Erin uttered a mild curse.

"And there's some speculation as to who did it."

"Well, you can tell me over breakfast. I'm starving this
morning."

"Oh! I'll get it!" Lilly said, rising. "It won't take but a
minute."

"I'll help."

Surprisingly, the offer came from Cade. "I can slice the
peaches while you get the eggs."

Lilly didn't feel like arguing, not when they'd been getting
along so well. Besides, she was getting hungry, too, and many
hands made light work, as Rose often said.

In the kitchen, she took a wooden spoon, lifted the eggs
from the hot water, and placed them in a brown crockery
bowl. She cut the buttered bread slices in half and arranged
them on a white stoneware platter.

"Shall I slice some cheese?" she asked, casting a glance over
her shoulder at Cade, who was sniffing a peach.

"That would be nice," he said. "D'ya want me to peel the
peaches or leave them?"

"I don't mind the skin, but you do whatever you like with yours and Erin's."

She set about slicing the cheese while Cade did the same with the peach. "Hm," he exclaimed. "What the devil is this?"

He reached into the basket and pulled out a folded piece of paper.

"Where did you find that?"

"It was under one of the peaches." He handed it to her. "I have a feeling it was intended for you."

She unfolded the note. The message was simple; the penmanship was exquisite.

MEET ME BEHIND DUSTY'S TONIGHT AT TEN.

She handed it to Cade. "He wants me to meet him out back at ten tonight."

Cade pointed the knife at her and shook his head. "Oh, no. I don't think so. The man is a potential killer."

"He may want to tell me something about Nora's death, McShane. Maybe he knows who killed her. Surely he wouldn't try anything right at my back door."

"And maybe he would. That's the problem with killers, lass. They don't think the way we do, and they don't have a sign hanging around their necks proclaiming to the world what they are. Besides, how do you know Monty wrote it?"

"Of course, he wrote it. He put it in the basket," she said, but even as she spoke the words, doubts began to surface. It certainly wasn't farfetched to think that he'd been the go-between for someone else.

Cade held the paper aloft and shook it. "Did ya notice the writing, lass? Do ya really think someone with his mental aptitude can write like this?"

That was an excellent point. "Then why can't you be just

inside the door, listening? That would be safe enough, wouldn't it? No matter who shows up?"

Instead of answering, he turned and began to slice the second peach. Lilly waited.

"You win," he said in a resigned tone. "I'll agree to that."

"Thank you." She exhaled a sigh of relief. It was comforting to know that he'd be nearby in case something went wrong. Then she smiled. "This could be our big opportunity."

"It could. But I intend for us to have a plan. And you will not pull any dimwitted stunts to try to be the woman of the hour. D'ya ken what I'm saying?"

"I do," she told him meekly. "Now, let's go tell Erin what's happened."

They showed Erin the note, explained who Monty was, and ate their simple breakfast.

"I think I've seen that man. I'm certain he passed me and Eli while we were walking around town last night." She perked up suddenly. "Yes! Marshal Davies stopped him, and they talked a while. Then the man went into one of the saloons down the street. I don't know how long he was there. Eli and I went into the Silver Slipper for a drink."

"Does he look like a killer to you, Erin?" Lilly asked.

Lilly didn't know if it was a trick of the light or if the color drained from the other woman's face. "Most killers don't look like killers," she said, verifying Cade's statement.

Sighing in defeat, Lilly picked up a piece of the peach, sprinkled some sugar on a slice of buttered bread, and folded it around the fruit. The McShane siblings looked at her as if she'd lost her mind. "It's very good," she told them, taking a bite of her sweet.

She felt a dribble of juice dripping from the corner of her mouth and licked it up. "There's something I don't understand."

"What's that?" her partner asked, but he seemed distracted, staring at her mouth.

"If they don't have any evidence connecting Monty to Nora's death, and if Monty and Nora spent as much time together as everyone claims, why does everyone think he's the one who killed her?"

Erin sat there for a moment and then looked from one partner to the other. "I might know the answer to that."

"Listen and learn," Cade said, taking a swig of his coffee.

"When a man can't perform in bed, he can become very disturbed. Not only is it infuriating, it's embarrassing, and he feels less a man. If it's something that's been going on for a while, it's possible that with some sort of twisted reasoning, he could reach a point where he refuses to believe it's his fault and—"

"—starts blaming the women," Lilly said, interrupting Erin's hypothesis.

Erin nodded. "Yes. What do you think, Cade?"

"It sounds logical. A man could build up a lot of rage over time, and if he's slow, as the grocer said, it's very possible that he's incapable of understanding the subtleties of the man-woman relationship. Which is why I want to be nearby tonight. Who knows if he'll try to haul you off to the bushes and see if he gets a different result than he has before."

"Or he might be luring you there for Eli Wilkins to nab and take somewhere else," Erin suggested.

"Well, aren't the two of you little Sally Sunshines?" Lilly quipped, though her heart was beating fast just thinking about the scenarios they'd suggested.

"Cade's right, Lilly. Illogical people are unpredictable. It's better to have a plan and not need it than to go into a situation unprepared."

The siblings exchanged a look that Lilly couldn't begin to identify. "I understand," she said. "I bow to your superior knowledge and experience."

"Well, that's a first," Cade said, popping a slice of peach into his mouth. He looked at his sister. "Are you willing to try to weasel information from Wilkins?"

"Fine. He only has one thing on his mind, but I can handle him."

"How are you going to keep putting him off, when he knows . . ." Lilly couldn't say what was in her mind.

"When he knows what I do for a living?"

Lilly nodded.

"It's an art, and Anne Boleyn was the master."

"Anne Boleyn?"

"You know? Henry VIII's Anne?"

Lilly nodded, wondering what the second wife of the scandalous British monarch had to do with handling Elijah Wilkins.

"The story is that smart Anne kept Henry dangling for years, and when he married her, he lost interest in no time. There's something exciting about the sparring and the waiting, I think," Erin said.

Thinking back to the verbal banter she and Cade had shared, Lilly tended to agree. The intimate back-and-forth was stimulating.

"Don't worry about me," Erin said. "I can handle Eli Wilkins."

CHAPTER 14

True to his word, Cade dressed after breakfast and announced that he was headed outside the Acre to the local equivalent of the Oriental Saloon to see if he could round up some poker players.

Much to Lilly's chagrin, Elijah Wilkins sent word that he would stop by to pick up Erin to take her to lunch. Lilly was beginning to doubt Erin's sanity. Or at least her common sense, and told her as much while Erin was preparing for her engagement.

"Why is it you're so worried about me and not yourself?" Lilly demanded. "We can't prove it yet, but we're almost certain Wilkins is the one who's really behind Nora's murder. He's dangerous, Erin, and you're putting yourself at risk every time you go off with him."

"D'ya think I don't know that?" she said, twisting her ebony hair up into an elaborate knot atop her head. "But then, that's a chance I have to take for Cade."

What did she mean by that? "For Cade? Why? The two of you don't even seem to like each other."

Erin turned to face Lilly with tortured eyes. "You couldn't be more wrong. I love my brother dearly, and I owe him."

"Explain, Erin," Lilly begged. "As his partner, I need to understand why he says and does the things he does. It would make things much easier. I know he ran amuck after his wife was killed. What happened to her? Why do you owe him? Why is there so much enmity between the two of you? He's no prude. Even though your . . . way of life disappoints and angers him, he just doesn't seem like the kind of person who would let it keep him from someone he loved."

Erin stared at Lilly as she spoke her piece and then turned and leaned closer to the mirror, touching her finger to the tip of her tongue and then smoothing it over a dark eyebrow. "You're with him every day. Why are you asking me?" she said. "Ask him."

"I did. Some of it. He said your story wasn't his to tell."

Erin straightened and turned from the mottled mirror. Almost absently, she rubbed at the scar on the inside of her wrist. Though her words were soft, her eyes were filled with pain. And defiance. "He doesn't know my story."

Lilly wasn't certain how to respond to that, so she said nothing. After a while, Erin turned back to the mirror and gripped the edge of the dressing table tightly. The expression in her eyes was almost reminiscent.

"He thinks I took up the life because Ma needed the help after Josep was killed, and I could make more prostituting myself than working at any of the factories."

Their reflected gazes met. "That wasn't the reason at all." She released her hold on the dresser's edge and turned toward Lilly. It was almost as if Erin wanted to make certain Lilly understood everything she was about to say. "I did it because I thought it was all I was fit for."

"I don't understa—"

"It was Josep," Erin said bluntly.

The three words told Lilly everything. "Josep . . . defiled you?"

"Every chance he got." Erin turned back to the mirror and held on to the table once more, almost, Lilly thought, as if Erin needed the support. Instead of looking at herself, she looked down at her white-knuckled grip. "He was gross and flabby and stank of cheap cigars, stale beer . . . and unwashed man." Her head moved back and forth, as if to negate the memories. "Dear sweet heaven, I despised that man. Him, and what he did, and myself."

Then she gave a shaky laugh, straightened, and looked directly at Lilly. Her eyes were glassy with tears. Lilly suspected she hadn't cried in years.

"I don't know why I told you that. I've never told anyone, and I hardly know you."

"No one?"

Erin shook her head.

"Not even Cade?"

"Especially not Cade. He never asked. By then, the nuns had him on the straight and narrow, and he was busy being the good son. Mr. Righteous. Main provider. Judge and jury."

Lilly's heart smarted with regret. She'd been guilty of that, too. *Oh, the ways we hurt others because of wounded feelings and pride and self-righteousness!*

"And even after so many years, he's never asked why and never gotten over it?" she ventured.

"There was a time he might have."

"What happened?"

"Glenna was killed, and it was all my fault."

After her stunning announcement, Erin had said she had nothing else to tell and needed to finish getting ready for her lunch with a man who was, at the very least, peddling human beings for money, and at the worst, a killer.

Knowing Cade would never tell her the details of his wife's death and wishing she could persuade Erin to confide more, Lilly had left the room, wondering how her new friend managed to push aside her fears and worries and go off with some man she really didn't know. Wondering if it was because she had a death wish.

Lilly shuddered at the insanity of even thinking such a thing, but as she went downstairs to clean up the breakfast dishes, she remembered Nora's saying in her letter that some of the women sought out death, feeling it was a better choice than what they had in life. It was a hard concept to accept, but then, Lilly had never dealt with anything like what they had suffered.

Almost as if her thoughts had brought her around, Lilly heard a knock at the back door and found Bonnie standing there.

"Bonnie! I wasn't expecting you."

"Hello, Lilly." Bonnie glanced over her shoulder, and Lilly stepped aside for her to enter. "Come in."

"Is Miss O'Toole here?"

Lilly's mind raced. She needed some answers, and Bonnie was the only person she knew well enough to question. If the previous night was any indication, any conversation would be difficult, if not impossible, while Bonnie was working. Having her here, away from everyone, might be the only chance to start a conversation that could lead to Nora.

Lilly knew keeping their identities a secret was essential, but things would be much easier if she could just start asking questions, the way she'd done in Vandalia.

Her decision made, she said, "She is, but she has a luncheon date."

Bonnie looked surprised. "Oh, I won't trouble her then. I'll come back another time."

Lilly reached out and placed a hand on Bonnie's arm. "No,

that's all right. She should be ready in a bit. I'm sure she'll have time to speak with you before Mr. Wilkins gets here."

Color fled Bonnie's face. "Elijah Wilkins?"

"Yes," Lilly said innocently. "Is something the matter?"

Bonnie looked as if she might bolt at any second, but then she relaxed. "Eli Wilkins is trouble with a capital *T.*"

"Really?" Lilly said, feigning surprise. "How so? He's been very helpful in answering Erin's questions about reopening this place." She gave a little laugh. "And believe me, Erin can handle herself when it comes to unpredictable men."

"Oh, he knows all the answers, but you be sure and tell her that she shouldn't trust anything he says. Nothing."

"Really?" Lilly smiled. "He's so fascinating in a rough, manly sort of way. I think she's enjoying his company."

"He's fascinating, all right," Bonnie said. "And he uses his looks and his charm to lure women into the life."

"What do you mean, he lures women? I've never heard of such a thing." Barely able to hide her excitement, Lilly took hold of Bonnie's arm and pulled her toward the table where Lilly and the McShanes had had their breakfast. "Sit and tell me all about it. There's coffee left from breakfast. I just warmed it up. Would you like some?"

"Well . . . yes. That would be nice. Thank you." Bonnie took a seat at the table, and, in a few moments, she and Lilly were sitting across from each other, their hands around their cups. "I don't mean to be nosy," Lilly said, "but what do you mean Wilkins lures women? He told Erin he could get whatever she wanted for her clients. Is he talking about a certain kind of woman? What?"

"Maybe. But it doesn't have to be a woman," Bonnie stated flatly. "Whatever your heart desires. Man, woman, child. Any size, any nationality."

Lilly sucked in a shocked breath.

"You're in the business. You know there are some ritzy

ladies who like a night out on the town now and again, and the good madams find out about their wildest fantasies, and Eli gets what they want."

"I have seen a few of those," Lilly lied.

"Velvet had a Chinese woman a year or so back, because one of her regulars said he'd heard they were obedient. She didn't speak much English, so she couldn't talk to the other girls. Everyone felt sorry for her and tried to help however they could, but she was so determined to get away that Eli started giving her morphine."

"Morphine?" Lilly tensed. She'd known the life was bad, but every day she learned more and more about just how bad. "What did Rosalie say?"

"I imagine she's the one who told him to do it. It's not un-usual," Bonnie said. "A lot of the girls use it because it's the only way they can survive."

Lilly pressed her lips together to stop their trembling. She could not imagine living in a drug-induced fog just to be able to tolerate your life. "That's . . . terrible."

Bonnie gave a nod. "Needless to say, she didn't last long. She couldn't have been more than sixteen."

"Sixteen! But she was just a child. What happened?"

"One afternoon, we were sitting out on the balcony, and she climbed over the rail and tried to fly."

The image that filled Lilly's mind was sickening. She visu-alized a petite, dark-haired girl with her arms outstretched, leaping over the railing. Imagined she heard the appalling thud as the body hit the unyielding Texas ground. Pictured a broken body lying sprawled in the street, and a trickle of blood oozing from her mouth and soaking into the grit beneath her.

"Didn't anyone try to stop her?" she said when she found her voice at last.

Bonnie shook her head. "We didn't see her. It was almost dark, and the rest of us had gone inside to finish getting ready.

Kim stayed behind. She could barely function, she was so full of morphine, but she managed to throw herself over the railing somehow."

"Unbelievable."

"Oh, there are plenty of tales."

"Like the dove found nailed to the outhouse wall?"

"Yeah. Like Dottie."

They were silent for long moments, each lost in thought, none of them pleasant.

Bonnie stared down into her coffee. When she spoke, her voice was small, hollow sounding. "It's funny, you know, how it stops bothering you after a while."

Lilly's head came up in surprise, like a deer that hears something in the woods. Was it possible that Bonnie and the others suffered the same things she feared? "What do you mean?"

"The first time something like that happened, I couldn't eat for days, but then it happened again and again, and the shock starts to diminish each time." She gave a sorrowful laugh. "It's so commonplace now that all us old-timers have started picking out which of the new ones will destroy themselves. We even place bets on how long it will take them to get a belly full."

Seeing the horror on Lilly's face, Bonnie smiled. A sorrowful, remorseful smile. "Believe it or not, I used to have a good heart."

"I believe you still have a good heart."

"Thank you for that. What about you?" she asked Lilly. "Did you or Miss O'Toole ever consider murdering yourself?"

Lilly thought about the scars on Erin's wrists that she kept covered with gloves when she went out in public. "No!" she said. "I'd never ever consider something like that. But," she added truthfully, recalling her conversation with Cade, "I have felt that hardness you were talking about creeping into my soul. I know it's a sort of self-preservation tactic, but I don't like it."

"No." Bonnie brightened. "Do you remember me telling you that you were different somehow? And that I liked you?"

"Yes."

"At the time, I thought you reminded me of someone, but I didn't know who. Now I remember."

"Oh?"

"Yes. There was this woman who was here just two or three months. The two of you look nothing alike, but there's something about you that reminds me of her. A sort of inner strength."

Inner strength? Lilly was aware that she was often considered hardheaded and stubborn. "Inner strength" sounded much nicer.

"Nora was a tough little thing," Bonnie said.

Expecting she would need to work the conversation to her friend in some roundabout way, the shock of hearing Nora's name spoken so casually caught Lilly off guard. "Was?" she asked in a low voice.

"Yes. She's gone now, too, but she went fighting all the way." Bonnie laughed. The notion seemed to please Bonnie no end. "She gave them merry hell before they finally got her."

"She sounds . . . interesting," Lilly said. "If she gave Velvet trouble I'd like to hear about it. Let me warm up our coffee, and then you can tell me about her."

With the cups refilled, Lilly settled in, ready to hear what had happened to her friend. "Tell me about this Nora."

Bonnie's eyes reflected her memories. "She was tiny and had frizzy blond hair and was feisty and smart. So smart . . ." Her voice trailed away. "She was one of the ones Eli lured here with his mail-order bride con. From what I've seen, there are a lot of women looking for a place to start over."

"A woman alone doesn't have too many choices, but it doesn't appeal to me," Lilly mused.

"Me either. I want to look at a man square in the eye so I can gauge for myself if he's lying or not."

Unfortunately, that wasn't always a good measuring stick, Lilly thought, remembering her own circumstances.

"Nora tried to escape after Eli sold her to Velvet. Running is common with newcomers. When he found her, she got a beating to teach her a lesson. As thrashings go, it could have been a lot worse. Just something to teach a dove a lesson. The madams don't want to hurt us so badly we can't work. Velvet is no exception."

"She's all heart, isn't she?"

Bonnie gave a short bark of laughter. "That's Velvet, all right." Bonnie took a swallow of her coffee. "Nora had no choice but to do as she was told, but she never gave up. She started trying to get the girls to leave. She told them they were the victims, that Jesus loved them, and that it was wrong for men to take advantage of them. She convinced a bunch of them that there was something better out there if they'd just walk away and go someplace to start over. Somehow, she managed to find out where Eli stashed some of the kids and she saw to it that they got out of town."

It sounded like something Nora would do.

Warming to her topic, Bonnie began to speak again. "The good Lord knows we need any kind of hope we can latch on to. The girls started refusing certain customers, defying the madams when they thought they could get away with it." She laughed. "I called it the Nora Rebellion."

"What happened?"

"Velvet let her go. Of course, no one else wanted her working for them, so she managed to get out, which is what she wanted. She moved in with one of her regulars. Not long after that, a kid from one of the other places just walked away. He walked down the middle of the train tracks and didn't get out of the way of the 2:10. He left a note behind that said he was going to go away and start over somewhere, just like Nora said they should."

Even though she knew from Nora's letter that children were being sold, too, Lilly gasped at hearing one had died trying to get away.

Bonnie peered into the depths of her coffee mug. "Eli brought in some more kids soon after that. It was the last straw for Nora. She was like a woman on a mission. Her whole purpose in life was to see the Acre shut down.

"She'd walk up and down the street with her Bible, telling anyone who'd listen that only a depraved person would force innocent children into such a dreadful life. She stood on the street corners and lectured about fornication and adultery and the wages of sin. . . ."

Hearing how militant her friend had become was a surprise. Lilly hadn't known that Nora was so vocal in her belief. No wonder she'd been silenced.

"She was a fighter," Bonnie said, smiling at the memories. "She put up signs at all the legal businesses saying that the Acre was a cesspool of evil and wickedness and should be shut down. She'd even march inside and tell the owners they should stand behind her."

Oh, Nora! You foolish, foolish girl!

"B. B. wrote a couple of articles about what a great thing she was doing, and he put out a plea, asking for help from anyone who might know about the children and where they were being held."

Lilly held her hands up, palms out to pause Bonnie's story. "Wait. Who's B. B.?"

"B. B. Paddock. The managing editor of the *Fort Worth Democrat*. He's all about making Ft. Worth grow, and he doesn't have much use for the district. He's done his best to try to put things right by printing rabble-rousing editorials now and then."

"I don't imagine that went over very well."

Bonnie chuckled. "You imagine right. Between B. B. and Nora, Davies had no choice but to do his job. So, like the good lawman he claims to be, he arrested a couple dozen women, and, as usual, they were out of jail by noon the next day."

"That's ridiculous!"

"Maybe so," Bonnie said. "But it's how things work around here. Then, just to prove he was doing a good job, Davies went out to Eli's to look and see if he was hiding any kids there. Of course, he didn't find a thing."

"Do you think they'd been there?"

"If you're asking if I have evidence of anything, the answer is no. If you want to know what I think, then I'd tell you that my gut says yes. Eli's got this dump out at the edge of town, and he's hardly ever there, so it's an ideal spot to stash a couple of kids until he can get a deal arranged."

"Deal?"

"Yeah. He sells to the highest bidder. We heard there was a bidding war going on between at least three of the houses for those poor kids. Thank God, Nora got them out of town before that happened."

Lilly was having a hard time processing everything Bonnie was telling her. She'd never thought of her sparkling, fun-loving friend as militant in any way, yet Nora had run a small revolution for good in one of the worst areas in Texas. Lilly felt a glimmer of hope. Since none of the madams had made a deal for the children, it was possible that none of them had been molested before Nora got them away from this hellhole.

"I imagine Mr. Wilkins was furious."

"All hell broke loose. No one knew what had happened. Anyone with half a brain figured it was Nora, but no one had seen a thing." Bonnie paused. "You know, now that I think about it, I guess it could have been any of the women, considering how riled up everyone was." She grinned at Lilly. "I don't suppose we'll ever be sure, but my bet's on Nora."

Lilly *knew* Nora had been behind the escape, but since she was supposed to be ignorant of the whole affair, there was nothing she could tell Bonnie. "How on earth could she manage that?"

Bonnie shrugged. "No one knows. Everyone agrees that if it was her, she had to have had help."

"Do you think it was the man she was living with?"

"Monty? He's not bad to look at, and he's sweet in his own way, but he's not smart enough to help with anything that complicated."

"What happened to Nora?" Lilly probed.

"Things were quiet for a few days, but it felt like something was about to happen, if you know what I mean. Like the calm before the storm you always hear about. That's about the time that Dottie was found hanging on the outhouse wall."

Lilly's eyes widened. "A warning to Nora—or whomever—that they could be next?"

"That's what I think. Let me tell you, everyone was on edge after that." Bonnie's eyes took on a haunted look. "I mean, things happen to whores all the time. You sort of get used to it, you know? But this was different. It put the fear of God in everyone."

It certainly put the fear of God in Lilly.

"Then a few days after the kids escaped, a gang of cowboys ambushed Nora in an alley." Bonnie gave a little shudder of horror. "I can't imagine what she went through."

Nor could Lilly. Once again, horrific images paraded through her mind.

"When she didn't come home, Monty got worried and went looking for her. When he found her, she was in a real bad way, but he got her to his place somehow and did his best to put her back together. She came around a few days later and told Monty she wanted to talk to the marshal, so Monty went and got him."

Lilly placed her elbows on the table and leaned forward. The information she was getting from Bonnie was invaluable. She couldn't wait to tell McShane and Erin and get their impressions of the story.

"Monty told everyone that she told Sam she knew who was behind her attack. He said he'd look into it, and, two days later, when Monty got back from work, she was dead."

"She just didn't make it?"

"No, she was recovering okay. She might have made it if it weren't for the bullet to the head."

CHAPTER 15

Thankfully, Erin came downstairs soon after Bonnie's grue-some announcement. Lilly needed some time to process every-thing she'd been told, which was a lot. She told Bonnie good-bye and excused herself so that the two women could talk pri-vately.

Both women were gone when Lilly came back downstairs. Although Erin didn't seem at all concerned about spending time alone with Elijah Wilkins, Lilly couldn't stop the nagging worry that cropped up whenever she thought of them alone, together. She'd seen evil up close when she'd come face-to-face with Preston Easterling earlier in the year. The expression in Wilkins's eyes bore a strong resemblance.

She'd just boiled a potato with the jacket on for lunch and was sitting down to eat it with more of the brown bread and cheese when she heard someone at the back door. Had Bonnie forgotten something? Taking the napkin from her lap, Lilly went to answer the door, a smile on her face, ready to greet her new friend.

The door swung wide, and her smile disappeared. All thought

of joking fled as she gaped in disbelief at the man standing there, his eyes wild and his hair standing on end.

Monty Newton.

Everything good Bonnie had told her about Nora's rescuer was forgotten while Cade's fears and warnings whirled in Lilly's mind. She and the little man stared at each other for long seconds. She was afraid to speak. Almost afraid to breathe.

When the alleged murderer spoke, he said only, "Are you Nora's Lilly?"

After a morning spent just looking around the Acre, Cade headed to the Gentleman's Corner, hoping to find a good game and some new information. The popular Ft. Worth saloon, which was located on a busy corner outside the Acre, was everything he'd heard it was.

Large cream-colored medallions, reminiscent of ancient coats of arms, were scattered over the sage-green wallpaper. On the wall behind the bar, on either side of a huge mirror proclaiming the name of the establishment, fancy sideboards shelved the liquor and beer spigots. Signage promoting popular lagers hung here and there, and a wall clock to help the gamblers and drinkers keep track of the time was placed in a place of prominence.

The elbow-high bar boasted five decorative corbels, which were good for little besides adding interest and class to what would otherwise be a plain front. A copper footrail bordered the base, and polished copper spittoons were placed at strategic points along the bar's length.

A glass case ensured freshness for a variety of cigars— everything from American made in the south to Philly-produced Spanish "segars," crafted from the most excellent Cuban tobacco, to the ever-popular Havanas, which discriminating smokers had been enjoying since Cuba had been opened to international trade in 1821.

The prized cigars, which were shipped from St. Iago, Cuba, were usually packaged in boxes of 1,000, 500, or 250, and shipped in wooden crates of 5,000 or more. Knowing that many saloons and eating establishments offered their customers a choice of smokes at little to no cost, Cade wandered over to have a look at the offerings.

"Help yourself," the barman said, swirling a spotless cloth across the counter's shiny surface.

"Thanks."

The barkeep slung the towel over his shoulder. "New in town or just passing through?"

"I'm not sure yet," Cade said, picking up one of the cigars and passing it beneath his nose. Deciding that if it tasted as good as it smelled, it would do, he bit off the end and spat it into the spittoon sitting near his foot. Then he took a match from a holder, struck it on the sole of his boot, and lifted it to his cigar, puffing on it until the end glowed red.

Nice.

"Beer?"

He only hesitated a moment. "That would be grand."

"You're not from around here," the waiter said, as he drew a mug of dark beer.

"No." Cade took another pull on the tobacco and blew a stream of smoke toward the ceiling. "I'm from Chicago. I work for a lady who may want to reopen Dusty Knowles's old place in the Acre. A special friend gave her the place."

"Lucky lady."

"Time will tell."

The man grinned. "Bouncer, are you?" He set the beer down on the counter.

"It's that obvious, is it?"

"Only if you know this business as well as I do. I'd heard someone was in town checking things out. What's holding her back?"

Cade drew on his smoke. "She's a pretty smart woman and has done all right for herself, but she wanted to come have a look and see if she wants to try this, or just leave well enough alone. Chicago can get mighty rough, but from what we've seen and heard since we've been here, it seems tame compared to the Acre."

The bartender laughed. "I won't deny that it's bad from time to time, but some of the things are exaggerated, believe me."

"That's nice to know."

"She could always fix it up and sell it."

"I hadn't thought of that," Cade said with a considering nod.

"It's something to consider. A lot of fellas with plenty of money come through here, and I hear them saying they'd like to have their own place, but they don't want to take the time or deal with the headaches of renovating."

"I'll mention it to her. Selling might appeal to her more than reopening. Like I said, she's heard a couple of things that made her uneasy."

"Don't tell me. Let me guess," the barkeep said. "Dottie. She's the whore they nailed to the outhouse wall, and then there was that other one that was raped by some rowdies in an alley and left to die."

"That's it."

"I heard about both of those incidents," the bartender said. "You can't keep much secret in a neighborhood that's as connected as the Acre is. I've been here six years, and I've seen some guys drink too much and get mad, and I've seen them get mean and uncontrollable, but what was done to those two is something else. That's nothing but pure evil."

"I'd have to agree." Cade set out a theory to see if he could get any new information. "It doesn't take much. Get a bunch of cowboys together who've been in the saddle too long, give them something to drink, and they lose whatever decency they had. A pretty girl comes along, and the next thing you know you've got a woman raped repeatedly and left fer dead." He took another puff of the cigar and slouched against the counter. "D'ya think they'll ever find out who did it?"

"The gang of men, no. She was in too bad a shape to tell the marshal anything at first, so they were probably long gone. There wasn't much he could do. There are some who say the man who found her in the alley finished her off."

"I've heard that, too, but I'm not buying it."

"Really? Why's that?"

"Why would the poor devil save her and nurse her back to health only to kill her?"

"That's a good point." The man shrugged. "She'd really been stirring everybody up. Maybe it was one of the locals who was upset over her trying to change the status quo. Who knows?"

"Who knows?" Cade repeated. It was something to think about. Every comment, every fact he learned had the potential to lead him down a trail that would lead him to Nora's killer. No tidbit of information was too small to reject.

"Now Dottie's a whole other mystery," the server said.

"I'm not sure I understand."

"No one knows who killed her, either, and some folks think it was one of the madams. Or one of the girls."

"Surely the competition can't be that stiff."

"The brothel owners are very protective of their girls, and they believe in payback for any perceived disloyalty."

"And how does this relate to this Dottie?"

"So, a while back, Dottie and another dove got into it over some man they were both convinced was going to carry them off to a new life."

Cade feigned surprise, though he'd heard of it happening. "Does that happen much?"

"Now and again," the barkeep said. "Some of the ranches are pretty far from town, and a man likes a little female company, so they'll marry one of the girls and they're both happy.

"Anyhow, the two girls got into it on the street one evening, and the next thing you know they got to rollin' around in the dust like a couple of danged cowboys, screaming and gouging eyes and pulling hair. Dottie, the one who got killed, bit a chunk out of Millie's chin, so scuttlebutt has it that Millie killed her for revenge."

"What's your opinion?"

"If Millie killed her, she had to have had some help. She's a little bit of a thing. There's no way she could have nailed Dottie to a wall without help."

Cade sipped his beer, wondering if he would ever stop being surprised by the depths of depravity people could sink to. Was there anything too heinous for them to do to one another? "So, you don't think it was Velvet or Rosalie behind that killing?"

"It's hard to say. I do know they hate each other. Always have."

"Why is that?"

"Elijah Wilkins. He supplies for them both. He supplies for almost every place in town, so things get a little strained now and again over perceived unfair treatment."

"Sounds like he's playing a dangerous game."

"Definitely. But on the other hand, he's got a pretty good thing going."

Yes, he did, Cade thought. Figuring he'd gotten all the information he could about the events surrounding Nora's death without arousing any suspicions, he turned his back to the bar and leaned against it. "Are there any good games in the back?"

"There are always games in the back," the bartender said.

Cade paid for his beer, lifted his cigar in a little salute, and picked up his mug. "Thanks for the cigar. And the talk."

"I hope it helps your boss make her decision."

"I'm sure it will."

CHAPTER 16

Lilly stood staring at the man believed to have killed her friend, her mind racing. Bonnie had given her a new perspective on the kind of man Monty was, but Lilly was having a hard time totally discounting the fact that many people in town thought he'd killed Nora. What was he doing here? She didn't realize she'd spoken the question aloud until she heard him saying, "I saw everyone leave, and I thought now would be a good time."

A good time for what? Murder? The random thought ran through her mind before she could stop it.

"I see." Well, that made sense if you wanted to meet with someone alone. Perhaps Monty Newton was smarter than anyone realized.

"I need to know if you're Lilly, Nora's friend."

"Why?" she asked, buying time. For what, she didn't know. She had no idea when Cade or Erin would be back.

"If you're Nora's friend, I'm the one who helped her get the letter posted. She told me you'd be coming to help her. She said you were terrible smart and pretty and that you had red hair. She wanted me to watch out for you. Are you her?"

Despite his rambling, Lilly's fears began to ease. There was no menace in his eyes or his demeanor. His stance was tense, but in no way threatening.

"Yes, I'm Nora's friend."

Relief replaced the anxiety in his eyes, and he looked as if the weight of the world had been lifted from his narrow shoulders. "What took you so long to get here? Nora's dead."

"I came as soon as I could," Lilly said, deciding it wouldn't do any good to go into a lengthy explanation. "I heard about Nora. Can you tell me what happened?"

"Everyone thinks I hurt her." His eyes filled with tears. "I wouldn't do that to her. Not Nora. I tried to make her better. She was my friend. I liked her."

"I liked her, too." Knowing McShane would have a conniption if he found out, she asked, "Would you like some coffee?"

"Coffee is for breakfast," Monty said. Then, after thinking a second, he said, "Sometimes Nora would want a cup in the afternoon, so I guess it's okay."

Smiling tentatively, Lilly stepped aside. "Take a seat there at the table," she said, gesturing toward the main room. "I'll make a fresh pot."

After she stirred up the fire and set the coffee on to brew, she joined Monty in the other room. She found him thumbing through the Pinkerton novel she was reading.

"You must really like detective novels," he said.

"Why is that?"

"This one has been read a lot."

"Yes, it has. What about you? Do you like Mr. Pinkerton's stories?"

"I ain't got much use for readin'," he said, then grinned. "Nora told me about the 'eye that never sleeps.' She said you worked for them. But you sleep, don't you?"

"Yes, Monty, I sleep."

"Boy, you are smart," he said with an even wider grin.

"Why is that?"

"I never told you my name, but you knew it."

Lilly laughed so that she wouldn't break down and cry. There was something incredibly refreshing about Monty Newton. An innocence and purity of thought not often found in so-called "normal" people.

"I have a confession to make, Monty," she said. "The grocer told me your name."

"Oh. Well, are you smart enough to find out who kilt Nora?"

"I have some people helping me," she told him, "so I certainly hope so."

A card game was the last thing on Cade's mind. Ignoring the players, he chose a seat at an empty table and went to take a book from the shelf that he had no intention of reading. Then he sat down to think.

As he'd known it would, his talk with the bartender had given him new perspective. He'd wondered if Nora's death and the vicious slaying of the other woman—Dottie—were connected in some way. That line of speculation had been put to rest, at least or until some new bit of evidence brought him back to it.

Unlike most of the town, he didn't think Monty Newton had anything to do with Nora's murder, for the reasons he'd explained. Erin and the others might speculate that Monty had gotten angry with Nora because of his sexual limitations, but if that was the case, why befriend her? Why wait until he'd saved her life to kill her? No, it just didn't add up.

There were only a few reasons for murder. If it wasn't about the sex, that left gain. Who stood to profit from Nora's death? She had no money, and it wasn't as if she was such a great hooker that she'd be murdered to cause harm to Velvet's business.

That left revenge. His gut told him that revenge was the basis for her killing . . . even for the rape. The question was, who hated her enough to want to get back at her? Velvet or one of the others? Any of the madams would have been furious over her trying to get the women to leave.

Or maybe it had something to do with helping those kids escape. If so, that could implicate any of the people who were interested in acquiring them. And was the rape connected to her war against the Acre, or just one of those unfortunate things that happen in places like this? It wasn't called Hell's Half Acre for nothing.

From what he'd heard about her, Cade could see Velvet setting up the rape, but why go back later and finish off the job when it seemed apparent that if Nora lived, she would suffer for the rest of her life? So far, the only person with a direct connection to the children was Elijah Wilkins, who boasted that he could get "whatever the client wanted." If he was robbed of his chance to sell them to the highest bidder, that would certainly be enough reason to kill whomever had robbed him.

Another question nagged at Cade: Did the houses keep children around just in case someone came along who wanted one, or had they been acquired for someone special, someone who liked abusing children for his own sick pleasure? If so, who could it be?

Good question, McShane. Good luck in finding that out. In a place where secrets were guarded and people injured and killed for much less, it would take some real sleuthing to unearth that person.

This was one of the times he didn't mind having Lilly as a partner. He was a big enough man to give credit where credit was due. The fact was that, because of their feminine qualities, women thought differently than men. They looked at a situation through a different lens. In a case like this, that was a good thing.

Lilly.

He sighed. He still hadn't decided how he felt about being her partner. Over the weeks, his initial resentfulness had grown into a grudging acceptance. He was accustomed now to her presence, yet her combined innocence and hardheadedness was enough to drive a cigar store Indian crazy. She baffled him. Angered him. Could annihilate his anger over her impulsiveness with her determination and her drive to do the right thing.

Doing the right thing was important to her, and something she'd said about lack of choices in life had him thinking about his relationship with his sister. Had Erin thought that prostitution was her only choice when they were younger? If so, why?

He'd been so furious and ashamed when he found out, that all he'd done was lambast her and try to make her guilty enough to give up that life and repent. That hadn't worked. Age had taught him that it never did. Repentance had to come from inside. From the heart. There was no turning away until you were convinced that you were wrong and realized that there was a different, better path.

They were both adults now, and his own experiences had taught him that things weren't always black-and-white. As he'd told Lilly, there were a lot of shades of gray in between.

Spending time with Erin made him realize how much he'd missed her. Was it time for him to get past his anger and try to establish some sort of relationship with her again? His bruised heart whispered *yes*. The devil sitting on his shoulder said, "What about Glenna?"

A sharp pain clutched at him. Although it was approaching two years since she'd been killed, the grief from losing her was as fresh as it had been when he'd stood staring at the smoking, burned-out shell of their home.

When the officials had come to look for her in the ashes, Seamus and Madden had had to forcefully remove Cade from the area. Madden, his older brother, had given him a sharp upper-cut to the chin to knock him out so they could haul him away.

They knew him well. If he'd seen the charred remains of her body, swollen with child, he might never have recovered.

Sweet Meagan had insisted that he did not need to be alone, so he'd gone home with Seamus. His sister-in-law had given him the children's room, and he'd pulled the curtains shut and collapsed onto the bed, weeping for the loss of a future. Of fatherhood. Of the chance to grow old with the woman who had captured his heart with her first hesitant smile.

Leaving Cade to his sorrow, Seamus had gone to break the news of Glenna's death to their sisters. When he'd gotten to Erin's, a neighbor said she'd been rushed to Cook County Hospital after attempting to take her life.

Cade was still wild with grief and wondering how he would get through the rest of his life when Seamus returned with the news. Despite his feelings about how his sister made a living, Cade loved her, and the possibility of losing both her and Glenna was unbearable.

He recalled how all the McShane siblings had descended on the charity hospital. The moment he'd seen her lying so still and white beneath the sheet, he'd almost broken down again.

"Excuse me, sir."

The sound of the man's voice pulled Cade from his dark pit of memories. Feeling somewhat dazed, he said, "Yes?"

"I hate to disturb you," the well-dressed, pudgy man said, "but we need another player for a game of monte. Are you interested in joining us?"

Not really, but it would be better than wallowing in misery and bitterness. He slammed the book closed and smiled. "Yes, I believe I am."

As it turned out, his sister had lived, but he'd lost her anyway.

CHAPTER 17

Cade got back to Dusty's soon after lunch. When he opened the front door of the boardinghouse, he saw Lilly sitting at one of the tables, her hands clasped together as if she were waiting for him, a tattered copy of one of Allan Pinkerton's dime novels lying next to her. She must have read those blasted books dozens of times, but she still brought them with her wherever they went. He'd have to see if he could find her something new.

He was about to ask what she'd been doing to pass the time, when he realized there was no smile of welcome on her face. Instead, she looked troubled. Vulnerable.

"Did you win lots of money?"

Sensing that something was amiss even though she seemed fine outwardly, he answered more sharply than was called for. "No!"

"Well, my goodness. There's no need to sound so grumpy about it," she said in a testy voice.

That was much more like her.

"Did you manage to get any new information?"

"Aye, I did," he said, tempering his tone.

"Tell me," she urged, gesturing toward one of the chairs.

"I've decided that we need to go somewhere outside of town and work on your self-defense skills."

Was that surprise in her eyes?

"Right now?"

He rested his forearms on the tabletop and leaned toward her. "Yes, now. There's plenty of daylight left."

"What brought this on after all this time?" she asked.

"A combination of things, I suppose. Hearing all the stories about what can happen to women here made me realize we shouldn't put it off. We've been busy the past few months, and this is the first time we've had so much spare time on our hands."

"That's true."

"And then, you have that meeting with Monty tonight. . . ." He gave a nonchalant shrug. "It wouldn't hurt if you had a few tricks up your sleeve."

"There won't be a meeting with Monty tonight."

"What? What happened?"

"He came while you were gone." She cast a glance over her shoulder. "I told him to wait in the kitchen until I let you know he was here."

Cade's initial reaction was raw terror. His second was anger. What was the silly chit thinking, asking a potential killer inside? If something had happened to her, he would never have forgiven himself for leaving her alone.

She reached out and placed a hand on his forearm.

Common sense reasserted itself, and as he realized that she was unscathed, the panic abated. Aware that his hands were trembling ever so slightly, he pulled free of her touch, curled them into fists in his lap, and reacted in the age-old way of men: respond to fear with anger. "Did ya think I'd shoot him?"

She smiled then, but just a little. "I wasn't sure."

Feeling old suddenly, Cade scraped a hand down his face. "Go get him."

Lilly went into the kitchen and returned a couple of minutes later with the man they'd seen in Velvet's a few nights before.

Cade stood for the introductions.

"Monty, this is my partner, Mr. McShane. He's going to help me find the man who hurt Nora. McShane, this is Nora's friend, Monty. The one who found her in the alley."

The men shook hands, and Monty took one of the empty chairs.

"What can you tell us about what happened?" Cade asked. He knew that a lot of what Monty would tell them would be a repetition of what they'd already learned in bits and pieces, but hearing it from him might add new information. It would certainly give the episode cohesiveness. He'd been there and witnessed much of what had happened, and he had no reason to lie . . . unless he was guilty, and Cade just couldn't see that.

"Nora was my friend," Monty said. "She didn't make fun of me the way the other girls did. And she didn't mind that I . . ."

"We understand," Cade said. He didn't really want to get into Monty's problems. "So, the two of you spent a lot of time together."

"Yes. As long as I paid Velvet, I could spend time with Nora. Mostly we talked."

"Talked? About what?" Cade asked.

"Everything. She told me about performing on stage and about her friends. She told me about Lilly."

Cade glanced at his partner. "Did she?"

"Sometimes she would sing funny songs to me. We laughed a lot. She talked to me about God. She didn't like being here, but she couldn't get away," Monty said. "Velvet found her and saw to it that she got a whupping."

"Who hurt her?"

"Most likely Elijah Wilkins. He does whatever Velvet tells him to."

"Does he now?" Cade said, sharing a look with Lilly. "Do you think he killed her, Monty?"

Monty shrugged. "Probably. He isn't a nice man."

"What can you tell us about the children?" Lilly asked.

"It made Nora real mad when she heard about that."

"Where did they come from?" Cade pressed.

"I'm not sure," Monty said with a shake of his head. "Nora told me that sometimes those kids on the orphan trains were handed over to men like Elijah. Ain't that awful? Anyways, he went on a trip and come back with two of them in tow."

"Did he take them to Velvet's or one of the other houses?" Cade asked.

"Oh, no. He kept them at his place, but when the sheriff went to look for them after Nora raised Cain, they weren't there." A sly smile lit Monty's eyes. "I know where he took them, though."

"How do you know?" Lilly asked.

"I followed him to that old warehouse over by the train tracks, and then I helped Nora get them away from here. She said it was our good deed." He smiled again. This time the smile was pure and sweet. "Jesus loves children, you know."

An hour or so after Monty left, Erin returned. Unlike Lilly and Cade, she'd learned little from the time spent with Wilkins, except that both Velvet and Rosalie did their best to keep the marshal happy, which Lilly and Cade already knew.

"Nothing else?" Cade asked.

Erin shrugged. "He's convinced that he is God's gift to womankind, and intent on proving it to me."

Cade looked furious, and Lilly felt her stomach sink. Something in the statement held a note of menace.

"I certainly hope you didn't ply your trade in hopes of getting information in return, sister dear," Cade snapped, taking the bait she'd offered.

She laughed. "Give me a little credit. You may not believe it, but I am somewhat discriminating. I stopped 'plying my trade' with men like Elijah Wilkins a long time ago. He has nothing to offer me except a few dollars and a roll in the hay, and I don't need either. His kind are a dime a dozen. Besides, my guess is that he isn't nearly as . . . accomplished . . . as he thinks he is."

"Enough! I really don't care to hear any more about your opinions of the man's . . . prowess. Real or imagined." Cade's voice was sharp, gruff.

Erin smiled, a bright smile that failed to reach her eyes. "Fine. How did the two of you spend the morning?"

Anxious to change the subject, Lilly said, "Your brother went to find that card game he mentioned earlier, and my meeting with Monty Newton was moved up to this morning."

"What?" Erin's eyes widened in surprise. "How did that happen?"

Lilly gave a shake of her head, as if she still couldn't believe what had happened. "He showed up at the kitchen door."

"And she let him in. Silly woman."

Lilly glared at him. "He didn't seem like the kind of person who would try to attack me. I had him wait here until McShane came back, and then we asked him a few questions."

"What did he want?"

"Mostly, he just wanted to make sure I was the friend Nora had been expecting. She'd described me to him, and he'd been waiting for me to arrive. He asked me what took me so long to get here, and wanted me to assure him that we would catch her killer."

"And you don't think it was him?"

"I really don't, Erin."

"I agree," Cade said. "Sit down, sister. Let's see what else we've learned today, and then I want to get your opinion on a couple of things."

Lilly and Erin exchanged astonished looks, then Cade's sister said, "You spent quite a while with Bonnie before I came downstairs earlier today. I'm sure you didn't chitchat about fashion."

"No, we didn't. Waiting for you gave me the perfect chance for a good talk. Somehow the conversation turned to her friend, Nora, and, when I mentioned that I'd like to hear about her, she told me the whole story. It was as if God arranged the whole meeting."

"Perhaps He did," Cade suggested.

"Perhaps. Anyway, she told me how Elijah had lied to get Nora here and about her running away when she found out what he really wanted. He gave her a beating at Velvet's request. She started talking to the girls about God, and encouraging them to leave, to go somewhere else and start over."

"Well, that was foolish!" Erin snapped. "It sounds as if your friend had a lot of guts and little sense. I've spent enough time with him to know he has a vicious streak a mile wide, and I get the feeling that he likes the power he has over women."

Lilly understood what Erin was talking about. She'd witnessed it while working the New Orleans case.

"Nora *was* gutsy," she said. "And when she got something in her head, she wouldn't let it go." Lilly went on to tell her companions how those efforts had gotten Nora fired. When she told them about the child who'd run away from one of the other houses and been hit by the train, both Erin and Cade were shocked.

"Are you saying that there was a child—a boy—who took her advice and left?" Erin asked.

Lilly looked from one to the other. "Yes. He had a sister, and she blamed Nora for his death because Nora had filled his head with a lot of nonsense about having a better life. Of course, Nora already blamed herself."

"Did you get the sister's name?" Cade asked.

"No, why?"

"We need to have a talk with her," Cade said.

"What on earth for?" Erin asked.

"If she blamed Nora, it's very possible that she had something to do with the things that happened to her . . . including her death."

"Oh."

"Did Eli bring the two new kids to town after that?" Erin asked.

"Soon afterward."

"Does anyone have any idea where he finds them?" Cade asked.

"Any number of places, I imagine," Lilly said. "Monty said that Nora thought he might have gotten them from an orphan train."

"I've read that those poor children often wind up in horrible situations," Cade said.

"When she heard about the new children, she took her protests to the streets and gave the information about the children to the newspaper. It seems the editor was happy to print the story, since he's been campaigning to clean up the Acre for a while now."

"There's too much money to be made—legally and illegally—for the law to shut things down," Cade said.

"You're right," Erin said with a nod. "And I know exactly where this is headed. Nora was waging a one-woman war against the system, and it resulted in her run-in with the gang of cowboys."

"That's my theory, too," Cade said. "Revenge. There are any number of people who might have been behind it, including Wilkins or any of the madams who were dealing with dissatisfied women. That's why we need to talk to the boy's sister. She certainly had reason to want Nora to pay."

"Good point," Lilly said.

"Whoever came up with the idea, it was brilliant," Cade mused. "It could have been any of a dozen different groups who come and go. They do the deed, leave town in a day or so, never to be seen or heard of again. It would be nearly impossible to place blame on anyone, since men have raped and killed women without any provocation for years."

"Do you think Nora was aware that she was putting pressure on people who had a lot to lose and wouldn't take kindly to what she was doing?" Erin asked. "She sounds so innocent and idealistic."

"According to the letter Lilly received, Nora was determined to shut the place down," Cade told his sister. "Her single-mindedness might have blinded her to the consequences of what she was doing. I'm not sure she thought things through or understood the lengths the businesses would go to, to keep the status quo."

"She stirred up a hornet's nest," Lilly added. "From what Monty told me, Davies was forced to look into the claims about the children, since he was getting bombarded by Nora in the streets and Paddock in the paper. Davies made a trip to Eli's, and the kids weren't there, and that was the end of that." There was no sense mentioning that Davies had done a half-hearted job. Everyone at the table knew that. "Monty found them at a warehouse, he and Nora helped them out of town, and here we are."

"Here we are," Cade echoed. "The barman did confirm that it was around that time that they discovered Dottie's body. I don't think there's any significance beyond it's acting as a warning."

"I'm not sure I'm following you," Lilly asked.

He told them about the fight between Dottie and Millie,

how Dottie had disfigured her opponent, and the bartender's theory that Millie was responsible for the killing.

"Until I heard that, I had the mind-set that the madams are responsible for a huge part of the violence, but a lot of these women have become hardened through the years. That's another reason we need to talk to the boy's sister. Millie, or any of the others, might have had reason to kill Dottie, as long as they had some help. And anyone who can kill someone and nail them to a wall would have no problem putting a bullet into someone's head."

Lilly cringed at his brutal assessment. Erin didn't say a word, but she looked confused.

"He's saying not to count anyone out," Lilly explained. "When you think of violence and punishment, it's natural to think of Velvet or Rosalie, or even Eli Wilkins. But there are all sorts of undercurrents in this place, all sorts of rivalries. It isn't unreasonable to imagine one or more of the other women instigating the attack on Nora and then finishing her off when it looked as if she might survive."

"Revenge," Erin's eyes grew dark.

"Most likely," Lilly said. "Monty claims Nora knew who was behind it all, and that she told the marshal. Word has a way of getting around."

"Indeed, it does," Cade agreed. "The marshal could have mentioned it to someone while he was having a drink somewhere, never knowing he was signing Nora's death warrant."

"A harmless mention?" Erin said, meeting her brother's gaze.

"It's possible," he said with a lift of his shoulders. "Sometimes the most innocent comments have terrible consequences."

Erin nodded. "Yes," she said, "I know."

She stood abruptly, saying that she wanted to rest until suppertime. Lilly's troubled gaze followed her retreating figure up the stairs. "She's behaving strangely, don't you think?"

"She's behaving like Erin."

"Be serious, McShane. She was fine. She seemed to be enjoying the exchange of ideas, and then, in an instant, she turned as white as a ghost and stopped interacting with us. Something we said hit a raw spot."

"I can't worry about Erin's sensitivity. We were talking about her business. Maybe something touched what little bit of conscience she has left."

Lilly glared at him.

"Look, lass, she was ever touchy about things. She'll be fine by suppertime. Now, where do you think we are in the investigation after getting all this new information?"

"I don't think Dottie's death has anything to do with Nora's. I believe that Elijah Wilkins not only procures for most of the town's bawdy houses, but that he's the one who handles all of Velvet's, and maybe Rosalie's, problems. My dear friend became a problem. I think our man is Wilkins."

"He's got the temperament for it. Goldie says he asks for her once in a while, and that he likes to play rough."

The image that rose in her mind sent a shiver of revulsion through Lilly. "One more reason to think he's our man. Now all we have to do is find the evidence we need to put him in jail."

CHAPTER 18

Lilly rose early. Cade was adamant that they start on her self-defense lessons, since Erin's arrival had interrupted them the previous afternoon. Recalling the almost intolerable heat of the previous day, she'd asked that they go early in the morning. He'd agreed readily enough.

Deciding that she needed a cup of coffee to sip on while she got ready, she went downstairs in her robe. Cade was already in the kitchen, pouring himself a mug. Instead of his usual dark suit, he wore brown twill pants and a light blue chambray shirt, the clothing he'd adopted for his role as an Irish immigrant during their stint in New Orleans.

He frowned at her. "We need to get started."

"I know. It won't take me but a tick to get ready."

"Fine. Dress comfortably. You'll need something that won't . . . bind. You wouldn't happen to have any trousers, would you?"

She offered him a grim smile. "Indeed, I do. While I was digging up that dratted grave, I discovered that skirts and petticoats are not conducive to some tasks, so I purchased some

Levi's," she said with a proud lift of her chin. "I also joined the Rational Dress Society."

She waited for the masculine censure she was sure must come. To her surprise, she saw a hint of a smile lift one corner of his mustache. "Of course you did."

Less than half an hour later, they were on their way. While Lilly dressed, Cade had gone out and rented a buggy, and they now headed north toward the Trinity River.

"How far are we going?" Lilly asked, looking at him from beneath the rim of the slouch hat she wore to protect her face from the sun.

"Until I think we're far enough out of town that there won't be any curious eyes and nosey questions."

He finally saw a place with some shade and pulled the gelding to a stop. After jumping down and tossing the reins over a low-growing bush, he swung Lilly to the ground. Dressed as she was in men's attire, it felt strange to help her, but the action was ingrained in his upbringing, no matter how she was clothed.

He began rolling up the sleeves of his shirt while taking in the absurd picture she made. Two of her assignments had proved she needed to learn the art of self-protection, but he was already regretting his decision to teach her. He feared spending time in such close proximity was not the wisest idea. A state of affairs both annoying and troubling.

While she drank from the canteen he'd brought, his gaze moved over her. Her vibrant red hair had been scraped back from her face and twisted into a tight knot, yet instead of detracting from her looks, the severity of the style accentuated the curve of her jaw, the delicate sweep of her cheekbones, and her small ears. Fierce independence and intelligence shone from her brown eyes as she stared out at the land surrounding them.

She had paired her new men's breeches with a white shirt,

quite possibly made for a boy, since it fit her narrow shoulders nicely. Her boots looked worn; they'd had dried mud scraped from them, probably from the grave she'd dug up on her first assignment.

Seeing her dressed in such a boyish way helped him understand why society looked down on women wearing men's clothing. The boy's shirt was buttoned to the throat and at the wrists. There was nothing tempting about any part of it, yet tempting it looked. The Levi's, which were belted around her small waist, made her legs look a mile long and accentuated the slimness of her thighs. Though they were in no way close-fitting, they showed all her curves, and he had to admit that she had a nice shape.

His innate honesty wouldn't allow him to deny her allure, and that same straightforwardness reminded him that feeling an attraction to her—or any woman—was taboo. He'd learned the hard way that caring was a weakness the enemy could use against you, and that weakness could lead one down a path far too close to hell.

But he was a man, not a saint, and he was not immune to the appeal of a beautiful woman. With his Pinkerton career already compromised by his previous behavior, to even think of Lilly beyond the boundaries of their work would be the height of folly. Thank goodness, he was a professional and knew well how to turn off his emotions and concentrate on his work.

"Didn't your parents teach you that staring is rude?"

The sound of her voice jerked Cade from his unwelcome thoughts. "I'm sorry. Actually, I was thinking." Without missing a beat, he said, "Ready to get started?"

"Yes."

He led her to a more open space. "You have a gun, you say?" he asked over his shoulder.

"Yes, a derringer."

"Did ya bring it?" He turned to face her, walking back-

ward. He couldn't help the taunting smile on his lips as he recalled how many times she'd needed the weapon only to realize she'd left it somewhere.

She glared back at him. "It's ungentlemanly to bring that up."

"Never claimed to be a gent," he said, and pivoted back
around. Lilly took a few running steps to catch up with him,
and he turned to look at her. "I'm sure you know they are
only effective at close range."

"Yes. Pierce was quite thorough with his lessons."

Cade didn't doubt that. From what he'd seen of Lilly's father figure, Pierce would be thorough in anything he under-
took. "Would you use it on someone?"

"What?" She stood stock-still, her eyes widening in disbelief.

He paused, too, and crossed his arms across his chest. "If
you haven't thought about it, you should. It's one thing to
carry a weapon, another to be of a mind to use it. What if
someone laid hands on you, and, say, tried to push you down a
staircase or—God forbid—rape you, could you pull the trigger
to save your own hide?"

She frowned and gave a slow nod. "I might have to think
about it a moment, but I think so, yes."

"No! That is unacceptable, yet that's what most women say
they'd do. In that split second while your moral upbringing is
struggling with the pros and cons of killing someone and your
will to stay alive, your assailant could already have fixed your
flint. That's the one thing you've got to remember. No thinking. No hesitation ever, or you're dead. Or worse."

All the color leached from her face. "But that's so . . . cold.
We're talking about willfully taking a life."

"Bloody right we are," he said, his relentless gaze boring
into hers. "Your life or his. Whose do you want it to be?"

The troubled expression in her eyes deepened, and she
nodded. "I see. You're right."

"Good," he said. "So, what do you think your greatest disadvantage is if you come under attack by a man?"

"My size and strength of course," she said without a moment's hesitation. "In most instances, it would be like pitting David against Goliath."

"Good analogy. So, like David, you need a version of the slingshot—some skill that will even the odds a bit."

"And what would that be? Boxing?"

He laughed. "Regular ring techniques would be useless. I'll teach you how to fight like a guttersnipe. Or a woman."

"And you have intimate knowledge of how they fight?"

"Yes, to both. And if some of the brawls I've heard about and seen since we've been here are any indication, when push comes to shove, they both fight alike—dirty."

She blinked. "Dirty?"

"Yes. Of course, the best deterrent is to stay away from places you know are unsafe, but you and I both know that you're unlikely to do that."

"I just try to do my job," she countered.

"You have a partner to help you in those situations," he reminded her. She started to reply, but he held up a silencing hand. "Let's theorize that an assignment takes you to a neighborhood that is less than savory. You think you hear someone behind you, and, when you look, you see he's coming."

He was pleased to note that she was fully engaged in what he was saying. "When a person is under attack, things happen in the body. Your first response will be fear. Your pulse will race, and the adrenaline will flow."

Lilly nodded.

"You start thinking of what you should do, or how to get away. Sometimes, the fear gives over to fury, and that's a good thing. Whatever you do, don't let the fear get the best of you. It saps your determination. It's crucial that you stay focused on the anger and the belief that you're up to dealing with whatever he may try to do to you. What's the first thing you do?"

"Run?"

"Yes, if you can. But before you run, there are other things you can do. You scream your lungs out for starters. With any luck, someone will hear and come to your aid, or the fellow will turn and run away."

"And if he doesn't?"

"If he gets his hands on you or tries to strike you that hate and anger I was talking about will surface. It's a funny thing, but it seems our mind finds a place where the need to protect the body takes over. It's a proven fact that a person will defend himself the best way he can until one of you wins."

He could tell she was mulling things over by the concentration in her dark eyes. Good. She was taking this lesson seriously.

"Try to keep out of his grasp. Resist however you can. Kick, hit, scream, pull hair, try to gouge out his eyes. If you simply can't break away, you can try going as limp as a dishrag."

"Why?" she asked in amazement. "Isn't that like giving up?"

"No. Because you aren't giving up. You're changing tactics. He won't be expecting that. Sometimes, the sudden drag of the dead weight unbalances the captor, and there's a possibility he'll loosen his hold on you. That's when you try to slip out of his grasp, or use your elbow to hit him in the belly, or kick him in the shins. Come here. Let me show you."

She neared him, an uneasy expression in her eyes.

"Turn around."

She complied. Cade moved behind her and took her in a bear hug, pinning her arms to her sides. He felt the heat of her body pressed against his. The slight breeze sent the flowery scent of her cologne swirling around him. For the space of a heartbeat, or perhaps two, she relaxed against him, and then she stiffened and tipped back her head to look up at him.

"Not fair! I can't move."

He gave her a grim smile. "That's the point, colleen."

Though he knew now why she hated the term, there were times he used it on purpose. Like when they were arguing about something, or when he was teasing her, or like now, when he wanted to get her riled up.

"*Don't* call me colleen!" Before he realized what she was doing, she leaned over and clamped her teeth onto his nearest arm.

Cade swore, and his fighting reflexes kicked in. He spun her around to face him, his fists raised in a gesture as automatic to him as drawing his next breath. They stood there, glaring at each other, both breathing as if they'd run a long distance.

There was no fear in Lilly's face, only fury. Slowly, he lowered his hands and rubbed his arm. Suddenly seeing the humor in the situation, he began to laugh. She'd done just what he'd told her to do.

She didn't laugh, but she did smile. Impishly. "Let's do it again."

And they did. Again, and again. He held her, and she struggled with everything in her. Her frustration was palpable, but he refused to give her an inch she didn't earn. Then, without warning, she went as limp as a dishrag.

He took her sudden weight with a grunt and bent slightly at the waist. She took the opportunity to slip out of his grasp and turned to face him with a triumphant smile and a saucy little curtsy.

Placing his hands on his hips, he smiled back. "Not bad, colleen. Not bad at all. If your back is to them, you can always try to kick, too. Anything. Just keep them off guard. And remember, not everyone who comes at you will be as big as I am."

"That's good," she said, breathing hard.

He grinned wider. "They may be bigger."

Instead of taking the bait, she muttered, "Job's comforter." Then, "Let's do something else. Something different."

"Fine. Remember that since you're at a disadvantage because of your size, it's good to go for their eyes. No matter how big you are, all eyes are equal. Biting"—he rubbed his arm and grimaced—"scratching and hair pulling and eye gouging are all acceptable in a street fight. Always be looking for an opening, for some way to inflict pain, and find yourself a chance to get away."

She nodded, soaking up every word.

"The nose is good, too. Make a fist and whack them as hard as you can." He rubbed his nose that had been broken a time or two. "I can tell you from personal experience that it hurts like the devil. And it doesn't take long for it to interfere with yer breathing."

"What if they get me down on the ground?"

"Like this?" he asked, and before she knew it, she was lying flat on her back and he was sitting astride her, her arms pinned above her head. Once again, he was aware of her, not as a partner, but as a woman. A striking, contrary, desirable woman. The look in her eyes told him that she was aware of him, too. . . .

Suddenly, she began to buck and kick and growl out her rage.

"Whoa, there, lass! What's the matter with you?"

She stilled at once. "I can't get you off."

"Well, don't panic. Just remember that the same rules apply. Go for the weak places, the unprotected areas. And whatever you do, don't give up."

An hour later, neither of them was smiling, and the canteen was empty. "That's enough for today. Let's get back to town and get a bath. We'll come another morning," Cade said.

He grabbed the tail of his shirt, which had come untucked

during one of their scuffles. He pulled it up to wipe his face, revealing a taut portion of his abdomen.

Heat that had nothing to do with exertion swept through Lilly. She pushed back a lock of sweat-soaked hair and wiped her dirty face on the arm of her once white shirt. "I'm ready for a break."

The training was physical, even intimate in many ways. Not since their time in New Orleans, when they'd been forced to share a room, had she felt so vulnerable, so aware of him. She'd hoped that resorting to a more businesslike approach to their partnership would ease the tension between them. Until today, she'd thought it was working.

Be honest with yourself, Lilly. Even though you know it can go nowhere, you are attracted to the man. Accept it, guard against it, and carry on. She could almost hear Pierce's voice echoing through her brain, telling her that the "show must go on" no matter what.

She understood the concept. She only hoped she could do it.

Late that night, Lilly lay in bed, listening to the revelers in the street and wishing sleep would find her, halfway wishing she'd gone with Cade and Erin. It wasn't that she was afraid . . . exactly. Uneasy was a better description. After their lessons earlier in the day, she'd declined going with them to the bars and bawdy houses, which left her alone in this big, empty saloon with its creaks and groans.

With everything they'd encountered since arriving in Ft. Worth, she knew Cade was right in insisting that she learn to take care of herself. Not since digging up the grave at Heaven's Gate had she felt so empty and exhausted. A long, hot soak when they'd come back from the river hadn't done much to revive her. She still felt as if she'd been dragged through the streets behind a wild mustang. Even a dinner of Texas steak had failed to boost her energy.

She flopped to her back and released a huge sigh, remembering all the falls she'd taken. It would take much more training before she mastered that one. When he'd finally called an end to the physical battering and given her a hand up, she had seen the glimmer of approval in his eyes.

Somehow, it had been enough. Or was it? Recalling how he'd shackled her wrists above her head and held her still beneath him caused her heart to pick up speed. When she'd begun fighting him, he'd been surprised. He'd had no way of knowing that a memory, fleeting and bittersweet, had flashed into her mind. Tim, holding her down just that way on the soft feather bed and then leaning forward and taking her mouth in a gentle kiss meant to cajole her into a good mood and a loosening of her purse strings. As usual, thinking of Tim had made her see red, and she'd begun to struggle.

No! No! She didn't want to ever feel that way again. If she ever trusted her heart to another man, it would not be the likes of Cadence McShane. No, the next time, she would choose wisely. She would look for someone steady and dependable. Not someone who would go jaunting around the country getting himself into scrapes of one kind or another.

Someone, perhaps, like Simon.

She rolled over and slammed her fist into the softness of her pillow. Good grief! She didn't want Simon or Cade or anyone. Not at the moment, anyway. *So why does it matter what Cade thinks of you? Why do you want him nearby?*

A rationalization came swiftly, though perhaps it was not as truthful as she pretended. She wanted to make him proud of her. She hadn't wanted this partnership and had fought it for months, but the fact was, she was a better agent with him guiding her. Though she knew that the militant women in the world would no doubt despise her for it, she wanted his approval. Wanted him to think of her as an equal, to feel she was pulling her own weight. To be happy that they were working together. Her laughter sounded loud in the darkness. Perhaps happy was too strong a word. *Accepting* might be better.

Somewhere in the night a gun was discharged, and, despite herself, she gave a startled jerk. This was not a good place, and she would be glad when they got enough information to put Elijah Wilkins behind bars and could go back home.

And then what, Lilly? You'll just be given another case as bad or worse than this one. What did you expect when you got on your high horse and decided to pursue criminals? That it would be roses and dewdrops?

What had she expected? Had she been so determined to prove that she was smarter, more noble than the average woman after being duped by Timothy Warner? Or had she really believed she could make a difference? Pierce had told her that she couldn't save all the misused women, but she'd insisted that she could save a few, and she had done that. Unfortunately, not Nora.

You saved them, but at what cost? No matter how much she thought about the good she did putting men behind prison bars, she could not rid herself of the notion that she was losing her humanity along the way.

Now Cade wanted her to look deep inside herself and be willing to pull a trigger to shoot someone. Shooting at empty peach cans and rocks was far different from aiming at a body that breathed and moved. The very thought made her cringe, yet she knew she did not carry the little gun for decoration. Cade was right. If she didn't intend to use it, she shouldn't have it.

Which brought her back to the question that had been plaguing her for a while now: Was she cut out for this work? She couldn't deny that she loved the freedom of being a detective. She'd already been to three parts of the country that she might never have seen if not for William Pinkerton.

She liked the challenge, the pitting of her instincts, skills, and intelligence against unknown criminals. She liked getting a new piece of information and trying to figure out how it fit in with all the other pieces she'd collected to create a picture of what had occurred. And she loved the thrill when she knew she had it figured out and went to get the villain. She loved hearing William sing her praises, seeing the gratitude in the victims' eyes, and hearing their litany of thanks.

She did not like seeing the evil purpose behind the crimes she exposed. Hated knowing that people could sink to such depths of sinfulness and depravity. But it was there. Had been since the creation of Adam and Eve, and would be until time came to an end. So then, the question became: Was she willing to deal with one to have the other?

Could she look upon the ugly things she saw in her work as just part of her assignment, something to be written up at the mission's end, turned in and forgotten? Most important, could she be surrounded by so many bad things and still live a good and meaningful life? In the end, it boiled down to one simple question: Did the good she accomplished outweigh the bad?

CHAPTER 19

The next few days meandered by, each in the same fashion as the previous one. The wind that seemed to blow most of the time and provided at least a modicum of cooling stopped. The sun beat down without mercy, scorching the already dry Texas earth. Two or three horses galloping down the street created a small dust storm. Temperatures and tempers rose. It didn't matter what place they chose to patronize, at least one fight a night broke out among the regulars or the girls.

Bouncers cracked jaws and smashed heads, and once Lilly saw a madam reach down and grab one of the girls rolling around on the floor by the hair and jerk her upright. Then the madam marched her out the door and plunged her head in the watering trough, yelling at her to cool off. There was a shootout in the street. Fortunately, both parties were so drunk that neither had a chance of hitting the other. A window was shattered during the fracas, and Marshal Davies arrested both offenders and hauled them off to the jail. Just another night in "Paris."

Neither of Lilly's associates had learned anything of importance, but Bonnie had told Lilly that Velvet was starting to comment on the length of their stay, grumbling that Erin ought to know by now if she wanted to open a business or not.

Hoping to ease any growing speculation about why they were staying so long, Cade started the rumor that Miss O'Toole had decided to reopen the dance hall. Hoping to add credibility to the lie, Erin dragged Lilly all over Ft. Worth as she pretended to look for fabric and furniture, feigned interest in paintings and knickknacks, and even consulted a pseudo-French designer about redoing her bedroom. Lilly was amazed at how believable Erin's performance was.

While they "shopped" for furnishings, Cade continued to cultivate his relationships with the bartenders, gamblers, and bouncers. He'd tried to make contact with the sister of the boy who'd been struck by the train, but no matter how often, through whom, or how many ways he tried to approach her, she remained close-mouthed about the incident, which begged the question, why? Was she afraid of accidentally incriminating herself, or had she been warned or threatened by someone else?

Lilly persisted in trying to chat up the girls wherever they went, but many of them refused to talk for fear of making their bosses angry.

Monty made no more visits and left no more notes. It was as if he'd dropped off the face of the earth.

After eleven days in the district, they were no closer to pinning Nora's murder on Elijah Wilkins than they had been when they first arrived. This was the hardest part of an investigation. When it seemed that there were no more ideas to check out, and everything came to an abrupt halt.

Desperate for some new avenue to investigate, and against Cade's wishes, Lilly and Erin visited the office of Mr. B. B. Paddock with the *Fort Worth Democrat* on the pretext of finding the town's most gifted sign painter. What they were really looking for was information about Nora's marches against the evils of the town, and, if Mr. Paddock were in an expansive mood, to see whether or not he had any thoughts about who might have killed her.

They found the newspaperman setting type in preparation for the upcoming weekly edition. Erin lost no time introducing herself, sauntering up to him with a gloved hand extended. "Mr. Paddock, I presume."

"I'm B. B. Paddock. How may I help you?"

"I'm Erin O'Toole, and this is my assistant, Miss Long. I'll be opening Dusty Knowles's old place soon, and I'd like an eye-catching sign for the front. I thought you might know someone who specializes in fancy script." She flashed her most seductive smile. "And, of course, I'll be wanting some advertising nearer opening day."

The disapproval in the journalist's eyes was evident. Considering his feelings about the Acre, Lilly imagined that the last thing he wanted to hear was that another bawdy house would be opening. To his credit, he remained professional. If he refused to deal with all the rascals in town, he'd have no business. It was his job to advertise for those who wanted it and print the newsworthy happenings, not to cut off his nose to spite his face by refusing their patronage.

"If you're looking for someone to paint a sign, Lionel Stevens would be your man, but he's been under the weather with his arthritis for a while now." The newsman thought for a moment. "Your next best man for the job is Monty Newton."

Lilly and Erin exchanged stunned looks. "Isn't he the man who hangs out in the bars? The one who isn't quite . . . right?" Erin asked.

"The one they say killed that woman who tried to shut down all the houses?" Lilly added. "What was her name?"

"Nora Nash," Paddock said. "She worked her heart out, but it's not going to happen. Not until we get someone in office who isn't in bed with the crooks in town. Literally."

So much for not sullying a lady's ears, Lilly thought. But then, to him, she and Erin were not exactly ladies.

More intent on a potential customer than gossip, Paddock walked over to a large drawer that held sketches and, riffling through them, pulled out two. "This one is Lionel's," he said, proffering a rendering of a woman's hat done all in flowers and ribbons. Flowing script proclaimed the newest ladies' attire could be bought at Le Petite Boutique. Lilly thought it was quite nicely done.

"Monty's." The newsman showed them another advertisement. This one with fancy lettering and a drawing of a ladies' walking dress. Lilly thought it was well-done, too, and as impossible as it was, there was something about the simple drawing that seemed familiar. In truth, most of the newspaper advertisements were much the same. As a novice, she didn't see a nickel's difference between Lionel Stevens's work and Monty's. She shrugged aside the thought. It wasn't as if Erin was really going to order a sign or buy any advertising.

Forcing her mind back to the case, she asked, "What do you mean about the law being literally 'in bed' with the crooks?"

Paddock shrugged. "It's no secret. The marshal has been close to Velvet for years. In fact, I heard they planned to marry about ten years or so ago. No one knows what happened, and they're still close, but that doesn't keep him from cozying up to Rosalie."

"It sounds as if he has a good thing going," Erin said.

"Oh, he does. And so do they. That's why it's so hard to clean things up. They have an 'I'll scratch your back if you scratch mine' mentality. Add Wilkins to the mix, and you've got a real mess."

"I've met Mr. Wilkins," Erin said.

"Well, watch him. There isn't an ounce of loyalty in him. He'd cut his own mother's throat if she got in his way."

Lilly saw the flash of uneasiness in Erin's eyes before she said, "Thank you for the warning."

The newspaperman seemed to realize that he'd said far too much about the town's shady business dealings and changed the subject. "You don't worry about Monty. He's peculiar, and a little slow, but he's harmless, and he can copy about any fancy lettering you might have in mind. The problem is finding him. No one's seen him in a week or more."

Back outside in the heat of the day, Lilly tried to calm the rapid beating of her heart. *Had* something happened to Monty? He'd said he intended to lay low, but knowing that she wasn't the only one who'd noticed his absence around town was unnerving.

"Well, what did you think?" Erin asked. "We'd heard Davies and Velvet were close, but planning to get married? That's interesting. I wonder what happened?"

Something about their conversation with Mr. Paddock needed further consideration, but Lilly couldn't put her finger on what tidbit was bothering her. There was the news that Velvet and the marshal had once planned to marry, which was fascinating in an unsettling sort of way, but whether or not it had any bearing on the investigation remained to be seen. She'd have to get Cade's take on it.

Now, she turned to her friend and said as much. "I'd like to know more about that, too, but I'm not sure it's important to the case. I still think Wilkins and Davies hold the key to what goes on here."

She stopped and reached out to take Erin's hand. "Be careful, Erin. I know you're capable and smart, but this man sounds like a fiend from hell."

For once, Erin had no glib comeback. Instead, she nodded and gave Lilly's hand a squeeze. "Thank you. Cade is lucky to have you."

Erin turned and began to walk briskly down the street, leaving Lilly to wonder what she'd meant by the unexpected comment.

"Paddock as much as said it's the quid pro quo between the marshal and the madams that contributes to the inability to clean things up."

She and Cade had eaten their supper and more or less caught each other up on what they'd learned. Much to Lilly's dismay, Erin had gone to eat with Wilkins, reassuring Lilly that it was just a meal in a public place and that she would see them later.

Lilly had suggested Cade and she go to Velvet's, because she wanted to ask Bonnie if she'd seen or heard anything from Monty. Cade was drinking his usual sarsaparilla, and Lilly had forgone her dessert in favor of a glass of port.

They were discussing the relevance of Monty's disappearance and the news of Velvet and Marshal Davies's previous plans to marry when Bonnie approached.

"Good evening," Lilly said. "Can you sit a minute?"

"No," she said, leaning toward Cade so that it would look as if she were engaging him in a conversation. "Velvet's been on a tear all day."

"What about?" Cade asked, smiling up at her as if she were the most fascinating thing in the world.

Playing the game, Lilly pasted an angry look on her face and reached over to grab his shoulder. As he turned toward her in feigned irritation, Bonnie planted her hands on her hips and said, "What do you think? She's furious because Erin is reopening The Thirsty Traveler. She got word from somewhere today that your friend had gone to meet with that Frenchy, what's her name?"

"Simone Delacroix."

Bonnie ran her fingers through Cade's hair, and he turned

back to her. "Monty needs to talk," she said with a seductive smile.

"We were just going to ask you if you'd heard from him," Cade said, as she sat down on his knee. "We were getting worried about him. Do you know what he wants?"

"Haven't a clue."

Lilly got up from her chair and marched around the table, grabbing Bonnie's arm and jerking her off Cade's lap. "Leave him alone, you two-bit tramp!" she yelled, trying to keep the charade going. To her shock, Bonnie responded by slapping her. Hard.

A feral sound, something between a growl and a snarl, came from Lilly's throat, and, before she realized what she was doing, she reached out and caught her friend by the hair. Cade was there in an instant, grabbing Lilly around the waist and ordering her to let go. "A little too much realism, lass," he murmured in her ear.

Coming to her senses and horrified by her actions, she released her hold on Bonnie at once.

"Velvet's watching," Cade said. "She's sending the bouncer over. Let's go before we get pitched out on our ears." He grabbed Lilly's hand and dragged her toward the doorway.

Once they were outside and down the street, he turned to her with a wide grin. "Great acting, Miss Long."

"Why thank you, Agent McShane." When she started to place a palm against her cheek, she realized he still held her hand. "I wasn't expecting Bonnie to get so realistic."

The semidarkness added a seductive note to his laughter. "It didn't look like acting when you tried to pull out her hair."

A rush of remorse swept over Lilly. "I'm ashamed to say it wasn't. When she slapped me, I don't know what came over me. Six months ago, I'd never have behaved in such an appalling fashion, but now this . . . this life seems to be rubbing off on me."

He stopped and faced her. "When you took this job, you were tough in a lot of ways, Lilly, but in others, you were a complete innocent. You know that. What's happening to you is the natural, normal progression of learning the business, of learning to take care of yourself. If Bonnie had been a real adversary, your actions would have been the right thing. Good job."

She heaved a heavy sigh, and he released her hand. "If you say so. Are we going to practice in the morning?"

"Yes. Same time."

They were almost back to The Thirsty Traveler when a man stepped out of a shadow-shrouded alley. Cade stepped in front of Lilly, his derringer already in his hand.

"I was afraid you wouldn't get my message."

"Monty!"

"You should announce yourself," Cade told him, depositing his gun back into the inner pocket of his jacket. "You almost met your maker."

"That 'ud be all right with me." Monty backed further into the shadows, and Cade and Lilly followed, trusting their instincts about the man.

"Do you have some information for us?"

"I sure do. I was loading up some garbage out back of Rosalie's this afternoon, and she has a couple of new girls. She started telling them about Dottie and Nora, and I heard everything, because I was just outside the kitchen door."

"Why would she do that?" Lilly asked.

"Probably trying to scare them into doing what they're told," Cade replied.

"That's right. When they asked her who'd do such a thing, Rosalie told them that I was a suspect, and that she'd heard that some people were beginning to say that Velvet had Eli finish Nora off for trying to turn the girls away from the life."

Which was exactly what Lilly and Cade thought. Velvet the mastermind; Wilkins the assassin.

"Then she laughed and told them it was probably me, even though there was no proof, because Eli had been with her all night, drinkin' and carousin'. She said he was still sleeping it off the next day when they found Nora. She had to wake him up to tell him."

Cade and Lilly looked at each other in the semidarkness.

"Do you think she's telling the truth?" Cade asked.

"Can't see why not," Monty said. "She's had a thing going on with him for a long time. Velvet, too."

"We'd heard that. So, it's true?"

"I'd say so." Monty started backing toward the far end of the alleyway. "Guess you can mark Eli off your list."

"I guess we can. You watch your back, Monty. You'll be the main suspect now."

"I know. I been tryin' to lay low, but I'm gonna have to be real careful until you find the killer."

He turned and started to walk away. Lilly placed a hand on his arm. "How will we find you?"

"You won't. I'll find you. One more thing. There's talk that some young girl who lives a few blocks away is missing. That's all I know. There'll probably be something in the papers tomorrow." With that, he spun around and sprinted down the dark passageway into the even darker night that lay beyond.

"There goes our case," Lilly said, preceding Cade back to the street.

"I'd say so, but I'm not sure I believe Rosalie."

"Why would she lie?"

"It wouldn't be the first time a woman has lied to protect a man, and, if Wilkins is guilty, her saying he was with her puts him back in the 'I owe you' column. It's all about protecting each other and their crooked activities."

"I understand that part, but I thought Davies was with Rosalie."

Cade chuckled. "Rosalie is with whomever Rosalie wants to be with on any given night."

Lilly thought about that and knew he was right. Rosalie wasn't the kind of person to let the truth stand in the way of what she wanted. "Well, even though she's given Wilkins an alibi, there's still Velvet. She had plenty of reason to get rid of Nora."

"You're right. We need to keep tabs on her."

"What do you think about the missing girl?"

"If she's really missing and hasn't just run away, there's a possibility that someone is working overtime trying to get replacements for the kids Nora helped escape. We'll know more tomorrow."

CHAPTER 20

Erin was still sleeping when Lilly and Cade left the next morning. Their hasty departure from Velvet's after the scene with Bonnie had caused them to miss her. Lilly had heard Erin's footsteps coming up the stairs at some time during the wee hours of the morning. Her heart had broken just a little, and she'd even cried herself to sleep, thinking of what Cade's sister and all the other women who were entrenched in the life had been through.

When Lilly had awakened at dawn, both her heart and her body felt weighted down with sorrow. She was ready to find Nora's killer and go back to Chicago. This assignment was wearing on her in more ways than she could ever have imagined.

Cade had the coffee made when she went downstairs, and they grabbed a hunk of cheese and a dense white Irish bread made with saleratus and buttermilk that Lilly had bought at the store the day before.

Since they were interested in seeing what everyone was saying about the missing girl, they left extra early so they could be back by the time the newspaper hit the street. Cade suggested that they find a place closer to town, and when they saw a deserted cabin well off the road, he decided it would be a good spot.

While they were still a good distance away, Lilly noticed two horses out front and mentioned it to Cade.

"That looks like the marshal's mare," he said, pulling the buggy to a stop.

She shaded her eyes with her hand and tried to make out the horse's markings. She knew little about horses and had never paid attention to what the lawman rode.

Cade handed her the reins.

"What are you doing?"

"I want to sneak up there and see if I can find out what's going on."

"Why?"

"Don't you think it's unusual for the marshal to be meeting someone at this ungodly hour?"

"I suppose it is," she said, frowning. Then her face cleared. "Do you suppose he's meeting someone he shouldn't be or trying to hide something?"

"That would be my guess. Take the rig back to that road a half a mile or so back. Go down it until you can't see the main road and wait for me."

"Why?"

"If you can't see the road, no one who's going down the main road can see you."

"Oh. B—"

"No buts. Just do as I say. I don't want you in the middle of things if they catch me."

"I don't want you in the middle of things, either," she said before she could stop herself.

"Then I'd better not get caught."

She scowled at him, but he'd already jumped down from

the buggy and was sprinting toward the cabin at an angle, moving from one scrubby bush to another.

Turning the rig around, she headed back the way they'd come. It didn't take long to reach their rendezvous point. She hopped down and tied the reins to a nearby bush and began to pace. How long should she wait before going for help?

Who would you get, Lilly? The marshal is here.

She shook her head and tried to concentrate on what they'd learned. Not much. It would be helpful to know if Nora's molesters had found her by accident, or if the incident had been planned. Who had sneaked into Monty's place while he was working one of his many odd jobs and shot her while she was recovering? Now that they'd learned their chief suspect had an alibi for the night Nora was killed, they were back to Velvet. After all, Nora had worked for her, and Nora had gone out of her way to try to bring down the operation.

Another question that needed answering was which sick individual in town had sent Wilkins after innocent little girls . . . or boys? From what she'd observed, Wilkins's taste appeared to run to older women, but one never knew. Who was he supplying? He was the kind of man who'd have no qualms about snatching young girls off the street, buying them off trains, or selling them.

He was also the kind of man who would have no problem persuading lonely spinsters to leave their comfortable worlds and embark on a journey to a place he described as wonderful and wild. A place where they would build a future and share all sorts of amazing experiences. At least, that was the picture he'd painted for Nora.

Lilly doubted he had much formal education, but he was just the type of man who made up for that with cleverness. He was also immoral and persuasive enough to pull off something like the mail-order bride deception, especially since it was done long distance. Yes. If nothing else, Lilly had him pegged for that.

She paced and chewed her bottom lip and worried for more than an hour before she saw Cade loping toward her from a different direction than she'd expected him. He looked unharmed, and she sighed in relief.

His shirt was wet with sweat, and his face was red. Breathing hard, he reached the buggy and fumbled beneath the seat for the canteen of water, downing at least half of it. Then he poured the remainder over his head. She waited, knowing that he'd speak when he was able.

"They were inside the cabin," he said at last.

"Who is 'they'?"

"Would you believe me if I told you it was Elijah Wilkins?"

Lilly stared at him, speechless. "Why on earth would the two of them be meeting in secret? They're supposed to be on opposite sides of the law."

"That's the question, isn't it? I'd guess they don't want anyone knowing they're conducting some sort of business, since they *are* on opposite sides of the law."

Lilly gave a soft snort of laughter. "With what we've heard about the marshal, that's debatable. How close did you get?"

"One of the windows was broken out, so I took a page from Robbie's book and—"

"You didn't sneak inside!"

He gave a weary laugh. "I don't think the cabin would have been big enough for the three of us. No. I just stood next to the window. I could hear every word they said."

"And?"

"Despite what Wilkins and Davies are telling Erin, Velvet and Rosalie are worried that she'll start up a business that will put theirs to shame. And Wilkins said he wasn't sure Erin would go along with paying for protection. He told Davies she was a snooty whore and thought she was better than the rest of them."

"What did Davies say about that?"

"That if she didn't pay, she wouldn't last long. Everyone pays. One way or the other. They pay for everything."

She saw his blue eyes darken. "What?"

"Wilkins told him not to worry about it. That he'd see to it that Erin paid. And soon."

Maybe it was just a statement, but Lilly thought it sounded a lot like a warning. Or a threat.

Considering the information Cade had gleaned, they decided to go back to Dusty's. On the drive back to town, they discussed the significance of Wilkins and Davies's conversation.

"Maybe they aren't connected," Lilly said. "Everyone in town has implied that if you want to stay in business, you ante up to Davies on a regular basis. Maybe Wilkins just wanted to let him know that Erin might not be so agreeable."

"Then why come all the way out here? He could have told Velvet or Rosalie, and they could have passed it on." Cade shook his head. "No, one of them had something else on his mind, and I missed it. They'd been there for a while."

"How could you tell?"

"I risked a peek. Thank heaven neither of them was sitting facing the window. They'd been drinking coffee. Wilkins kept yawning and rubbing his eyes and saying how tired he was. Davies said that if the scratches on his face were any indication, he must have had a tough night."

An image of Erin inflicting those scratches leaped into Lilly's mind, and she closed her eyes to block it out.

Cade swore beneath his breath. "I'd love to know what they were talking about before I got there."

"So would I." She glanced over at him. "Will you tell Erin what they said?"

"Of course, I will. She's my sister. I don't want anything happening to her."

"If it hasn't already."

Cade shot her a sharp look. "What do you mean?"

"It was very late when she came in last night," Lilly offered. "Or this morning."

"Holy Mother of Pearl!" he grated, reverting to the phrase he and Robbie had adopted when they were upset about something and didn't want to curse in front of someone. "I thought she said . . ."

"Calm down, McShane! I'm not saying anything happened, but I can't tell you it didn't. Erin is very smart, and she's accustomed to handling all sorts of unruly men. I think she'd be extra careful after what Mr. Paddock said about Wilkins."

"What did he say?"

"That Wilkins would cut his own mother's throat if she got in his way. Erin seemed genuinely troubled."

"As well she should be."

Despite having been up until all hours the previous evening, Erin was having a cup of coffee and eating a slice of the buttered bread with a little jam when Cade and Lilly returned. Though she seemed a bit subdued at first, the moment they spoke to her, she looked up with her usual, derisive smile. "Well, you children certainly missed your curfew, now didn't you?"

"I thought that was you," Cade said before Lilly had time to think of a snappy rejoinder.

"It's a little late to be getting so protective, don't you think, Cadence?"

Lilly had heard enough! She had no siblings, but she wanted to think that if she did, she would not alienate them because of something that had happened in the past. Erin and Cade were family, and they should care enough about one another that nothing this side of the grave could separate them. Lilly would have given anything to have known the baby who had died when her mother was murdered. She would give anything to be able to visit with Pierce and Rose, to ask their opinions on the case and hear the love in their voices.

"Stop it, you two!" The sharpness of her voice cut through their caustic banter like a hot knife through butter. "I don't know what the problem is between you, but I think it's time to discuss it as two grown people, and not like schoolyard children who've had their feelings hurt."

Erin looked stunned by the outburst.

McShane glared at her. "How many times have I told you, colleen, that you need to keep your nose out of my business?"

"I'd love to, if you didn't insist on conducting it in front of me!" she shot back. "Now both of you shut up unless you have something to say about the case."

Cade glared at her, a look in his eyes that said he would like to thrash her. She drew herself up to her full height and looked from one McShane to the other. "I'm going to get some coffee," she said in her most genteel voice. "Would you care for some, McShane? We have a lot to discuss."

He didn't speak, but answered with a single nod. "Good," she said. "Now sit down and behave until I get back."

After fetching the coffee, she stood in the doorway for a moment looking at two of the most stubborn people she'd ever met. They were sitting there, studiously avoiding looking at each other. To her surprise, Cade looked properly chastised. Erin looked heartsick. Exhaling a weary breath, Lilly carried the cups to the table and sat one in front of her partner.

He glanced up and met her eyes. "Thank you."

"You're very welcome." She took her seat and sipped at

the dark brew. "Did you tell Erin what we saw on our way to practice?"

"No."

Lilly turned to his sister and began to relate what they'd seen on their way to the river. Erin listened intently. When Lilly got to the part about Wilkins's "tough night," she saw a strange expression cross Erin's face. Lilly deliberately left out the part where he'd claimed Erin would pay. Cade was supposed to break that news to her.

"If you're wondering if he was with me, the answer is no. He pushed. I pushed back. He told me I was awful high-and-mighty for a common tart. I told him I wasn't common, and he slapped me."

Cade looked as if he could bite tenpenny nails in half.

"Then he called me some nasty names and told me just what he wanted to do to me. What he would do to me. Then he left. I was afraid to come home, because I thought he might still be out there somewhere waiting for me, so I stayed with Bonnie until almost daylight."

"They were talking about not being certain you'd ante up for protection," Cade told her, looking her square in the eye. "Davies said that if you didn't pay, you wouldn't participate. Wilkins said you would pay."

Seeing the alarm in her eyes, Lilly reached out and covered Erin's hand with hers. "Don't worry about it. You're not really going to open this place up, so it's immaterial."

"I don't think Wilkins makes idle threats," Cade told them. "Be careful, Erin."

The gentle warning was not quite an olive branch—more like an olive leaf. At least it was a start.

Erin nodded.

"I'm glad you're okay," Lilly said gently.

To her surprise, Erin's eyes filled with tears. "Yes. Me too.

Mr. Paddock was right. That man is evil incarnate, and I will be careful, Cade, I promise."

Sensing they were both anxious to get away from the personal, Lilly looked from one to the other. "We may not be any closer to finding Nora's killer, but we've certainly stirred things up."

"Aye," Cade said. "That we have."

"And whether he killed Nora or not, we know for a fact that Eli is in the thick of everything," Erin said, regaining some of her composure. "While I was with Bonnie, I asked her if she knew about Velvet and the marshal's planning to marry a few years back, and she was shocked. She said she'd see what she could find out."

"Do you think you can trust her?"

The women looked at Cade as if he'd lost his mind.

"Why would you think we couldn't?" Lilly asked. "She's volunteered information to us since we got here. Why question her now?"

"Maybe it's my natural distrust. I can't help wondering why she's helping us. What does she get out of it?"

"I think she has a good heart," Lilly replied.

Cade rolled his eyes heavenward. "The harlot with the heart of gold?"

"Something like that."

"Freedom."

Both Cade and Lilly looked at Erin. "She's helping us in hopes that when I open this place I'll hire her. She gets freedom from Velvet and her abuse. I'd squeal on someone for a lot less."

Cade nodded. "Fine then. That makes sense. It's just that the corruption here is so deep and far-flung it's hard to know whom to trust."

"I agree," Erin said. "But I do believe Bonnie. She wants

out. Bad. She told me that she's been hearing for years that Davies is partners with the evil twins."

As unbelievable as it seemed, Cade smiled at her new name for the two madams. "Business partners?"

"Yes."

"Well," he said, after thinking on it for a moment, "if it's true, we know why he looks the other way when they get into trouble. He's protecting his investment."

"Did Bonnie have any other bits of gossip to pass on?"

"A couple of things," Erin said, nodding. "She told me that it's rumored that Davies has strange sexual inclinations."

Lilly and Cade looked at each other. Did those "strange inclinations" include children? Was the marshal's involvement in the illegal activities deeper than they suspected?

"Do you think Bonnie would be more specific if you asked?"

"She might try to find out for us. All she said was that the times she's been with him, he wanted the regular stuff. She did tell me that she's almost certain Wilkins set up Nora's rape. In fact, he was going from place to place talking to all those cowboys who had just got in off the trail." Erin looked from her brother to Lilly. "So, what's next?"

"We're at a standstill," Lilly said. "We have a lot of theories and many potentially guilty people. What we don't have is proof, and it seems that everything we find out just muddies the waters more."

"I think we need to take another hard look at everything," Cade said. "Lilly, do you have something to write on?"

"Yes. I brought a small tablet."

"Do you mind getting it? I think we should make a list of all the suspects and the information we have about them and see if we can make any connections."

"That's an excellent idea," she said. "I'll run up and get it."

"Bring Nora's letter to you, too. Maybe we missed something important in it."

Lilly found the tablet and rummaged around in her reticule for the letter Nora had sent her. She was almost to the stairs when she remembered that she had one of the letters Wilkins had sent to Nora when he was "courting" her by mail. If they were lucky, maybe there would be something useful in it.

Feeling hopeful, she placed the items on the table and sat, ready to take notes of their conversation. She drew a line down the middle of the paper and put *Nora* on one side and *brides/children* on the other. On each of four pages, she wrote the names of Davies, Wilkins, and Velvet and Rosalie.

In less than half an hour, they'd listed every bit of information they had on both topics and the four suspects. It helped to see everything in one place, but no one came up with any new theories.

"Let's look at her letter," Cade said. "Erin hasn't heard what's in it."

Lilly handed the note to his sister, and when she finished reading it, she said, "I'm assuming Monty is the friend who helped her."

Cade nodded. "He told Lilly that he's the one who found the children when Wilkins had them moved, and he was the one who helped Nora get them out of town."

"That makes sense," Erin agreed.

Lilly read the missive aloud, and then they each looked it over carefully to see if anything stood out with closer scrutiny. Nothing new occurred to them, and she laid the correspondence aside.

"What's the other letter?" Cade asked, indicating the envelope lying on the table.

"A letter Wilkins wrote when he was courting Nora," Lilly said, removing it from the envelope.

"How on earth did you wind up with it?" Erin asked.

"Pure accident. The night we had dinner together, she was so excited about her new romance and going to Texas that she insisted on reading parts of his letters to me. She was in love with the idea of open spaces and cattle grazing and having her own home.

"She left the restaurant before I did, because her troupe was leaving the next morning on the first train out. I'd had such a lovely time that I decided to have another coffee and think about how wonderful it had been to see a familiar face.

"When I went to pay my bill, I heard a waiter hurrying after me. He was waving something in his hand. It was one of the letters. She must have dropped it as she was putting them in her reticule. I had no way to give it back, and for some reason I couldn't bring myself to part with it."

"Hopefully, there's something useful in it," Cade said.

Lilly unfolded the plain white paper and smoothed the pages flat. "Shall I read it aloud?"

"That's fine."

Lilly's gaze dropped to the pages spread out before her. "'*Dear Nora,*'" she read, "'*It was so good to get your letter. I can't wait for you to . . .*'"

Her voice trailed away, and she scanned the written pages.

"What's the matter?" Cade asked.

Without answering, Lilly picked up the letter from Nora and looked from one to the other. She shook her head and then placed both letters on the table.

"Lilly . . . what is it?"

She lifted her stunned gaze to his. "The writing is identical. These letters were written by the same person."

CHAPTER 21

"The same person?" Cade scoffed. "That's impossible. One is *to* Nora, the other is *from* her."

She pushed the letters toward him. "Look for yourself."

Cade examined the pages with care. Then he handed them to Erin and stood. "This calls for a stiff drink. Since that's impossible, I need more coffee. Anyone else?"

Both Lilly and Erin held their cups aloft.

When he returned a few moments later carrying the blue spatterware pot, he said, "Erin? What do you think?"

"As impossible as it may be, it looks the same to me."

The trio sat in silence, thinking about this new discovery.

"Just so I'm clear," Cade's sister said after a while, "are we thinking that Wilkins wrote the letters to Nora, as well as the one to Lilly, asking her for help to get away and catch the offenders?"

"That's how it looks."

"But that's impossible, isn't it?"

Lilly looked at Cade. "What do you think, McShane?"

"I'm not sure what I think," he confessed. "Let's say he is

the culprit. Why would he write the letter we assumed was from Nora to you? Why ask that you come to Texas to help her?"

"Well," Erin said after a few moments of hard thinking, "maybe Nora talked to him about Lilly, and he was hoping to get her out here, too."

"Hm," Cade said. "An interesting concept."

Lilly's thoughts were running rampant; she was replaying old questions, thinking about conversations, considering everything in a new light. Something important was just beyond reach.

"If that's the case, he knew somehow that she worked for the Pinkertons," Cade ventured, "because the letters were sent there."

"True, but if they talked about Lilly, Nora probably told him her friend was a Pinkerton," Erin offered.

"Yes," Cade agreed, "but why risk bringing the most powerful law enforcement agency in the country down on your head? It doesn't make sense."

"Excellent point," Erin said. "I'm all out of theories. So, if Wilkins didn't write the letter, who did? It's someone who knows how to write well."

"Monty."

It was the first time Lilly had spoken in several seconds, and the conviction in her voice couldn't be ignored.

"What?" Cade and Erin said together.

"Monty wrote both letters."

"But he's . . . slow to say the least," Erin said.

"Is he? Or is he a better actor than anyone thinks?"

Cade regarded her with a thoughtful expression. "Go on. Back up your theory."

"All right. I'll try." Lilly turned to Erin. "Do you remember when we spoke with Mr. Paddock about a sign, and he suggested Monty?"

Her eyes brightened. "Yes."

"Mr. Paddock said that Monty could copy any script and showed us an advertisement he'd been working on. Something about it nagged at me, but I didn't know what it was until today. Subconsciously, my brain connected it with Nora's letter, but I didn't know then where I'd seen the writing before. And now, we see that the letter we assumed *she'd* written to me was written by the same person who wrote Wilkins's letters to her."

Confusion was written all over Cade's face. "Are you saying that Monty—not Wilkins—is behind the mail-order bride scheme?"

Lilly laughed. "I don't know what I'm saying, but my gut says the same person wrote both of those letters. And I think both of you think the same thing. I believe that person is Monty."

Erin nodded. "If he's acting, he's very good. And why pretend to be mentally lacking if you aren't?"

"I haven't a clue," Lilly said.

Cade rubbed his palms together. "Okay, ladies, let's look at this from a different angle. What if Monty wrote the letters *for* someone else, someone who couldn't write, maybe? Like Rosalie or Velvet or even Wilkins."

"Oh, I like that!" Lilly said with a wide smile. "Wilkins is crafty enough to put the plan together, but he doesn't have what it takes to execute it."

"Exactly. So, he gets Monty to write the letters for him. Let's suppose that Monty doesn't understand what he's doing. He writes what Wilkins tells him to, picks up a little money, and all is well. Until Nora. She's different. Maybe she helped open Monty's eyes to what Wilkins was doing."

"That makes sense," Lilly said. "We know she spent a lot of time trying to be a good influence. . . ."

"Which got her fired and beaten and raped," Cade reminded them.

Lilly began to understand where he was headed with his

theory. She nodded in sudden understanding. "And she nearly died from it all."

"And she reached out for help from her sickbed, so to speak."

Erin caught up admirably fast. "But she was in such bad shape that she couldn't write, so she had Monty write what she told him." Erin rounded out the speculation for them. She looked very proud of herself.

Cade and Lilly looked at each other and smiled. Finally, something was beginning to make sense.

"I suppose the next thing we do is try to find Monty and see if we're right," Lilly said.

"That might be easier said than done."

Just then, a timid knock sounded at the kitchen door. Cade jumped up to answer it. When he came back, Monty trailed behind him.

He looked troubled, nervous.

"I thought you might like to know they found that girl that went missing."

"Thank God!" Lilly breathed.

"She's in real bad shape, though." He swallowed hard. "Reminded me of Nora after she got so beat up."

"You've seen the girl?"

"Yes, sir."

"Was she able to say who it was, or describe the man?" Cade asked.

"She was trying to tell the marshal what he looked like, and they wanted to see if I could draw a picture of him, but Doc had given her so much morphine she didn't make no sense at all. I don't expect she's long fer this world, poor thing."

"Sit down, Monty," Cade said. "We'd like to ask you a couple of questions."

His forehead puckered into a frown, and he looked from one to the other. "Am I in trouble?"

Lilly reached out and touched his arm. "No, Monty. We only

want to ask you some things about when Nora was hurt . . . before she died."

"Oh. Okay, then." He took a seat next to Lilly.

"After those men did those things to her, and you were helping her get better, did she ask you to write a letter for her?"

"Sure did," he said, nodding. "She wanted me to write a letter to you." Pride shone in his eyes. "They'd broke her writin' hand, and she wanted to let you know she was hurt and all, so I wrote it and even took it to the mail."

"I thought you told me you couldn't read, Monty," Lilly said. "And to my knowledge, if you can't read, you can't write."

"No, ma'am," he said. "I never did say I couldn't read. I said I had no use fer it. That's 'cause I don't do it very good. I can draw, though, and I can write better'n most people in town. It's just a talent I got," he told them proudly.

"Yes," Lilly said. "It is definitely a talent."

"What about Wilkins?" Cade asked. "Can he write?"

"Eli?" Monty laughed. "He don't read nor write a lick, but I'm the one who's 'slow.' "

"Did you ever write any letters for him?" Cade asked.

"All the time," Monty confessed. "Every time he gets a letter back from one of those gals he writes to, he pays me to write an answer. I make out pretty good from that."

"He's still doing it?" Erin asked.

"Yes, sir. I wrote a letter to an Emily a couple of weeks ago."

"Swine," Erin muttered beneath her breath.

Lilly arched an eyebrow at her. "Does this mean you won't be having lunch with Mr. Wilkins anymore?"

"It does. It also means that I'm rethinking another offer that was made to me recently, if it's still open."

"A new lover?" Cade quipped, even though Lilly's eyes were shooting daggers at him.

"In a manner of speaking."

"So," Lilly asked, looking from Erin to Cade. "What are our plans for today?"

"I'm staying close to home," Erin said. "And then, whenever I do go out, I'm going to avail myself of my brother's bodyguard abilities."

"I think that's an excellent idea," Lilly told her. "Monty? Will you be okay for a few more days?"

"I'm real careful, Miss Lilly. I'll be fine, but I'd best be goin' now."

That afternoon, Lilly decided to pay a return visit to the newspaper office and see if Mr. Paddock had any further information about the marshal and Velvet planning to marry at some time in the past. Erin stayed at the saloon. Between Paddock's warning, what she'd been told about Wilkins's threat, and her own altercation with him the night before she was properly frightened.

When Lilly arrived, the newspaper editor was bringing a roll of newsprint from a back room to the press.

"Hello, Miss Long," he said, wiping his hands on his ink-stained apron and then extending one in greeting. "It's good to see you again."

"Thank you, Mr. Paddock."

"What can I do for you?"

"As you know, Miss O'Toole is planning to reopen The Thirsty Traveler, but she is a peace-loving woman and is accustomed to running an honest establishment."

Seeing his skepticism, she smiled. "I know that's a hard concept to believe in this neighborhood. She has genuine concerns."

Paddock nodded.

"It seems that every day we're here, she hears of some new criminal enterprise, or of other heinous happenings."

"It's true that there is always something afoot."

"Well, Miss O'Toole finds it quite disturbing." Lilly pasted a look of horror on her face. "Just this morning she was told that the marshal has business dealings with at least two of the madams in town, and that they get preferential treatment. She has also heard that he once had a very serious relationship with Velvet Hook and that they had once planned to marry. I'm sure you understand that she's afraid of getting treated unfairly by Marshal Davies, if all these things are true."

She smiled sweetly at the newsman, who was not immune to a pretty woman's wiles, soiled dove or not. "The only person I could think of who might tell me the truth about these matters was you."

Paddock nodded. "I appreciate your faith in me, Miss Long, and I wish that I had a definite answer for you; however, all I can say is that, though I've heard those same rumors, I have no confirmation that there's any truth to them."

"I see. Miss O'Toole is also somewhat concerned about competing with Rosalie and Velvet. She has already heard that neither of them is pleased about her reopening Dusty's old place. And, we've heard that they can be somewhat, uh . . . vindictive."

Paddock smiled. "Which means that you've heard the gossip that Velvet was responsible for Miss Nash's death, not Monty. Again, it isn't something I can confirm, but, in my mind, she had far more reason to harm Miss Nash than poor Monty."

Lilly's heart seemed to stall. Though she and Erin and Cade had talked about this very possibility earlier, to hear it from such a reliable source gave it credence.

"That's troubling, to say the least."

"I won't deny that it's something to be cautious about. I'd tell Miss O'Toole to think long and hard about this new venture."

"I certainly will," Lilly assured him. She extended her hand. "Thank you so much. I didn't intend to keep you from your work, so I'll let you get back to it." At the door, she spun back around. "Oh. What about the young girl who was attacked? Is she making any improvement?"

"No, ma'am. Not that I'm aware of."

"Does the marshal have any idea who did such a horrible thing?"

Paddock shook his head. "As with Miss Nash, it could have been anyone."

Lilly was halfway out the door when the newsman's voice stopped her. "By the way, did you hear the news about Billy the Kid?"

"No," Lilly said. The gunslinger's reputation was known far and wide, as was his total disregard for the lives of others. "Did he shoot someone else?"

"Nope. Pat Garrett finally ambushed him on a ranch in New Mexico. He's dead."

CHAPTER 22

Longing for something cool to drink, Lilly trudged down the street, sweltering in the heat of the July sun. Droplets of sweat dared to trickle from her hair down her temple. Sweating! *How unladylike,* she thought with an inward smile.

Sadly, her trip to the newspaper's office hadn't yielded much useful information, except that, eventually, criminals met their deaths, and the speculation about Velvet.

She wasn't sure where they went from here or how they would unearth the truth about either of the crimes they were working on, but she was well aware that their time was running out. Erin wouldn't be much use if she didn't snap out of the fear that had taken hold of her, and, even with the pretense of reopening the saloon, they couldn't stay much longer without the locals becoming more suspicious.

Preparing herself mentally for another night sitting in a dance hall and pretending to enjoy herself, she unlocked the door to Dusty's and stepped into the shady interior.

Erin was nowhere to be seen, and she wasn't in the kitchen. Hoping she wasn't disturbing a nap, Lilly ran up the steps, calling her friend's name. There was no answer. Frustrated, she went to the door to Erin's room and froze. The door stood open. The lock had been ripped from the jamb, and splinters of oak lay torn from it, as if someone had kicked the door open.

Every fiber of Lilly's being screamed that something was wrong. Terribly wrong.

Erin kept her room immaculate; now it looked as if a storm had swept through it. The bedding was a mess. Part of it hung off the edge and onto the rug. Most of the personal belongings that had been artfully arranged on her dresser now lay on the floor. The fancy iron bed had been pulled from the wall on one side. The fireplace poker lay on the floor at the base of the armoire.

Erin was gone, but she hadn't gone peacefully. Lilly had a good idea who had taken her.

Trembling in fear, she backed out of the room, her mind whirling. She had no idea where Cade was or when he would get back, but she knew she couldn't leave Erin in Elijah Wilkins's clutches any longer than necessary. Horrible visions of what he could be doing to her flashed through Lilly's mind in a succession of sickening, jerky images.

Think, Lilly, think!

Where would he take her? His place, of course, but she had no idea where that might be. How could she find out? Monty knew, but she had no notion of where he was or how to find him.

Marshal Davies? No way this side of Hades.

Think, Lilly!

Bonnie. Bonnie, or maybe even Goldie, might know where Wilkins lived. It was worth a chance. She started down the stairs, then turned and ran to her room. This time she wouldn't leave her derringer behind.

She rummaged around in her underwear drawer, asking herself if she was really thinking about confronting Elijah Wilkins, a man who regularly beat women who disobeyed their bosses. A man who sold those women into a horrible existence. A man who might be a killer.

Yes, she was. She grabbed the little gun, shoved it into her skirt pocket, and slammed the drawer shut.

McShane will have a fit.

Well, then, he would just have to have one! There was no way she could sit here and wait for him to show up before going to look for Erin. Lilly dashed down the stairs, her earlier lethargy gone. She was headed for the door when she realized it would be smart to let Cade know where she'd gone. Very smart, in fact.

Running across the room to the table where they'd been sitting earlier, she picked up the pad and snatched the pencil. Her hands shook as she printed:

WILKINS HAS ERIN. GONE TO HIS PLACE
TO FIND HER.

Short and to the point, but it would work. She left it propped against one of the mugs sitting there and raced back across the room and out the door.

Since Velvet's was only a couple of blocks away, it didn't take long to get there. Breathing hard, Lilly pushed through the swinging doors and scanned the interior. She didn't see any of the girls milling about, but Charlie was behind the bar, polishing glasses.

She didn't even stop to think if it was wise or not before calling his name and crossing the room. He turned and smiled when he saw her. It looked like a smile she could trust.

"Hello, Lilly. How are you?"

"I've been better," she told him.

He must have seen the panic in her eyes, because he came

around the end of the bar and took both her hands in his. "What is it? What's wrong?"

"Someone came to Dusty's while I was out this afternoon, and, when I got back, Erin was gone. There'd been a struggle. I think Wilkins has her."

Charlie muttered a low curse. "I imagine you're right. Bonnie told me that Erin was pretty upset last night, and I don't think there's anyone with a lick of sense who would deny the man's a monster. What do you need me to do?"

"Can you tell me how to get to his place?"

"I can, but there's no way I'm letting you go alone," he told her.

"I'll be fine." She heard the bravado in her voice, but her insides were quivering with nerves and fear. "I have training. . . . I'll tell you more, later."

"Lilly . . ."

"Please. I need you to stay here in case McShane comes in. If he does, tell him where I am and tell him to hurry. If he doesn't come, I suppose you can call Davies."

"No. Not him. I'll come myself and bring a couple of the boys."

Bouncers. Perfect.

"And we need some law we can trust here in a hurry."

Charlie's head bobbed up and down in understanding. "I'll go down the street and telegraph the Dallas sheriff."

"Good. Thank you. Now tell me how to find Wilkins's place. I want to get there before anything bad happens."

Wilkins's street was outside the Acre, several blocks past the train tracks. Even with Charlie's directions, Lilly got turned around once or twice.

When she reached the little house, she wasn't surprised to find it neglected and run-down. Sitting on a narrow city block, amongst a patch of knee-high weeds, the entire structure canted to one side, a silent testimony to rotting floor joists. Several boards at the bottom had decayed, and several cedar shingles were missing. Its only noteworthy feature was the trees around it, one of which had dropped a limb onto the roof.

Lilly had no idea if Wilkins had brought Erin here and left her, or if he was in the house. She had no proof that Erin was even here. She recalled McShane telling her that, before an agent went running into a building or a room, he should look around for possible ways of entry and escape. With that advice in mind, she decided to look around before choosing how to go inside.

She glanced over her shoulder to make certain there was no one to see her snooping around. Unless someone was peering through a grimy window, she could nose about to her heart's content. She started in the front and went to the side window. Through the dirty glass she saw that the room was the parlor. Like the exterior of the place, it was disgusting. Even from where she stood, peering through the filthy, wavy glass, she could tell that no one had used a broom on the floors in heaven knows how long. Erin was nowhere to be seen, so Lilly eased through the weeds to the next window.

She had to stand on her tiptoes to see through this one, since the lower glass had been broken out and wood reused from a case of canned beans had been nailed over the opening. She saw nothing inside but a rough, wooden table, four chairs with woven seats, and a shelf.

No Erin.

Reasoning that the room at the back was a bedroom and that if Wilkins was here, he had to be in that room, she ducked around the corner, where there was even less likelihood of anyone seeing her window peeking.

With her front against the house, she inched closer to the

window, which had been left open to allow the halfhearted breeze to circulate the stifling heat of the day. A quick peek into the room told her the bed sat near the window. A second look let her know the room was empty . . . except for the woman lying half-naked on the dingy sheets. Erin! And if her condition was any indication, Lilly had arrived too late. . . .

The afternoon was more than half gone when Cade returned from making his daily information rounds. He'd learned nothing of value and was looking forward to a nice meal with his sister and Lilly. As far as he was concerned, they could stay in and play cards for the evening. Though he had never thought he'd admit it, he'd had about all he could take of bawdy houses, saloons, and gambling establishments. At least for a while.

When he unlocked the door and stepped inside, he was greeted by silence. No sounds filtered down from upstairs or the kitchen. Wondering where the two women had gone, he was on his way to get a drink of water when he noticed the note propped against one of the coffee mugs they'd used earlier. A feeling of uneasiness was already creeping through him when he snatched it up and read the note.

Wilkins had Erin, and Lilly had gone to try to help free her. Even as he headed for the door, his mind was filled with a jumble of thoughts, one following the other without rhyme or reason. His first was to wonder how Wilkins had nabbed Erin. She'd made it very clear that she intended to stay away from him, and Cade believed her.

Close on the heels of that came anger at Lilly for once again putting herself in harm's way. Would the stubborn chit never learn?

Where would Wilkins have taken Erin? How long had she been gone? How had Lilly found out? Did she have her gun? Would she use it? What did Wilkins intend to do with his sister?

Cade's vivid imagination gave him the answer in a single, sickening image. For all the bad blood between Erin and him, the image in his mind was almost unbearable.

Out on the sidewalk, he stood, undecided, willing his nerves to steady and his mind to settle down and concentrate on what to do first. Two of the people he cared about most in the world were in danger. He'd be of no use to them if he didn't get his thoughts together.

Lilly's note said she was going to Wilkins's place, but how would she know where to find it?

Bonnie. Bonnie was the only person she could trust outside of their small group. Without another second's hesitation, he started down the street toward Velvet's, praying that he would find his sister and Lilly before it was too late.

CHAPTER 23

"*Pst.* Erin . . ."

Erin stirred, but didn't open her eyes, one of which was swollen and had begun to turn a dark plum color. Her lips were puffy; drying blood ran from one corner of her mouth and trailed across her chin.

She was still partially clothed, but her skirts were bunched around her waist. Her blouse had been stripped away, leaving nothing but her chemise, which had been torn from one shoulder. Ugly bruises in the exact pattern of fingerprints marred her arms where Wilkins had held her.

Lilly felt tears slipping down her cheeks and swiped at them with an angry motion. She clenched her jaw. No one deserved what had happened in this room, no matter what her occupation. Erin needed help.

Being as quiet as possible, Lilly hoisted herself up and through the open window. As she hung there, half in and half out, she remembered being in this same position a few months previously. Only that time, she had been trying to get *out* of the room.

Somehow, despite her skirt and petticoats, she managed to

get one leg over the sill and ease through the opening. Inside, she stood and listened for any signs of movement. Nothing. At least nothing she could hear. Tiptoeing, she went straight to the pitcher and basin. Peeking inside, she saw that there was enough water to at least wash the blood from Erin's face.

The towel lying beside the bowl was filthy, so Lilly pulled her handkerchief from her pocket and poured some water over it. Then she straightened Erin's skirts and went to the side of the bed nearest the window, reaching out with a light touch to bathe her face. She stirred, but again, didn't open her eyes.

Gently, Lilly dabbed at the blood on Erin's chin, doing what she could to erase the outward reminders of the savagery she'd been subjected to. The inner reminders would always be there, lurking, waiting to rob her of the peace and happiness she might find in the future. After a while, her eyes opened. She seemed to have trouble focusing. Then she whispered Lilly's name.

"Sh."

As consciousness returned, Erin murmured, "What are you doing here? How did you find me?"

"Never mind that now. I need to get you out of here. Can you sit up?"

"I think so." With Lilly's help and a single moan, Erin levered herself into a sitting position. "The room is spinning."

"I don't doubt it. Just sit a minute." Lilly handed her the handkerchief so that Erin could do her own washing up.

"We need to get out of here," Lilly whispered. "Do you think you're up to it?"

Erin nodded.

Lilly wrapped her arm around Erin's waist and helped her to her feet. "Can you sit on the sill and ease out somehow?"

"Well, well, well. What have we here?"

The masculine voice froze them in place. Terrified, Lilly turned slowly. Erin seemed incapable of moving.

Wilkins lounged in the doorway, his shoulder leaning against the doorframe, regarding them with a lazy smile.

"Erin's leaving."

A puzzled expression entered his night-black eyes. "What's the matter, Erin? Didn't you like our little loving session?"

Erin stepped closer to Lilly, and for the first time it dawned on Lilly that the formerly self-confident woman was looking to her for protection. The realization was scary. Trembling like a leaf herself, Lilly stiffened her backbone and her resolve and moved between Erin and Wilkins.

"Love had nothing to do with what you did to her," Lilly said. "It was nothing but a pitiful display of strength by someone who wasn't man enough to get what he wanted any other way."

"Lilly . . ." Erin warned in a low voice.

Wilkins laughed, a rough, guttural sound. "Oh, this is gonna be fun," he said, lurching away from the doorframe and taking a few steps toward them. "I like a woman with fight in her, and you were always my first pick. Remember?"

"Go, Erin!" Lilly commanded, giving her a little push backward, but Erin seemed unable to take her eyes off the man advancing toward them.

Realizing that the situation was about to get ugly, Lilly reached into her pocket and pulled out her little gun, pointing it at Wilkins.

He laughed again. "You gonna use that fancy little peashooter on me?"

"If I have to. And believe me, I know how to use it," she bragged, but even she heard the uncertainty in her voice.

He gave a mock shiver and took a step closer. "Ooh! I'm scared."

A feeling of déjà vu came over Lilly. Being in a similar situation with Timothy Warner only a few months earlier. Looking back, it seemed like years since she'd faced the man she'd married and his gun. She didn't doubt that Wilkins was carrying one, hidden somewhere. It would behoove her to remember that.

While she tried to gather her thoughts and devise some sort of plan, he lunged toward her. *Stay out of his reach, Lilly.* Cade's instruction came rushing back. In a move as instinctive as breathing, she darted to the side.

All Wilkins managed to do was rip the sleeve of her blouse free at the shoulder. The expression in his eyes was dark and menacing. Predatory. He meant to hurt her, however he could.

For a moment, they stared into each other's eyes, watching . . . gauging . . . waiting to see what move the other would make. She was so focused on Erin's kidnapper, Lilly had no idea what Erin was doing or thinking.

Wanting to put as much distance between him and herself as possible, Lilly took a step back and discovered that her back was against the wall. A quick glance told her that Erin had edged from behind her to the narrow space between the bed and the wall. Neither of them was in a good place.

This wouldn't do. Hoping to get him away from Erin and herself out of an impossible spot, Lilly once again surged to the right. He followed. He was strong, but she was fast. The next few moments were spent doing an awkward, deadly dance of pursuit and evasion. The dangerous waltz continued for several seconds. Lilly was at the foot of the bed and closer to the door.

Don't wear yourself out. Make him do the work. Cade's voice again.

She planted her feet and leveled the gun at him. "We're leaving, Elijah," she said. "And you're going to let us, or I'm going to shoot you."

"I don't think so." And with that, he once again sprang at her. His arm swung to the side, knocking the gun from her hand. It went sailing through the air and landed on the floor near the window. Then he backhanded her with his other hand.

Pain exploded in her head, and she wondered if he'd broken her jaw. Timothy's blow had been nothing compared to this one. She staggered, and her shoulder hit the armoire, sending another wave of pain radiating throughout her body.

Once again, they stood staring at each other, both breathing hard. Lilly wanted to clutch at her aching head and rub at her throbbing shoulder, but she refused to give him the satisfaction of seeing that she was in any pain.

Once again, she tried to recall everything Cade had told her during their practice sessions. She knew that if Wilkins ever got hold of her, she would suffer the same fate as Erin. That could not happen. Was not going to happen.

She glanced at the bed and saw that Erin had picked up the derringer and was looking at it with tortured eyes. Dear, sweet heaven! Was she thinking of using it on herself?

"Erin, no!" Lilly screamed, hoping that the sound of her voice would bring the broken woman out of her stupor.

Something in her voice must have alerted Wilkins that he had another threat. He glanced toward the bed and, seeing that Erin had the gun, turned and started toward her.

It was the break in concentration Lilly needed. She forgot everything Cade had told her about trying to escape and spent no time looking for a weapon. Instead, screaming out her fury at the top of her lungs, she shoved away from the armoire and launched herself at Wilkins, hitting him in the back with the full force of her slender body. Her momentum sent him toppling over the footrail and onto the bed.

While he cursed and fought to free himself from the tangle of covers, Lilly ran around the end of the bed and grabbed both of his feet. She fixed her scuffed boots on the wood floors and yanked, sheer determination and adrenaline giving her the strength to pull him off the edge. His head made a satisfying *thud* as it hit the floor. She landed on her rear.

Roaring with rage, he scrambled to his feet. With murder

in his eyes, he swung a booted foot toward her. The sound of a gunshot mingled with her scream. . . .

Cade was standing on the sidewalk in front of the house, gauging the best way to gain entrance without giving away his presence. As Lilly had, he was making a visual survey of the house. He was about to peek into the window of the first room when he heard Lilly's scream and the *pop* of a small caliber gun coming from the back of the house.

All plans for a stealthy entrance fled. He leaped onto the porch and burst through the rickety door with ease, heading toward the place where the cry had originated.

The scene in the room made his blood run cold. Erin was on her knees in the middle of the bed, a derringer in her hands, looking at it as if she wasn't certain what she'd just done. He needed to let her know he was there. The last thing they needed was for her to shoot him as well.

"Erin?" he said sharply. "Are you all right?"

She looked up, a dazed expression in her eyes. "Fine," she said. She looked anything but.

Lilly was lying on the floor, Wilkins's prone body on top of her. Cade's vision blurred. For a second or two, he was incapable of thought. If someone had asked, he would have sworn that his heart had stopped beating, yet blood thundered in his ears. A panicked refrain ran through his mind. *Not again. Not again. Not again.*

Then he saw Lilly's fingers twitch, and his heart resumed its beating. Wilkins groaned. How badly they were hurt remained to be seen. Able to reason, Cade put his gun back into his pocket. Then he went to pull Wilkins off Lilly. From the looks of his shirt, Erin's shot had hit him in the shoulder. As Cade dragged him off Lilly, Wilkins muttered a curse. He'd live.

With the dead weight off her, Lilly drew in a shuddering

breath, and her eyes fluttered open. The confusion he saw there turned to anger. Or at least irritation.

"What took you so long, McShane?"

The memory of her saying the same thing to him when he'd found her in the Purcell attic brought a wry smile to his lips. "Ever the grateful one," he said, bending over and drawing her to her feet.

She grabbed him at his waist, and he kept one arm around her as he guided her to the bed. Then he took Lilly's little pearl-handled derringer from his sister, and the two women fell into each other's arms. Erin was sobbing uncontrollably.

Wilkins pushed himself to his knees. Cade grabbed him by his upper arm—on the side Erin's bullet had hit—and hauled him to his feet while the captive muttered dire threats beneath his breath.

"You're not going to do anything where you're going," Cade told him, and without another word, he drew back and gave the mad man a satisfying punch in the face. Wilkins crumpled onto the floor.

Seeing that Lilly and his sister were looking at him in question, he shrugged and said, "I didn't have any handcuffs." He hefted the fallen man over his shoulder. "I have a buggy outside," he told the women. "Lilly, can you help Erin so I can make sure this piece of rubbish doesn't decide to make a run for it?"

"I've got her." Supporting each other, Lilly and Erin preceded him down the short hall while Cade followed, giving the unconscious man hanging over his shoulder no more thought than he would a bag of grain.

CHAPTER 24

Cade stopped by the doctor's office and waited with Wilkins while the female physician—a rarity—put Erin in a small room and gave her a thorough examination.

Twenty minutes later, the stocky, no-nonsense woman returned and announced that his sister was battered and bruised and had been poorly used, but that she would be all right in a matter of days. Physically. Emotionally, what she'd been through would likely haunt her for years to come.

Torn between relief and sadness, Cade asked if the doctor would look at Wilkins's wound. She agreed, and they followed her to another small area where his blood-soaked shirt was cut away. When Cade informed the doctor that the wounded man was the one who'd assaulted Erin, the woman gave Wilkins a hard look and began to probe the bullet hole without benefit of any sort of spirits to help dull the pain. His moans, curses, and threats had no visible effect on her.

By the time she pulled a small fragment of fabric from the wound, Wilkins was sweating, and Cade was smiling.

"Tell me, Doctor Potter," he asked, while she bandaged the

injury, "is the young girl who was kidnapped and attacked still here?"

Potter glanced up from her work. "She's made great improvement over the past few hours, but yes, she's still here. Why do you ask?"

"Though it's only a guess on my part, there's enough similarity between her case and my sister's that I feel this man is responsible for her abduction, too. If it's all right with you, I'd like for her to have a look at him."

"Be my guest."

The confrontation between Wilkins and the adolescent was excruciating for Cade to observe; he couldn't imagine what young Carrie must be experiencing as she faced her captor with tears and shame bordering on hysteria. Moments later, carrying a signed statement confirming that Wilkins was indeed the culprit who had taken her, Cade informed Lilly he would be back for her and Erin as soon as he turned over their prisoner to the authorities.

Wilkins sat silent and sullen on the way to the jail. There was no ignoring the pointing and staring that accompanied them. Seeing the familiar scoundrel sitting in a rented rig, shirtless, handcuffed, and bandaged must be quite a sight. Cade could almost hear the whispers following them. And there was no doubt that the onlookers who darted inside one business or the other were telling what they'd seen and speculating about what was going on.

When he pulled Wilkins off the buggy and shoved him through the door of the jail, he found the sheriff's deputies playing some sort of card game in one of the cells and the sheriff, an aging man with a heavy white mustache, cocked back in his chair, reading one of the lurid tales from an old copy of *National Police Gazette*. The sheriff straightened and laid the magazine aside when the two men entered the small room.

"Where's Marshal Davies?" Cade asked.

"I don't have any idea. Someone sent a telegram saying we should come and pick up a prisoner and not to let Davies have custody of him. We came over on the train."

Good for Charlie. He'd been thinking.

"This is the prisoner, Elijah Wilkins. He acquires women and children for several of the houses in the Acre, and possibly murdered Nora Nash a few weeks back."

"That's a lie!" Wilkins shouted, speaking for the first time since they'd left the doctor's. "I didn't kill that whore."

Cade gave him a crushing look. "Guard him well," he cautioned the sheriff. "He has a lot to answer for."

"And just who in tarnation might you be?" the sheriff asked, rankling at being told what to do.

"Yeah!" Wilkins jeered. "Who in hell are you?"

Cade pulled his badge from his vest pocket. "Andrew Cadence McShane, Pinkerton agent. This is a Pinkerton arrest, and Davies has no authority over him."

The sheriff examined Cade's badge and handed it back, looking suitably impressed. Cade tipped his head toward Wilkins. "Lock him up, and I'll be back in a bit with my partner. Wilkins kidnapped my sister and assaulted her as well, and I'd like to see how she's doing."

By the time Cade walked back into the medical office, the tremendous stress he'd been under began to weigh him down. He needed to hear what Erin had to say, but already he knew what had happened. The truth of her ordeal left him feeling empty and sick.

He realized that when a man forced himself on a woman it was because he was trying to exert his power. Gain the upper hand. Show her who was boss. Erin had continually turned down Wilkins's advances, and in the end, he'd decided to show her that whatever he wanted, he would get, even if he had to take it.

When Cade entered the room, he saw Lilly in a chair next to the bed, her cheek resting on its edge, her face turned away from him. She must be as exhausted as he felt.

Erin was propped up with some pillows, sleeping. She'd been cleaned up. There was no trace of blood on her face, and her black eye stood out against the whiteness of her cheeks. Her tangled hair had been brushed, and she was wearing a clean nightgown. She slept, one hand beneath her cheek, the way she had when she was just a girl and their lives had been happy and innocent.

Innocence. He could barely recall those days, back when his da was alive and sang bawdy Irish songs when he was in his cups, while Cade and his siblings had danced the jig and his ma had scolded Padraig for being too loud, even though the smile in her eyes said she loved every minute of it. Remembering brought tears to his eyes, but he blinked hard and forced them back.

He must have made some noise, because Lilly raised her head and turned toward him.

He cleared his throat. "I'm sorry. I didn't mean to wake you."

"You didn't," she told him, matching her tone to his low voice. "I was praying."

"How is she?"

"Strong. Stronger than you know." Lilly stood. "Let's go outside, so we don't wake her."

"She'll probably sleep for hours if the doctor gave her a dose of laudanum."

"She didn't. Erin wouldn't have it."

"Don't go. I'm awake."

Erin's voice was low and weak and just a little lost. Again, Cade was reminded of their childhood when she would beg him not to leave her to go off with his friends.

"Are you sure?" Lilly asked.

Erin nodded. "Sit, Cade. I have a lot to tell you."

Though he was keen on hearing her story, he wondered if it was too soon, if she shouldn't rest longer before diving back into the vile memories. "Why don't we wait until tomorrow?"

"No. I want to tell you while it's fresh in my mind and . . . and while I have the courage."

He started to argue further, but she held up a hand to stop him. "I want to put it behind me, and to do that I need you to hear every ugly detail."

Uncertain if he could stand to hear it, or could bear to hear it standing, he sat, as she'd told him to do, resting his elbows on his knees, his clasped hands dangling between them.

"He came to the back door. I thought it was Bonnie, so I opened it."

She divided her attention between Cade and Lilly. Her telling was blunt. To the point. Devoid of emotion.

"When he started to push his way in, I managed to run to my room and lock the door. He kicked it in. We fought, but it didn't take him long to win that battle, either."

"Erin, you don't have to do this," Lilly said.

"Yes. I do." She drew in a deep breath. "He tied me up with one of the cords from the drapes, tossed me over his shoulder, threw me into the back of a wagon, and covered me with a bunch of burlap sacks. They smelled horrible."

If the tale hadn't been so dreadful, Cade would have smiled at that. The mind was a strange thing. She didn't mention Wilkins's beating her and how it must have hurt. Didn't say anything about the fear that had to have held her in its grip, or the dread that must have filled her, knowing what was ahead. Instead, she talked about stinking feed sacks.

"When we got to his place, we had another tussle. Of course, I couldn't win, but I swear I fought my hardest." She found Cade's gaze once again. This time he saw the shimmer of tears in her eyes. "I couldn't let it happen again."

"Again?" he echoed.

She didn't seem to hear. "It's my body!" she said angrily. "I should be able to give it to whomever I want, but he was just too strong, Cade. You know how strong Josep was."

"Josep?" What was she talking about? Lilly reached out and grabbed his hand. The expression in her eyes commanded him to hold his questions. To simply listen.

Instead of looking at them, Erin was now looking at the hands she was twisting in her lap. "When he'd slapped me until my ears were ringing and I couldn't fight anymore, he threw me on the bed, and . . . he just took what he wanted. It's so easy for a man to just take. He told me that if I told Ma, he'd tell her that I teased him and led him on. And he said that if I told you, he'd have you shanghaied."

Understanding crashed down on Cade, shattering his holier-than-thou judgments into a million pieces. Josep—their step-father—had taken his sister's virginity, her innocence, and her laughter. How many years had she lived with that betrayal?

"When?" he asked.

She looked up then. "It started soon after he married Ma."

"And she didn't know?"

"How could she? He'd catch me when she was gone off to work or running an errand. And sometimes his friends—"

Grief, ten years too late but gut-wrenching nonetheless, made it hard to think, hard to breathe. Not just Josep, then, but others . . . Cade held out a trembling hand to silence her. "For the love of all that is holy, Erin, no more. I can't bear to hear anymore."

"You can!" she said in a fierce, determined voice. "And you will. I've lived it; you can stand to hear about it second-hand!" Yet after the outburst, she said no more.

Finally, when the silence in the room had stretched to un-bearable limits, he asked, "Then why go into prostitution after he died? You were free to choose whatever path you wanted. You could have married and—"

"No," she cried. "Don't you see that I wasn't free, and I couldn't marry. Josep had taken my one gift. My only dowry. What did I have to offer a prospective husband? If I told him, he'd be disgusted. If I wasn't honest, and one of the others said something, then what?" She shook her head. "No. I'd not shame a husband that way.

"Prostitution seemed my only option. At least I could get paid for letting a man use me. At least I'd get something out of it." She laughed, a bitter sound that seemed to come from her very soul. "And believe me, they paid."

Cade started to speak, but she stopped him. "No! Don't go telling me what's right and wrong. I know all about it."

"No," he told her. "I wasn't going to say anything about that. I've sinned enough in my life that I'm not the one to cast stones."

"But you did."

"I didn't know, Erin. I didn't know. All I knew was that my beautiful sister had forgotten how to laugh and that she'd cho-sen a life that would bring the family dishonor, and no one could sway ya from it. Da always said we shouldn't do anything to bring shame to the family name. And then, when ya tried to kill yourself the same day I lost Glenna, I thought you'd taken a shortcut to hell."

"I didn't try to kill myself, though I had thought about it often, and never more than the day Glenna died."

"No?" he challenged, with a hint of anger. "Then what are those scars on your wrists?"

"They're from a very sharp knife, but I didn't do the cut-ting."

He felt Lilly's fingers tighten around his, his only reality in this ever-worsening nightmare his sister had sucked him into.

"So, someone did it to ya? Is that what yer sayin'?"

"Yes."

"That makes no sense."

"It does when it has to do with Glenna's death. Glenna's murder."

"Leave Glenna out of your story. Glenna was pure and good, and—"

"—and I'm just your slut of a sister trying to make up some tale so that you'll feel sorry for me, is that it?"

He shook his head. Torment filled his blue eyes. "I don't know what you're doin'."

"I'm tryin' to set the record straight as Seamus always says. And I mean to get all the horridness out in the open, so that maybe the two of us can move past it. There are things ya don't know, brother." As she spoke, her voice grew softer, almost pleading.

When he made no reply, she continued, "You blame me for Glenna's death, and rightly so, but I meant her no harm. Ya must know I'd never hurt the person my brother loved the most in this world."

Cade looked at her ravaged face, as if to gauge whether or not she was telling him the truth. "Then tell me what happened. Tell me what I don't know about that day."

"You know that MacKenzie Daily was takin' care of me then."

Cade nodded. He had sent Mac's brother, Roscoe, to prison for his involvement with a gang that had robbed several trains and killed a couple of passengers during the course of the robberies.

When he'd found out about Erin's taking up with Mac, he'd considered it nothing more than another way his sister was thumbing her nose at him, the family, and the world.

"At the time, I thought he was just another guy, but that wasn't the case at all. After a while, I realized that he was pumping me for information about you. Where you were working, where you lived, that sort of thing. Of course, I didn't tell him."

"Then how did he find out so he could burn down my house and kill my wife?"

Erin's already pale face turned as white as the proverbial sheet. "I told him, but not willingly. That day, he came, and he was really upset about something. He didn't waste any time. He asked me outright where you lived. When I refused to say, he decided to use his knife to make me more 'agreeable,' as he put it."

"Are you telling me that Mac Daily cut your wrists?"

"Yes. But not quick. Slow and painful." She licked her lips, and her violet eyes grew dark with memories. "At first it was just a prick, a little cut, and when I still wouldn't talk, he moved to the other wrist and did the same thing. He told me that I was going to sit in my chair and bleed to death, and that everyone would think it was because I'd grown tired of my pitiful life. Every time I refused to tell him, he made the cuts larger, until I finally gave in."

Tears slid down her face, and she swiped at them in anger, but her gaze was unwavering. She was determined to take the blame and punishment she felt she deserved. "There was so much blood, and, despite what you may believe, Cade, I wanted to live. I really did."

He couldn't speak. He was too immersed in the revelations. Yet despite the bizarreness of the tale, something about it rang true. He had an extensive background with the Daily boys, and the fact that they had a ruthless streak when it came to getting what they wanted was common knowledge. So, while Erin's tale sounded far-fetched, Cade knew it was just the sort of thing they'd pull.

"I was so worried after he left. I had no idea what was on his mind, but I knew it wouldn't be good. I went next door to Mrs. McCutcheon's and asked if she'd get me some help. And then I passed out. There were some men fixing potholes in the street. They took me to the hospital." A sudden sob burst from her. "I'm sorry, Cade. I'm so sorry."

She was asking for his forgiveness. Forgiveness for bringing shame to herself and the family. And for causing Glenna's death in trying to save her own life. Could he give it? Could he blame her for putting her life ahead of Glenna's?

No. Sweet heaven above, Erin had suffered enough. And for a long time. It was in his power to relieve her of at least part of her pain. As he'd said, it wasn't his place to judge her for how she'd lived her life. It was his place as her big brother to be there for her.

As for her blaming herself for her part in Glenna's death . . . well, hadn't he done the same thing? Wasn't that why he'd turned to drinking? To forget his guilt?

"That's why I couldn't let anything happen to Lilly."

He'd been so lost in thought that he didn't make the connection. "I'm not following you."

"I shot Eli because I knew that if I let anything happen to her, it would be my fault."

"That isn't true!" Lilly said, speaking for the first time.

"Isn't it?"

"No. It would have been my fault for going there."

"Why did you?"

Lilly shrugged. "I was doing my job. Trying to get to you before anything happened, but I was too late."

"You put yourself in danger because of me. I couldn't let anything happen to you, because I knew that if it did, Cade would never forgive me, and I would never forgive myself. Don't you see, Lilly? I couldn't be responsible for him losing a woman he cares for. Not again."

CHAPTER 25

Lilly and Cade left soon afterward to head back to the jail, but not before Cade and his sister had cried in each other's arms and begged for each other's forgiveness. She knew that as hard as the past half hour had been for them both, it was long past due. Something she felt would give them a sense of healing and a new perspective on their present situations.

Lilly hoped that knowing the truth would set Cade free of the burden of blame he'd placed on his sister and the torment he'd suffered. Maybe now, he could put the past in its proper place and look to the future, the way she was trying to do.

For the first time in months, she wondered what her future did hold. Since signing with the Pinkertons, she'd spent almost every waking minute involved in one assignment or another. In some ways that was good. It left little time to dwell on the past or dream of the future. But, with Erin's comment still ringing in her ears, Lilly couldn't help wondering if there was any significance to Erin's statement. Had she meant that Cade felt something for her? Something as strong as what he'd felt for Glenna?

The possibility stole her breath. No! He had made his love for his wife known in hundreds of ways over the past months, and he'd also made it clear that he had no desire for another woman.

While it was true that their initial annoyance at being forced to work together had faded, and they'd grown more comfortable as they got to know each other, that's all it was. A solid working relationship and respect for each other's skills. Spending so much time together was bound to have eased their initial tensions. Any partners would feel the same thing.

"I feel as if I've gone ten rounds in the ring."

She glanced over at him. He looked it, too. She knew he was referring to the gutted, empty feeling left behind after going through an emotional upheaval.

"You'll feel better tomorrow."

He glanced over at her. "I already feel as if a weight has been taken off my shoulders."

"Refusing to forgive is a heavy burden to carry," she told him. "And believe me, the forgiveness will do you as much good as it does Erin. I only hope she can forgive herself."

"Me too." He shook his head. "I can't believe that Josep . . ." He couldn't finish the sentence. "Now that I know what he did to her, her choices make more sense, as bad as they were." He cursed beneath his breath and faced Lilly with a look of self-loathing. "Why didn't I see it? I should have suspected something."

"Oh, no you don't! You're not going to rid yourself of one blame and take on another. Pierce told me that we can't solve every crime. We can't right every wrong. All we can do is give it our best. We're not perfect."

He glanced at her for a second, then he seemed to throw off his melancholy, and his rare, impudent smile appeared as he gave his attention back to the street. "Speak for yourself, colleen."

Who could resist that smile? Who could resist him when

he turned on his not inconsiderable charm? Not Lilly Long; however, she would be smart to remember that he *was* able to turn it on and off at will.

Her reply was a sharp jab in the ribs with her elbow.

He laughed and tucked her hand around his arm. "I just can't believe she kept all of it from us for so long."

"She didn't want to hurt you." Lilly grinned, wanting to keep the moment light. "Maybe she was trying to keep you boys out of jail."

His lips twisted into the semblance of a smile. "If I'd known, I'd have beaten Josep within an inch of his life." Cade glanced over at her once more. "Do you think he'd have done anything to me if she'd told me?"

She shook her head. "You were little more than a boy, and I don't know anything about Josep. Erin believed him. That's all that matters."

Cade pulled the buggy into a space in front of the marshal's office and tied the reins to the hitching post. Cade asked the sheriff if he would take his men to get a bite to eat so that Cade and Lilly could interview the prisoner in private. They were happy to do so.

Elijah Wilkins was locked in one of the cells, lying on the cot with his hands folded behind his head. He was still bare-chested, and, when he turned to see who'd come, Lilly noticed that the cocky expression she'd hated the first night she'd met him was still in his eyes. Wordlessly, he swung his feet to the floor and sat on the bunk, facing them with a challenging look.

Cade pulled a chair in front of the cell door and spun it around on one leg, straddling it and placing his arms across the back. "Did they give you anything to eat?"

"Why?" Wilkins shot back. "Are you concerned for my well-being?"

"Not particularly. I'm just doing my job. Are you ready to talk?"

"Why should I?"

"Because you're in a world of trouble. If you don't talk, someone will, now that they know you're in custody. That's how it works here, isn't it? Everyone covers his own tracks?"

Lilly could almost see the wheels turning in Wilkins's brain as he weighed the pros and cons of talking, picking and choosing just what to say and how much. "What do you want to know?"

"I want to know if you provide women for Velvet and Rosalie exclusively, or for whomever has a need."

"As long as I get the best deal, I'll sell to anyone," he said. "That's good business."

"You're a lowlife who deals in human flesh! Innocent women and children!" Lilly cried, unable to stand there and witness his callous disregard.

Cade motioned for her to stay out of it. "Are you the one behind the mail-order bride arrangement, or did you just work it for someone else?" he asked.

"It was my idea, and it was a good one, don't you think? I had no idea there were so many unhappy women back East looking for something different. Wanting to see more of America . . . wanting to find a *good* man and have a passel of kids."

"You had Monty write your letters," Lilly stated, forcing herself to a calm she was far from feeling.

"Sure did. They couldn't have read my hen scratching."

Lilly refrained from telling him she knew he couldn't read or write. There was no sense stooping to childish behavior. "Nora Nash was my friend."

"Who?"

Rage settled over her. Dark and biting rage. Nora had

meant so little to him, just one of many, that he didn't even know which one she was.

"Nora Nash. The actress."

Was that a hint of recognition in his eyes?

"Oh, yeah. That cute little spitfire with the curly hair. Now she was something else."

"She's dead." Cade's voice was as cold as ice.

"Yeah, you said that before," Wilkins said with a sorrowful nod. "Too bad. I liked her."

"And you had nothing to do with it."

"Nope."

"What happens when someone turns on you and says you did?"

Wilkins stood and approached the cell door, walking that swaggering walk, wearing that smug look. "Then that person would be a liar. I didn't kill her. I'm not denyin' I roughed her up some a time or two, but that's part of the job, you know? I just do what I'm told."

"What about the attack by all those cowboys?" Cade pressed. "Do ya know anything about that?"

"I didn't order it."

"Who did?"

"How do I know? You may not believe it, but I'm not in on everything that goes on in this town. I strongly suspect it was Velvet or Rosalie, and my guess would be Velvet. Your friend caused a lot of trouble when she started spouting all that Jesus stuff." He laughed. "I've never seen two madder whores in my life than Rosie and Velvet."

There was a noise behind them.

Cade and Lilly turned. Sam Davies stood in the doorway, taking in the scene with a troubled expression. She could only imagine what must be running through his mind.

"Miss Long. Mr. McShane."

Cade gave him a nod of greeting. "Marshal."

"What in blazes are you doing here, Sam?" Wilkins snarled.

"This is my office," Davies reminded him. Then, addressing Cade, he said, "I was in Dallas most of the day. Imagine my surprise when I heard the sheriff had been summoned to my territory. Then, the first thing I hear when I get back is that Eli has been arrested. I'd like to know by whose authority."

Lilly produced her badge from her handbag, and Cade pulled his from his inner coat pocket. Davies examined them closely. "You're both Pinkerton agents?"

"We are."

"I've never heard of a woman Pinkerton before."

"Well, you have now," Lilly said. "Perhaps you should sit down, Marshal. I'm sure Agent McShane has a few questions for you."

"Me? In case you haven't noticed, I'm the law around here. Not a criminal."

"You can spout your innocence from now 'til doomsday, but it hasn't escaped anyone's notice that you're pretty easy on some of the madams. From what we've seen, most of them should be shut down, but they aren't. Why is that, Marshal? A little payment at the first of the month?"

Davies's face flamed. Embarrassment or bluster? "How dare you question my ethics!"

"I'm not questioning them," Cade said, shaking his head. "Not at all. I'm tellin' ya that everyone knows that's your game."

"Tell me, Marshal. What does it cost to get away with murder?" Lilly taunted.

"I don't know what you're talking about!"

She strode right up to him, facing him with the full force of her wrath. "Really? How much time did you spend looking for Dottie's killer? Or was she just one less poor, pitiful dove you had to deal with?"

Davies looked as if he'd like to choke the life from her. "How dare you come in here with all your high-and-mighty ways. You don't know how hard it is to keep up with all the unrest in this town. If I tried to intervene in every grievance these women have with one another, I'd never get any peace."

"Really?" She turned away from him and sauntered back toward the cell. "Maybe the job is too much for you, Marshal." He opened his mouth to say something, but she turned and silenced him with a look. "We were just discussing my friend Nora's convenient death with Mr. Wilkins when you arrived. Perhaps you can shed some light on the subject."

She noted a flicker of recognition in his eyes. "Who is Nora?"

"She was a friend of mine who came here expecting to become Eli Wilkins's wife and was sold into prostitution instead. Would you happen to know anything about those illegal activities?"

Davies remained silent, but Lilly could tell he was weighing his next words.

"I still have no idea who she is."

Cade spoke up. "Do they mean so little to you, then, these women you've sworn to protect? Surely you remember Nora. She's the one who was found shot in the head at Monty Newton's place just days after she was accosted and raped by a gang of cowboys. Just two days after you spoke to her and she told you her suspicions about who'd arranged her attack."

"That is a bit of a coincidence, don't you think?" Lilly asked. "Wilkins says he didn't do it. What about you, Marshal?"

"I had nothing to do with it!" Davies shouted. "And I resent your coming in here and acting as if I'm some sort of cold-blooded murderer!"

"Fine." Lilly gestured toward the cell where Wilkins had gone back to his cot. "What's your relationship with Mr. Wilkins?"

"We both work here in town."

"What does he do?"

Wilkins leaped to his feet and grabbed the bars of the cell. "I'll tell you what I do!" he said in a voice laced with defiance. "I do just what you said. I get women for the houses. I give them a thumping when one of the owners thinks their behavior needs adjusting."

"And what about children?" Cade asked. "Do you find them for the perverted people who take their satisfaction from abusing them?"

"I have, on occasion."

"And you have no problem with that?"

He shrugged. "I'm a businessman, and it's just business."

"You are a most disgusting man, Mr. Wilkins," Lilly said. "Have you no sense of decency or morals?"

His mouth curved into an unconcerned smile. "Guess not."

"If murder is on your list of orders, do you do it?" Cade asked.

"I've never been asked to."

"Then you know nothing about Nora Nash's shooting?"

"I beat her when she tried to run away, but I didn't arrange for the boys to have a good time with her, and I didn't kill her."

Though there was no logical reason to do so, something in his tone made Lilly believe him. And, although he was slimy in his own way, she doubted that Davies had anything to do with it, either. He wouldn't want to get his hands that dirty. He was the kind who just wanted to get by, take the easy way out, not cause any waves.

So, if not Wilkins, who? Everything came back to Velvet. Nora had worked for her. Was it possible that when she took to the streets talking salvation and encouraging the girls to leave the life, Velvet had thought it might hurt her business? Had she ordered the rape to discourage Nora? Had she hoped she'd die from the abuse, and then, when she hadn't and had told the marshal she knew who had arranged her ambush, had Velvet decided to silence her wayward employee once and for all?

"The Acre is a small community," Cade said. "People talk. Someone in your position is bound to hear things. Let me remind you that you're looking at a long time in prison for what you've been doing. If you know who was behind Nora Nash's death, now would be the time to speak up."

Wilkins thought on that for a while. "It was Rosalie."

The sheriff and his deputies arrived and locked the stunned Davies into the cell next to Wilkins.

"A few more questions, and we'll be finished for now," Cade said to the deposed marshal. "We heard that you and Velvet were an item at one time and planned to get married. Is that true?"

"What does that have to do with anything?"

"You never know when some unexpected piece of information can take things in a whole new direction."

"We were."

"What happened?"

One corner of Davies's mouth lifted in a sarcastic smile. "Let's just say that she wasn't content to be the wife of a simple lawman. She wanted the finer things. And she objected to some of my . . . inclinations."

Lilly shot a glance at a frowning Cade. She felt her chest tighten. "Children?"

"I prefer not to discuss it without legal representation." Davies turned away, and Wilkins spoke up.

"I can answer that."

"By all means, Mr. Wilkins, you do that," she said.

"It wasn't him, and, for the record, neither Velvet nor Rosie deal in kids. They don't like complications. It's a couple of the other places."

"Would you please tell us what Velvet's objections were to you?" Lilly asked, turning to Davies again.

"Ask her."

"Fine. We will." Lilly considered what he'd said, trying to get her mind around the unusual relationship. "Despite your breakup, you stayed nearby and helped her all you could."

"Some feelings take a long time dying," he said. "And sometimes they never do."

Love was indeed a complicated emotion.

"What about Rosalie?" Cade asked. "We've heard the two of you share more than business interests."

"Everyone needs someone, Agent McShane. When Velvet dumped me, Rosalie more than satisfied my needs."

The sheriff left his deputies guarding the prisoners while he accompanied Lilly and Cade to the Silver Slipper to arrest Rosalie Padgett for the murder of Nora Nash.

Rosalie saw them the moment they walked through the front door. She turned a pasty white, but did not appear too surprised. No doubt the rumormongers were telling everyone within earshot about the Dallas sheriff being called in, and about seeing Wilkins handcuffed in the back of a wagon driven by that bodyguard fella from back East.

The trio headed straight for her. To her credit, she didn't try to flee or retreat. Her steady gaze zeroed in on Cade and Lilly. "I knew the two of you and your other friend were up to something. I suppose you're private investigators hired by Nora's family."

"Actually, Nora hired us to come and have a look at the abuse and corruption here before you killed her." Cade pulled out his badge and tipped his head toward Lilly. "Miss Long is my partner."

Rosalie couldn't hide her shock. "Pinkertons! You're both Pinkertons?"

"That's right. Now the sheriff here would like to take you over to the jail."

"Who squealed on me?"

Cade glanced around the room. You could have heard the legendary pin drop. Every eye was turned their way. "Wouldn't you rather discuss this in private?"

She sighed. "Sure. Let's go. Sam will get this straightened out in no time."

"I don't think so," Cade said.

"You have Sam, too?" she asked in an incredulous voice.

"We do."

Lilly watched Rosalie's disbelief turn to anger. Without another word, the sheriff took her arm and led her out of the saloon.

Back at the jail, Lilly and Cade bade the sheriff good night and, leaving the rig tied to the hitching post till morning, they headed back to Dusty's. It was well past midnight, and Lily couldn't recall ever being so tired.

"So, we're finished here?"

"More or less. It may take a day or two to tie up the loose ends, but you can telegraph William and tell him that we've found Nora's murderer and we'll be on a train headed back soon."

Lilly heaved a loud sigh.

"What's wrong?" he asked, turning to look at her.

"I thought finding out who was behind the mail-order bride scam and who murdered Nora would make me feel different. Better."

"What do ya mean?"

"I thought bringing the guilty parties to justice would make the pain go away . . . or lessen it somehow. But all it's done is make me mad enough to shoot Rosalie myself."

"I know how you feel. After they put Mac Daily away in the same prison as his brother for killing Glenna, I'd have gladly joined them there if I could have had ten minutes alone with them."

"What did you do instead?"

The twist of his lips was supposed to be a smile, but failed. "I went to the gym and punched a bag until sweat blinded me and my hands were so bloody and sore I couldn't use them for a week."

"Really, McShane," she said in her most severe tone, "that wasn't very smart."

His mouth curved in another of those wry smiles. "I would have to agree with you, Miss Long, even though it seemed like the thing to do at the time. You'll soon learn that every case is peculiar in some way, and each one leaves you feeling different, but one other thing I've learned is that revenge is something best left to the courts. And God."

"You know, McShane, sometimes your understanding of a situation surprises me." They walked a block in silence. "It's hard to believe that Davies claimed to love Velvet, but has something going on with Rosalie."

"Why does that surprise you? These people have no morals, scruples, or anything related to decency. As for Velvet and Rosalie, it's what they do, isn't it? Sell their bodies?"

"I suppose," she mused. "For some reason, I thought that, when you became a madam, you no longer had to indulge in that sort of thing."

"I'm sure they don't *have* to. If they do indulge, it's for something besides money."

"Like what?"

He chuckled. "If I need to explain, your Tim must have been lacking in the love department."

Lilly snorted in disgust. During the short time she'd been with Timothy, she'd had no complaints about their intimacy. What she did find appalling was that he'd professed to love her, which had been a lie. He had also used their lovemaking as a system of punishment, reward, and bribery.

"Love has nothing to do with it."

It was Cade's turn to stop. "Ya can't mean that?"

"Of course I do."

"Then ye're daft."

"Daft? That's rich, McShane. Can you honestly say that love played a part in your . . . physical conquests through the years?"

A long breath hissed from him. "I confess that you have me there. But when you do love someone, it's . . . different. *You're* different."

She wondered if he was speaking of his love for Glenna, but refrained from asking. And then she wondered if she would ever experience what he was trying to explain.

They were almost back to Dusty's, and then he asked, "How long do you think it will be before Erin can travel?"

"A few days, I imagine. I'm sure the doctor can tell us."

"Do you remember my telling Davies that one little piece of information can change everything?"

"Yes." She couldn't tell him that every word he'd said was imprinted into her mind.

"It's true."

"What are you getting at?"

"Erin. I always knew she'd told Mac where Glenna and I lived, and of course I blamed her for that, but finding out how he'd tortured her for the information made all the difference in how I looked at her part in the whole incident."

"Judging is like revenge, McShane," she said, curling her hand around his upper arm. "It's best left to the courts and to God."

CHAPTER 26

The conductor announced that the train would be reaching its destination in ten minutes, and, though Lilly was glad they were back in Chicago, she made no move to gather her things. Cade was sitting next to his sister, his arms folded across his chest, his head tipped back against the cushion, sleeping. Or pretending to.

Lilly had telegraphed William to tell him what had happened and then sent off a letter with more details. It was a tale that could not be told without recounting what Erin had suffered and how her abduction had led to Wilkins's capture. Lilly knew her boss would want to hear the tale in full, probably the following day.

Though she and her partners had spent a lot of time discussing the case and the possible outcome, Erin had been less talkative on their return trip than she had been before. Lilly knew she'd asked the doctor to post a letter to someone, and, if possible, Erin's sadness had seemed to worsen after that.

Lilly had tried to engage Cade's sister in conversation many times, and while she was pleasant, she showed little interest in having a true conversation. She had lost her sparkle and the air of vitality that made her the center of everyone's attention when she entered a room.

She had lost the essence of what made her Erin.

Once, when Lilly asked what her plans were when they returned, she'd said she had no idea, but that she didn't plan to go back to her old job. At least that was a positive thing to come from her horrifying ordeal. She suspected that Cade's forgiveness and the new, tentative bond they were forging had something to do with the decision.

When Lilly asked if the new avenue she'd mentioned pursuing involved a man, Erin had explained that the opportunity might no longer be available. An intriguing comment to say the least. Lilly couldn't imagine what that path might be; however, she felt strongly that whatever Erin decided for her future, it would be with the help and support of the entire family.

As for herself, Lilly was glad to be back, though she didn't know why. There was no one to welcome her, and she was not looking forward to returning to the small, cramped bedsitting room she called home between assignments. She really should make some friends outside her work, but how did a single lady go about doing that?

If she were careful with her funds, maybe she could start going to the theater on occasion. There were always book clubs, places where bluestockings met to discuss writings deemed too intellectual for the mere housewife. And art lessons. She'd always been quite good at drawing. And maybe she and Simon could go out for dinner now and again. That would be nice; he was the kind of man she could imagine in her future.

Part of her uneasiness had to do with her indecisiveness. Recalling her treatment of Henri Ducharme, and how she had wanted to shoot Elijah Wilkins and Rosalie for the horrible things they had done, made her wonder if she had what it took to be a Pinkerton.

This is exactly what Pierce meant when he told you the world outside the theater would eat you alive in a month.

Though it galled her to admit it, he'd been right. It had taken longer than his predicted month, but the longer she worked, the harder it became to separate herself from her experiences. Six months ago, she would never have wanted to shoot someone.

Oh, she knew she would never really do it, but the fact that it had crossed her mind was disturbing. It seemed that each case showed her a bit more of the evil in the world. She'd never realized how much ugliness was out there until she became an operative.

Still, there *was* good to be found. Like Mrs. Fontenot and her family in New Orleans, and Monty and Bonnie and Charlie in Ft. Worth. The thought of them made her smile. Before they'd left, Bonnie had told Lilly that she was leaving Velvet's, and she and Charlie were getting married and moving to Oklahoma to start fresh.

Bonnie had found her knight in shining armor. Lilly was beginning to think hers had been killed in battle. The thought brought a reluctant smile to her lips despite the downward turn of her thoughts.

"A penny for them," Cade said, leaning around his sister.

"I'm not sure they're worth that much."

Just then the train's brakes began to screech, and the giant beast came to a grinding stop. "Don't forget that William was supposed to let the family know we're coming in today," he told his sister. "I imagine they'll want us all to meet at Seamus's for supper. You too, Lilly."

"I don't know. . . ."

"C'mon, Lilly," Erin said, speaking for the first time in

more than an hour. "Maybe they'll be so busy picking your brain about the assignment they'll leave me alone."

"Are you certain you want them to?" Lilly challenged.

Erin looked nervous. "It's been a long time since we've all been together. I'm not sure what to expect."

Lilly smiled. "A lot of hugs, I imagine."

"C'mon, lassies, gather your things, and let's get off this tin monster."

Moments later, Lilly stood on the platform. She was looking around to see if she recognized anyone from Cade's family in the crowd when she heard Erin's gasp. Turning toward her friend, she saw that her gaze was fixed on a man standing beneath the eaves of the station. A tall, rather gangly man who stood shifting his weight from one foot to the other. A man dressed in a nice suit that looked as if he'd slept in it. A nice-looking man with a mop of messy blond hair and tortoiseshell glasses.

Simon?

What was he doing here? Had William sent him? Lilly started to take a step toward him, but at the last second, she realized he wasn't looking at her. His anxious gaze was focused on Erin, who stood as still as a figurine except for the white handkerchief she was twisting in her fingers. She didn't even seem to be breathing.

Simon and Erin? Was this the man Robbie meant when he said some swell had been around a lot? Was he the "lawyer" Erin had spoken of? Was it possible he was the change she'd foreseen in her future?

Simon finally made a move. He smiled. Perhaps the most magnificent smile Lilly had ever seen. It spoke of happiness, and love, and so much more. Erin smiled back. Tentatively, at first, and then, when he took a step toward her, she picked up her skirts and flew into his arms. He swung her around, forgetting his customary decorum, and they laughed together in pure joy.

Lilly felt the sting of tears and a suspicious tightening in her chest. It looked as if she would not be having any dinners with Simon unless Erin was along. Like Bonnie, Erin had found her knight.

Oh, well, Lil, you'd have made mincemeat of him in no time. The voice sounded familiar. Lilly could have sworn the thought came straight from Nora.

"Simon?" Cade's incredulous voice came from behind her. "My sister and Simon Linedecker?"

"Love is a complicated emotion, McShane," Lilly said, recalling Sam Davies's remarks the night of his arrest.

"Obviously." Still staring at the couple, he offered her his arm.

"I'm sending your bags to your room. Will the landlady accept them?"

"Yes. That's fine." She cast a look back at the lovers, who were smiling at each other in a rather silly fashion. "Isn't it wonderful?"

"What?" he said, sounding rather grumpy.

"Erin and Simon."

"It happens every day."

"Not to people like them," she said. "Do you realize what this means?"

"That I'll soon have a new passel of nieces and nephews, I imagine."

"Wouldn't that be great?"

"Not necessarily. Speaking of Erin, there hasn't been a private moment for me to thank you."

"For what?"

"It was a brave thing you did, going to try to help her that day at Wilkins's. Dimwitted and unwise as usual, but very brave."

She choked on a laugh. How very McShane. "Is that meant as a compliment?"

"Well, of course, it is!" he snapped, looking affronted. "What else would it be?"

"With you, it's hard to tell."

"You need to work on your street fighting," he added. "It sounds as if you still fight like a girl, but I was impressed when you said you pulled Wilkins off the bed and banged his head on the floor."

"Again, thank you, I think. And, in case you haven't noticed, I am a girl."

"Of course I've noticed." To her dismay, there was not a single ounce of familiarity in his tone or manner. She was his partner, after all.

"At least you remembered your gun," he noted. "That's an improvement. But Wilkins did manage to take it away from you."

"Please!" She didn't know whether she wanted to laugh or cry. "Stop."

"What is it?" he asked.

"I can't take any more praise."

"Aren't you a strange lass?" he said, looking at her with a baffled expression. "We're here anyway."

EPILOGUE

Pinkerton Offices

Lilly and Cade arrived at the Pinkerton offices promptly at nine. As usual, Harris was pounding away on his Remington typewriter, doing whatever it was Harris did to help the agency run in a smooth, professional manner.

"Good morning, Harris," they said almost in tandem.

"Miss Long. Agent McShane. I hear your trip to that terrible place—what is it called—?"

"Hell's Half Acre," Cade supplied.

"Yes." A little shiver shuddered through Harris. "Dreadful-sounding place! I hear it was a success."

Cade nodded. "We found out who was luring women out West, and we found out who killed Lilly's friend, so yes, it was successful."

"That's wonderful." Harris rose and led them to one of the inner offices where William was waiting to hear the details of the mission.

He greeted them with his customary handshake and offered them a seat. "So," he said, making a steeple with his fingertips. "You found the culprit."

"We found several of them, sir," Cade told him. "But I'm afraid it will take more than a couple of weeks to clean that place up. It will require lawmen who aren't taking money to look the other way, and a concerted community effort determined to rid the place of crime."

"It isn't called the oldest profession for no reason, Agent McShane," William said. "As long as there is a demand for some product or service, there will always be someone willing to provide it."

"That's true."

"Tell me what we have."

Together, Lilly and Cade told William everything they'd learned about Wilkins's obtaining women and children for sexual slavery. Cade explained Marshal Davies's prior relationship with Velvet, and how Rosalie had encouraged the group of cowboys who'd raped Nora. They told him it had been Rosalie herself who had killed Nora after Davies told her that Nora had put all the pieces of their ugly enterprise together, and that she knew that the golden-haired madam was the one behind her attack.

"Did you ever find out who murdered the other girl . . . Dottie?" William asked.

"We may never know."

"What about Davies's connections to Rosalie and Velvet."

"He did own a piece of both businesses," Lilly said. "Which is why none of the charges against them ever stuck for long."

"And his failed relationship with Velvet? Did you find out what ended that?"

Lilly looked to Cade for help. "We did," he said in a hesitant voice. "He wouldn't say, but, when we asked her, she said that he liked, uh . . . female domination, and she preferred, as she called them, 'manly men.'"

"Good grief!" William said, blushing to the roots of his

pomaded hair and casting an apologetic look at Lilly. He didn't quite meet Cade's eyes as he asked, "Am I to assume she had no problem with his taking up with Rosalie?"

"Apparently not."

"Well, life is interesting, isn't it?"

"It is, sir."

Lilly praised Erin for everything she'd done to help them, and it was Lilly who told William of the events leading to Wilkins's capture, while Cade sat stone-faced, his fingers gripping the arms of the chair until his knuckles were white.

William appeared truly touched by the tale. "That's unfortunate. I might have been able to use her now and again."

Lilly leaned forward. "Do you mean you might hire her, sir? Another woman?"

William had the grace to blush. It was well known that while Allan Pinkerton considered women to be a vital part of the work, his other son, Robert, and many others, thought they were ill suited for the job. At best, William had seemed ambivalent about the notion. At least until now.

"It had crossed my mind when you wrote to say how well she'd carried out her duties. But that won't be happening, it seems."

"Why is that?"

"She didn't tell you?"

"We had supper with her last night," Cade offered. "She didn't have a lot to say about anything."

"I see. Well, I hope I am not letting the cat out of the bag, but Mr. Linedecker came in yesterday before meeting you at the station and tendered his resignation."

"What!" Lilly couldn't hide her surprise.

"I believe Simon will make a fine addition to your family." William straightened some already tidy papers on his desk, signaling the interview was over. "Once again, I commend the two of you for the successful conclusion of your assignment, but before you go, I wanted to talk to you about the money that Miss Nash sent."

"Is there a problem?"

"Nothing beyond what to do with the balance. Since it didn't take as long as we anticipated, there is somewhere around one-hundred-fifty dollars left. I was wondering if it would be acceptable to the two of you to divide it equally among the three of you. It would make a nice wedding gift for Mr. Linedecker and Miss McShane."

"That's fine with me," Cade said. "As a matter of fact, you can give her my share as well."

"And mine."

Cade looked at Lilly as if she'd gone mad. "You could use that money."

"I could," she agreed. "But so could you. Simon was a great help when I was looking for representation for my divorce from Timothy, and I grew fond of Erin while we worked together. Those two could use some good fortune."

He nodded. "Fine, then. Mr. Pinkerton, please see to it that they get whatever money is left."

"I'll do that." William regarded the two of them with a solemn expression. "I realize you have barely had time to breathe between assignments, but I chose you for them because they seemed to call for a team." The expression in his eyes was thoughtful. "Miss Long, you must be feeling overwhelmed. The law-keeping business wears on you, even though what we do is worthwhile and needed."

How could he know how she was feeling? Lilly shot Cade a disapproving look. Had he said something to William about her doubts?

Cade shrugged, as if to say he had no idea where this was coming from.

"I want the two of you to take some time. I'll try not to give you any new assignments for at least a month. Lilly, why don't you find out where Pierce and his wife are and spend some time with them? It would do you good."

"Thank you, sir. That sounds wonderful."

"All right." William stood. The interview was over.

Out on the sidewalk, Cade turned to her with his hands stuck in his pockets. "So, it looks as if we're getting a break."

"Yes."

"Is there any significance in the fact that you didn't say anything to William about quitting?"

"Not really. I'm still thinking about it."

"I see. The time off will be good for you. Maybe a rest will help you decide what you want to do."

"I hope so. Did you say anything to William? Is that why he gave us this break?"

He sketched an *X* over his heart. "Cross my heart. I didn't say a word. William's a smart man. And very observant."

True.

"He's right, Lilly. The work is hard, and, unless you're one of those who eats and breathes it, the way I always have, it takes a lot from you."

"Even you?"

"Even me." Cade exhaled heavily. "Look, lass, I canna make your decision for you, but don't throw away a promising career because of one bad experience."

"Bad experience!" she challenged. "The man intended to—to have his way with me. That isn't something easily forgotten, as you heard your sister say."

He scrubbed a hand down his clean-shaven face. "I know. I'm doing a poor job of this."

"Yes, McShane, you are."

"What I meant to say is that there will be plenty of times you'll be in a pickle. Maybe something worse than that."

"My, aren't you Job's comforter," she said, crossing her arms over her breasts.

The sound that came from his throat sounded like a growl. He abandoned all efforts at trying to be sensitive with his advice. Sensitivity was not McShane's forte. "What I'm trying to say is that you were warned about the hardships, but you wanted to help women and said you could take it!"

He was right. Lilly recalled the arguments her family and even the Pinkertons had made before hiring her, but she'd come straight off Tim's betrayal and felt she had a noble calling to try to make wrongs right.

"What I'm tryin' to tell ya is that you signed up for danger. Helping victims and putting criminals away puts you face-to-face with violence. The things people do to one another . . . men and women . . . are often beyond our imagination, but those people who are injured deserve justice."

"Is that all?" she asked.

"No."

She gave him a questioning look.

For a moment, it looked as if he was trying to decide what to say next.

"What are you doing tomorrow?"

She hadn't expected that. Leave it to him to keep her wondering. "I have no idea. Why?"

"I thought if you didn't have anything planned, we could go to the gym, and I could teach you a few boxing moves. I've heard of this man in New York who thinks boxing is one of the best ways to stay fit and healthy. And he teaches it in a whole new way."

She looked at Cade as if he'd lost his mind. Hadn't he heard a word she'd said? She wouldn't need boxing moves and self-defense tactics if she went back to the theater.

Despite her doubts, she nodded. "Fine. Where and what time?"

If you enjoyed this Lilly Long adventure,
be sure to look for

THOUGH THIS BE MADNESS

by Penny Richards

Available at your favorite bookstore and e-tailors.

Turn the page for a quick peek!

CHAPTER 1

1881
89 Dearborn, Chicago
Pinkerton Offices

"I bloody well won't do it!" The declaration came from the man pacing the floor of William Pinkerton's office. "I'm a Pinkerton agent, not a blasted nanny."

William Pinkerton pinned the young operative with an unrelenting look from beneath heavy brows. "You haven't any choice, McShane."

Andrew Cadence McShane faced his boss with a defiant expression. "What? I haven't yet groveled enough for you and your father?"

William stifled his own irritation at the bold statement. McShane was a loose cannon, and if it were up to William, he'd fire the man on the spot. Indeed, Allan *had* fired him a year ago, for drinking and brawling and behaving in a way that was unacceptable to Pinkerton's code of conduct. But, claiming that he had his life together at last, McShane had come asking for his job back about the same time the young actress, Lilly Long, had applied for a position. Allan, who had always thought the Irishman was one of his best agents, had rehired him on a provisional basis.

"You know exactly what I mean," William said in a measured tone. "No one was holding a gun to your head when you agreed to the terms of our rehiring you, which, as you no doubt recall, was probation for an undetermined length of time."

Feeling a certain amount of uneasiness over his father's decision to hire McShane and Miss Long, William had suggested that McShane be assigned to keep an eye out for the inexperienced new operative on her first mission, which would—Lord willing—keep him too preoccupied to get into any more scrapes. Allan had agreed.

So while new agent Lilly Long tried to locate the Reverend Harold Purcell, a preacher who had stolen from his congregation and disappeared from his home near Vandalia, Illinois, McShane had kept tabs on her by pretending to be part of a traveling boxing troupe. He'd been no happier about the job than Miss Long had been about her missing person assignment, but they'd both known they were in no position to object, just as neither had any say about this new arrangement.

"Until we feel confident that you will not resort to your previous unacceptable behavior, you will partner with Miss Long."

McShane's eyes went wide with something akin to shock. "It was a barroom brawl, sir. I did not reveal any secrets or compromise my assignment in any way."

"We've been through all this before, McShane, and I refuse to revisit it." William's gaze shied away from the younger man's, which had lost its belligerence and grown as bleak as the stormy spring morning.

William cleared his throat. "Believe me, I understand that on a personal level you were going through an extremely rough patch at the time, and for that you have my sympathy, but you must understand that the agency cannot have our operatives behaving in ways that make us look bad. We have a sterling reputation, and we will do what we must to make sure it stays that way. If you continue to do well, you'll soon be on your own again."

All the fiery irritation seemed to drain from the younger man. "Yes, sir."

"Actually, this assignment is one that will be best served by a man and woman working together."

Seemingly resigned, McShane took a seat in the chair across from William's desk. "Tell me about it."

"I prefer to explain things to you and Miss Long together," William said. "She should be here any minute. But I will tell you this much. The two of you will be going to New Orleans."

The rain had stopped . . . at least for the moment, but thick black clouds still roiled uneasily in the sky when Lilly's cab pulled up in front of the five-story building that housed the Pinkerton offices. She paid the driver and, careful to step around the puddles, entered the structure with a feeling of elation.

Since returning from her first assignment just a week ago, she'd been riding the wave of her success in bringing her first case to a satisfactory conclusion and basking in the knowledge that she would continue to be employed by the prestigious detective firm. She'd been more than a little surprised when she received a message that morning stating that William wanted to see her at once.

Though she knew she had a long way to go before becoming a seasoned agent, the praise she'd received from both William and Allan was, to paraphrase the bard, "the stuff that dreams were made of." When her missing person assignment had evolved into solving a twenty-year-old murder, it had been satisfying to know that she'd helped bring about justice. And Allan, who loved correcting what he perceived as social wrongdoing, had been quite satisfied that things had been made as right as humanly possible. She was eager to embark on her next mission.

Pausing outside the doorway, she tucked a loose strand of red hair beneath the brim of the straw hat she'd purchased as a treat for herself the day before. The soft green of the grosgrain ribbons was the exact hue of her new walking dress with its high stand-up collar topped with the wide, heavy white lace that marched down the front. The off-the-ground hem of her narrow skirt showed the pointed toes of her matching shoes and was trimmed with a wide band of the lace.

She stepped through the door to the outer office, where William's clerk, Harris, pounded on the keys of the Remington typewriter, using the hunt-and-peck system. The morning sunshine behind him illuminated the long, thin wisps of graying hair that had been combed over to help disguise his balding pate.

Hearing her at the door, he looked up. "Good morning, Miss Long," he said with a polite smile. "You're looking chipper today."

"Hello, Harris," she replied. "I am chipper this morning. I'm anxious to get back to work."

Harris stood. "I'll just let them know you're here," he said.

Them. Lilly smiled. Oh, good. Allan was going to be involved in her next project. She had the feeling that the intrepid lawman supported her hiring, even though William was ambivalent at best about his father's determination to hire female agents.

"Miss Long is here," Harris said, moving aside for Lilly to enter.

When she stepped through the aperture, William was already coming around the desk, his hand extended in greeting. But it wasn't William who caught Lilly's attention. It was the man who had risen from a chair as she entered the room. It wasn't Allan Pinkerton who stood when she stepped through the doorway. It was Cadence McShane.

With her attention focused on the other man, she barely heard William's words of welcome. The last time she'd seen McShane was after the completion of the Heaven's Gate assignment. He'd made a cryptic comment and disappeared into the crowd. She thought she'd seen the last of him, so what was he doing here, she wondered as he took her hand in greeting. His palm was rough and warm, and his words and smile were pleasant, but the coldness in his sapphire-blue eyes was undeniable.

What the devil was going on? she wondered again, her lively imagination steering her toward a conclusion that was not the least bit acceptable. Seeking an answer to the questions churning around in her head, Lilly turned her puzzled gaze to William. Allan Pinkerton's son was noted for his speed in assessing situations, and he did not miss the query on Lilly's face or the disdain on McShane's.

"Have a seat, Miss Long," he said, gesturing toward the chair Cade had vacated at her arrival.

Clutching her purse in her lap, Lilly did his bidding.

"My father and I have decided on your next assignment," William told her, wasting no time getting to the point. "You and McShane will be going to New Orleans."

"What!" Lilly's gaze flew to McShane's. If the grim twist of his lips and the blatant annoyance in his eyes were any indication, he was no happier than she.

"Do you really feel this is necessary, sir?" she protested. "While I appreciate the fact that you were concerned about my inexperience, I understood the agency was happy with my work in Vandalia."

"We were extremely pleased," William assured her, "but one successful assignment does not afford you any vast field knowledge. While you were the one who rooted out the truth about the Purcells, if it had not been for McShane, you might very well be dead."

She could not deny that there was a kernel of truth in William's statement. She'd been trapped in the attic of the Purcell home, and though she'd been in the process of trying to free herself by jumping from a small window onto a steep roof, her plan might have gone very wrong. McShane had rescued her from a sticky situation.

"Keeping your youth and inexperience in mind, my father and I feel that, at least for the next few assignments, you and McShane should work together. It will give you a chance to hone your skills."

Lilly looked askance at the man now lounging with apparent indolence on the settee, though the set of his jaw and the jewel hardness in his sapphire-hued eyes left no doubt of his true feelings.

She made one last attempt to change the course of her task, indeed, the course of her life . . . at least for the foreseeable future. "And is Agent McShane agreeable to this arrangement?" she asked.

William's calm gaze flickered over the younger man. "McShane is a professional, Miss Long," he said in a no-nonsense tone. "He accepts his obligations and gives this agency his best." Though he was speaking to her, she could not shake the notion that his words were directed to her new partner as well.

Lilly sighed. Disappointment, anger, and frustration vied for supremacy. Clearly, neither she nor McShane had a choice in the matter, and to argue it further would only make her appear contrary and disagreeable. As she had with her first assignment, she would accept the situation, do her best, and hope that soon she would be trusted to go it alone.

With a lift of her chin, she said, "So we go to New Orleans." The statement told her employer that she had resigned herself to her fate and was ready to hear the details of the operation.

"Yes, actually, Miss Long, I believe you will embrace the case once you hear about it," William told her, stepping from behind the desk and handing each of them a copy of the journal they were given at the beginning of each case. The book held the name of the client, the situation, and the agency's ideas for following through. As per Pinkerton protocol, the persons seeking help would not be introduced to the agents or have any idea how the help they sought might come about.

"If indeed there is a crime involved, it is against a woman, so I know you'll derive a great deal of satisfaction from investigating it," William said to Lilly.

"A brief overview of what you'll find in the journal is this: Just days ago, we received a special-delivery letter from one Mrs. Etienne Fontenot, whose name is LaRee . . . LaRee Fontenot. She and the legitimacy of her concern have been confirmed by her long-time attorney, Mr. Armand DeMille."

William looked from Lilly to McShane. "Mrs. Fontenot believes that her grandson's widow, Patricia Ducharme, has been wrongly committed to an insane asylum by her new husband, Henri."

Lilly's irritation at being paired with Cade faded as she gave her attention to William's tale. "Are you saying she believes there is nothing wrong with her granddaughter-in-law?" Lilly asked.

"That is exactly what she believes."

"Why?" The question came from Cade, who, like Lilly, seemed to have lost his animosity as his interest in the case grew.

"Mrs. Fontenot is convinced that Patricia's new husband's, Dr. Henri Ducharme's, true purpose is to gain control of the family fortune, which, according to Mr. DeMille, is extensive and which all the Fontenot males have gone to great lengths to keep safe for future generations."

"I don't understand," Lilly said. "Wouldn't it pass down to the remaining heirs?"

"Indeed. Louisiana operates under the Napoleonic Code, which means that the closest male relative handles the business and monetary affairs of their womenfolk, who are considered little more than chattel to their fathers and husbands."

Lilly felt herself bristling. Once again, a male-dominated world sought to keep the fairer sex under its thumb. No doubt they felt that feeble female brains were incapable of comprehending, much less dealing with, anything beyond regular feminine pursuits.

"I see you take umbrage at that notion, Miss Long, as I suspected you would," William said with a nod and a slight smile. "As you know, social injustice is one thing that infuriates my father, so he was immediately drawn to this case. It's also common knowledge that he has strong beliefs in a woman's capabilities, or he would not hire female operatives.

"But I digress. When LaRee Fontenot's husband, Etienne, suffered a stroke at a relatively young age, he began to consider ways to insure the money he'd amassed stayed within the family. With Mr. DeMille's legal advice, Etienne transferred all his business holdings, as well as a house on Rampart Street and a plantation called River Run, to his son, Grayson, in whose capabilities he had complete trust. All this before his death.

"By all accounts, LaRee Fontenot was quite a lovely woman in her youth, and Etienne feared that after his death she would fall for some unscrupulous ne'er-do-well, who would take control of the family fortune."

"Let me see if I understand," Cade said. "Etienne hoped that by giving everything to his son before his own death, he could avoid the possibility of his family losing everything he'd worked so hard to gain, should his wife marry unwisely after he died."

"Exactly," William said, nodding. "He knew Grayson would be generous and fair in providing for his womenfolk, yet they would have no money of their own."

"It doesn't sound as if Etienne had much faith in his wife's ability to choose a suitable husband," Lilly said.

William smiled and shrugged. "In any case, LaRee Fontenot never remarried. According to DeMille, the arrangement worked well, and the same agreement was set up between Grayson and his son, Garrett, who lost no time expanding the family holdings—timber in this case—into Arkansas, where he made his home most of the year.

"Garrett was unmarried when his father passed away, and on a visit to his grandmother in New Orleans, he met and fell in love with Patricia Galloway. After they married, they went back to Arkansas to make their home."

"Is this the same Patricia who is now in the insane asylum?" Lilly queried.

"The same," William corroborated. "Garrett and Patricia had two daughters, Cassandra and Suzannah. He died four years ago with no son to inherit. Like his father, he felt that some women are as intelligent and business savvy as men, since his grandmother had regularly and successfully interjected her thoughts and ideas into the running of the various family endeavors."

"You said his grandmother *had* interjected her thoughts and ideas," Cade said. "Why isn't she still?"

"We're getting there," William said. "Bear with me."

"As a resident of Arkansas, Garrett was not bound by Louisiana law. In accordance with the Married Women's Property Act, which admittedly is haphazardly enforced, depending on who sits in the seat of power, Patricia became heir to everything the male Fontenots had amassed from Etienne's time until the present."

"Ah," Cade said with a nod. "And it was Patricia, not LaRee, who fell for the unscrupulous man, this Henri Ducharme."

"It appears so, yes," William told them.

"If Patricia and her daughters lived in Arkansas, how did she meet Ducharme and lose control?" Lilly asked.

"She was lonely in Arkansas without her husband, and she and her girls had moved in with Mrs. Fontenot. She and Henri met soon afterward. To the dismay of the entire family, they were married as soon as her year of mourning ended."

"You say that Ducharme is a doctor, and yet Mrs. Fontenot doubts his diagnosis in Patricia's case," Cade said. "Why?"

"Yes, Cassandra, the older daughter, confided to Mrs. Fontenot that her mother was mere months into her new marriage when she began to suspect she'd made a dreadful mistake and had put the family fortune in her new husband's grasping hands—Mrs. Fontenot's words, not mine," William clarified.

"I can certainly relate to that," Lilly said in a voice laced with bitterness. She ignored the questioning look her partner shot her way.

"According to Cassandra, it appears that her stepfather's sole intent in life is to spend them into poverty."

Lilly gave another huff of disgust.

"To further upset the family," William continued, "within ten months of the marriage, Patricia found herself with child—what is commonly referred to as a 'change of life baby.' The confinement was troublesome, and Patricia got little comfort from her husband, who constantly warned that something could go wrong because of her age."

"Job's comforter," Cade muttered.

William nodded. "As it happened, something did go wrong. The baby, a boy, was stillborn some eighteen months ago, which sent Patricia into a deep melancholy, from which, Mrs. Fontenot claims, she seemed to be emerging little by little, until she received another blow."

As Lilly listened, she thought of her own mother's murder that resulted in the death of the baby she'd been carrying. She wondered if she would always be reminded of their deaths at odd times like this, with nothing but a snippet of conversation bringing back the painful memory.

Cade leaned forward in interest. "What was that?"

"Four months ago, in an effort to cheer her mother, Cassandra urged Patricia to attend a suffragist gathering with her and her sister, Suzannah, who somehow became separated from them in the crush. They looked for her to no avail, and she was located two days later by some hobo in an alley. She had been molested and killed."

There was an apologetic expression on William's face as he looked at Lilly, but though her heart gave a lurch of empathetic pain for Patricia Ducharme's loss and Suzannah's suffering, she was no shrinking violet to go into a swoon from hearing such brutal truths.

"The murder has not been solved, and the New Orleans police have little hope of ever knowing who committed the crime. Needless to say, this tragedy on top of the loss of her infant son strained Patricia's emotions to the limit."

"It would strain anyone's emotions," Lilly said.

William nodded. "Henri claimed she was so overcome with grief and anger that she became abusive, striking him on several occasions.

"Mrs. Fontenot admits that Patricia's emotions seesawed between bouts of depression and something near normalcy, but she never witnessed the"—William referred to the letter in his hand—" 'howling, screeching creature hell-bent on physical injury.' That last was Henri's description as Mrs. Fontenot recalls it.

"Ducharme claims he had no recourse but to administer small doses of laudanum. Fearful of making her a fiend, he discontinued the drug after the funeral, at which time Patricia began to alternate between forgetfulness and belligerence. She began to imagine things that were not so and accused him of everything from hiding things to lying to her."

"The poor thing," Lilly said, thinking that it certainly sounded as if the woman's sanity had fled.

"And so he had her committed," Cade said.

William nodded. "A month after burying Suzannah, Henri committed Patricia to the City Insane Asylum there in New Orleans."

"I've heard of it," Cade said. "I thought it was for indigents, not the crème de la crème of New Orleans society. I can't imagine Mrs. Fontenot choosing such a place for a loved one."

"You're right, McShane," William said with a dry smile. "But there is a certain method in her madness, if you'll pardon the dreadful pun. Henri wanted to put Patricia in a state institution, but Mrs. Fontenot put down her foot and insisted that Patricia be placed in a private home or left in the city until her true mental state could be evaluated by professionals. That way she would be close enough for the family to visit, and"—his smile deepened—"with the Fontenot bank account, Mrs. Fontenot could arrange for special privileges and care for her granddaughter-in-law."

"I understand the special privileges, but not the other," Lilly confessed.

"By law—anyone, including policemen, family members, clergy, literally anyone—can leave someone for evaluation at the New Orleans facility for a certain length of time. If they get better, they're released, but if they don't, they're sent to the East Louisiana State Hospital in Jackson."

"From what you've told us, it seems Dr. Ducharme's fears are well-founded," Lilly mused. "Why does Mrs. Fontenot doubt his judgment?"

"She admits she has no proof that Henri is up to anything nefarious," William told them. "But with Cassandra's statement about her mother's concerns over her new husband and

Mrs. Fontenot's own feeling that too many disasters have befallen Patricia since her marriage, she feels she has justification
for her suspicions."

Lilly understood LaRee Fontenot's intuitive feelings perfectly. She recalled feeling that people were withholding the
truth during her previous investigation. She also remembered
the feeling of certainty that Cadence McShane was not the
person who intended her harm after she'd almost been run
down by a buggy, even though her intellect reminded her that
he'd been in the area when other dodgy things had taken place.

"Cassandra also believes that her stepfather is somehow responsible for Patricia's mental state," William was saying. "She
and her great-grandmother fear that Henri will bypass them
and send Patricia to an even worse place and that leaving her
in an asylum truly will drive her over the edge."

"So our job," Cade said, glancing at Lilly, "is to try to dis-
prove the notion of Patricia Ducharme's insanity?"

"Yes, and to do everything in your power to find out
whether or not Dr. Henri Ducharme is the villain Mrs. Fontenot
and Cassandra believe he is. And do it as quickly as possible."

Lilly was feeling a bit overwhelmed by the task set before
her and her disgruntled partner, especially since they needed
to move without delay. She shot Cade a sharp glance. His dark
eyebrows were drawn together in a frown as he looked over
the notes he'd been taking.

"Does Mrs. Fontenot know anything at all about Henri's
past?" she asked. "We could use someplace to start looking."

"The doctor is, by Mrs. Fontenot's grudging admission, an
attractive and charming man, forty-seven years old, and has
been married before. She has no idea to whom he was married," William supplied. "She believes the first wife died."

"Am I correct in assuming that we will be employed by
Mrs. Fontenot at the house on Rampart Street?"

William nodded. "You will be hired as a married couple."

Cade and Lilly shared a stunned look.

"We've arranged things so that it is almost a given that you will be hired."

Mouth set in a hard line, Cade nodded in compliance. "Who else lives in the house besides Mrs. Fontenot?"

"The doctor, of course, and an array of servants."

"Cassandra?"

"No," William said. "She met and married an attorney"—he shuffled the pages of the letter again—"one Preston Easterling, fifteen months after her mother married Ducharme. They live on the family plantation, River Run, a half-day's trip from New Orleans; however, they are frequent visitors to the house on Rampart Street."

"Does Mrs. Fontenot's attorney . . ." Cade paused, searching through his notes for a name.

"Armand DeMille."

"Yes. Does Mr. DeMille have any input about the family's finances, or has he discovered any financial shenanigans that can be attributed to Ducharme?" Cade asked.

"DeMille has been in the dark since soon after Cassandra married Preston, and Henri suggested that it made more sense to have all the family affairs handled by someone in the family. He turned over everything to Preston."

At the seemingly innocuous comment, Cade's head came up like a hound on the scent of its prey.

"I see you find that interesting, too, McShane," William said with a nod of approval.

"Very."

"I want you and Miss Long to become an integral part of that household," William instructed, looking from one to the other. "You will, of course, interact on some level with all the people we've discussed today, though as you know, not even Mrs. Fontenot is to have any idea who you are."

Agency policy dictated that the clients never meet the operatives working their case. It was a practice that made a lot of sense to Lilly. William's steady gaze met hers, then moved to Cade. At that moment, Lilly saw Allan Pinkerton's determination and drive reflected in his son's eyes.

"Within reason and the law, you are to use every means possible to find out everything you can about Dr. Ducharme. If he is as corrupt as the Fontenot ladies and Mr. DeMille seem to think he is, I want you to nail the scoundrel's hide to the wall."